Four Days in Michigan

Philip Zazove

Gallaudet University Press
Washington, DC

Gallaudet University Press
Washington, DC 20002
http://gupress.gallaudet.edu

Library of Congress Cataloging-in-Publication Data

Zazove, Philip, 1951–
Four days in Michigan / Philip Zazove.
    p. cm.
ISBN 978-1-56368-534-7 (pbk. : alk. paper)
ISBN 1-56368-534-5 (pbk. : alk. paper)
ISBN 978-1- 56368-533-0 (e-book)
ISBN 1-56368-533-7 (e-book)
  1. Deaf—Fiction.   2. People with disabilities—Fiction.   3. Michigan—Fiction.
4. Hearing—Fiction.   I. Title.
  PS3626.A96F68   2012
  813'.6—dc23

                                                           2011050065

Cover photograph by Philip Zazove
Front cover concept by Rebecca Zazove

∞The paper used in this publication meets the minimum requirements of
American National Standard for Information Sciences—Permanence of Paper for
Printed Library Materials, ANSI Z39.48-1984.

To Barb, whose love makes me the luckiest man in the world...

Foreword

Like many people, I'd always dreamed of writing a novel. Each time I read a good story, I felt the urge to sit down and compose my own. But the travails of life got in the way, as we all know. In my case, it was medical school, marriage, residency, opening a medical practice, and then family. Kids have a way of taking up every spare moment of one's life... and then some. If you have any, you know exactly what I'm talking about.

But the dream never disappeared. Finally, one evening, after the kids were put to bed, I decided to write a few words, just to get things started. Maybe by doing a little bit each week, over time I could write my novel.

Alas, if only it was that easy. But a story did start to take shape. I eventually finished my first draft and sent it around for comments. Then another draft. And another. And another. Each time, I like to think the story got better. You're holding in your hands the culmination of all those rewrites and improvements. I'm hoping you'll enjoy it.

Isaac Newton, when asked how he was able to come up with his revolutionary theories, said he was able to do it only because "I stand upon the shoulders of giants." Well, I too have been able to write this book (which is nowhere near the level of Newton's accomplishments) because of the help of so many others. Without them, this story wouldn't be. First and foremost are two people who've been there since the beginning, supporting my ambition to write as well as giving me wonderful feedback. One is my father, a much better writer than I can ever hope to be. He read innumerable versions of the story, each time giving me wonderful comments in the non-intimidating way that only he can. Dad, I love you. And second is my wife, a well-published writer in her own right. She helped by not only giving me constructive comments on the manuscript, but also by being the best mother and wife anyone could ever have. She's taught me so much about life and love. Barb, I love you.

Many others have contributed in various ways. My youngest daughter, Rebecca, perhaps the most imaginative person I know, came up with the surprise ending, which improved the story many-fold. Two other family members also gave me constructive criticism—Judy Reed, my sister-in-law, and Mark Coons, my brother-in-law, before his untimely death from cancer. I love you all as well. There are also friends who gave freely of their time and expertise. Two in particular, both with profound hearing losses of their own, were kind enough to read the manuscript when I was at an impasse and suggest improvements. Nancy Page and Deborah Wolter, I'm lucky to have you as friends. Thank you so much for your help.

Finally, but no less important, are the professional editors. Pam Check read two early versions of the book and made some wonderful comments. Ivey Wallace, editor at Gallaudet Press, encouraged me to make changes in how the story was structured that further improved the book. Lastly, Bob Middlemiss of Durban House Press made changes that resulted in a much more readable and compelling book. I am indebted to all of you for your help. Thank you.

As some of you know, I have a profound hearing loss. I was, to the best of anyone's knowledge, the first deaf person to be main-streamed in the northern Chicago suburbs, and one of the first deaf physicians in America. I have made it only because I was given the chance to succeed in a hearing world. Many deaf, Deaf (those who use sign language and are part of the deaf community), and persons physicians in America. I have made it only because I was given the chance to succeed in a hearing world. Many deaf, Deaf (those who speak sign language and are part of the deaf community), and persons with severe hearing losses don't have this opportunity—even today. If they had the opportunity, many more of them would become very successful citizens. Thus, I will be dedicating profits of this book to the Louise Tumarkin Zazove Foundation, a 501(c)3 nonprofit (www.ltzfoundation.org), which provides scholarships for deaf college students. By doing so, the Foundation aims to help these students have an equal opportunity to succeed.

I hope you enjoy the book. If you end up with a better understanding of what life is really like for those of us who can't hear, I've succeeded.

Prologue

"He's here!"

The message spread like wildfire through the house, and everyone hurried to the front window to see for themselves.

Chuck Winter exited the taxi, paid the driver, then paused at the curb as the cab drove away. It had been a long time since his last visit home to Springville. Too long, really. He studied the ranch house, bathed in the late morning sun. It hadn't changed since his childhood. The slate gray roof, tan bricks, and immaculate yard were icons of stability in an increasingly turbulent world. They also brought back bittersweet memories. Of growing up as the only hearing person in a Deaf family. Of always feeling different from everyone at school. And of the continual requests to interpret for deaf people in public, even as a young child. He'd made the right decision to leave Michigan after high school, to go off on his own. Still, it was nice to come home.

He pulled up his coat collar, near his now-whitening blonde hair, to ward off the autumn chill. Chuck glanced up and down the street. Minor changes were evident in several houses, and the stately Dutch elm trees that had lined the road were gone now, making the street look more barren than in his younger days. Otherwise the road looked exactly as he had remembered it. He sighed at the memories, then recalled why he had come back. Chuck took one last look down the street before heading up the sidewalk.

When a short woman with dark hair opened the door, he dropped his suitcase and hugged her warmly. "Good to see you," he told his oldest sister, Lisa, using his hands effortlessly to communicate in American Sign Language. She was approaching sixty years of age. Sadly, she also looked older.

"You too."

"How's Mother?"

She shook her head. "Not good. Dr. Benson doesn't give her much longer."

Before Chuck could reply, a large mutt nudged against him. He petted the dog as Lisa's husband came up, followed by their other sister Judy and her husband. Chuck hugged each of them in turn, as is typical when Deaf friends and family meet each other. Then there was a flurry of hands as everyone signed, and many minutes passed before Chuck hung up his coat and they entered the dining room. It was there that Lisa updated him about the situation.

"Mom's given up," she signed with a Midwestern accent. "She's refusing the chemotherapy, and a few days ago she even stopped eating. The only thing that seems to interest her is news about that senator from New Jersey. You know, the one she's always been interested in, who's been an advocate of Deaf rights ever since he was elected."

"Amazing. At a time like this, it's hard to believe she still cares about someone she doesn't even know." The others nodded. "What does Dr. Benson say about Mom not eating?"

"Not much he can do." Judy took over. "You know Mother. When she decides she's going to do something, no one's going to change her mind. And she's as stubborn as ever. She won't even go to his office anymore because she says it's useless."

"The doctor's been nice enough to stop by here," Lisa said. "Yesterday he told Mom she had at most a week left. That's when she asked us to get you. She wanted you sent to her room as soon as you arrived."

"Of course. After all, you always were her favorite." Judy's hands conveyed her feelings as much as her actual signs.

"That's not true."

"Yes it is."

Lisa moved between her siblings and held out an outstretched palm to each of them before signing. "Stop that! I know everyone's upset about Mom dying, but fighting isn't going to make her better. We should be supporting each other, not arguing."

"I'm just stating the facts, and you know it." Judy made a face. "And I never understood why, since you aren't even Deaf."

Chuck stood still. He wasn't Deaf, but he had grown up in the culture. And he knew it well. He'd been a big supporter of Deaf community advocacy over the past two decades. So they no longer had to stay quiet, out of sight. So their rights under the Americans with Disabilities Act were met. So they had interpreters when needed. He even capitalized the D in the word "Deaf," just like his family did when they referred to a Deaf member of their community, to differentiate themselves from deaf persons who didn't sign.

Lisa turned to Chuck and gestured toward the bedrooms. "You'd better go see Mom. All day, she's continually asked when you'd get here."

He nodded, deciding to ignore Judy's putdown, and walked down the hall, the dog leading the way. His mother was dying from colon cancer. It had been discovered two years earlier, well after his father's fatal heart attack. She'd actually had the abdominal pain for months before but had attributed the discomfort to stress, and went to see Dr. Benson only when the bleeding started. By then, it was too late.

Chuck pushed open the door to his mother's room, knowing she wouldn't hear him knocking, and looked in. Sitting up in bed, propped up by two pillows, Sandra Winter was staring at a picture in her hands, lost in thought. She looked much more emaciated than she had at his last visit. Her face was gaunt, her body a mere wisp of its former self. Despite her debilitation, Chuck was pleased to see she still retained her elegant bearing.

The slight breeze created by the opening of the door alerted her. Sandra lifted her eyes and, when she saw who it was, let out a cry of pleasure. He walked over, and they hugged tightly.

"I'm so glad you're here," she signed, finally letting him go and setting the picture down on the sheets. He could tell the arthritis in her fingers was worse by the way she moved them.

"How are you feeling?"

"Not good. I'm ready to get this over with."

"Mom, don't give—"

She cut him off with a wave of her hand. "I'm in constant pain, I can't eat, and I spend most of my time lying in this bed. Why go on? There's nothing left for me in life. So I don't want to hear any more of that—from you or anyone else. But before I die, there's some unfinished business I need to take care of. And it involves you."

Her son raised his eyebrows as he put his right forefinger in front of his mouth and moved it forward, the sign for, "Really?"

"It's a long story, though, but only for you to see." She pointed across the room. "Close the door so no one else can watch, then pull up that chair here. It'll take awhile."

As Chuck did as she requested, his mother caressed the dog by her bedside, then picked up the picture on her bed and stood it lovingly back on the bedside table. She smiled at her son as he sat down next to her.

"Comfortable?"

He nodded.

"Good." Her fingers began to move earnestly despite the arthritis. "Then let's start at the beginning."

September 1942

Day One

One

It began in Springville, a town thirty miles northwest of Detroit. A couple stood on a front porch, clinging to each other, until he pulled back, glanced at his watch, and signed, "I really have to go. I'm going to miss you so much."

"Me too. Two months seems like forever. I wish I could afford to visit you in New York."

He nodded as he bent a clenched fist forward at the wrist, the sign for yes, and repeated that motion several times. "The good news is my dad says that once I learn this part of the business, I shouldn't have to spend much time there again."

"Good. And remember, Jacob, the Tigers play in Yankee Stadium in two weeks. Don't forget to go see them."

"Don't worry. There's no way I'll miss that." He kissed her, then signed, "Have you decided what you're going to do?"

She shook her head.

"Sandra, it makes total sense that you're upset at how things turned out, but you need to move on now."

"It's not that easy. I devoted my entire life to becoming a veterinarian, and did so much more than any other deaf person ever has to do that. To not even be given a chance just because I'm deaf, well, it hurts."

He saw the tears. "I know. Remember, I'm deaf too."

She nodded. It wasn't that Sandra was ignorant of the long odds she had faced. She'd experienced the same discrimination all deaf people do. People ignoring her. Stares when she signed in public. Neighbor kids taunting her. Difficulty getting summer jobs. Feeling like an outcast from society. But she had believed that could all be overcome, and besides, she was plain stubborn. She'd always been so, even as a child, and telling her she couldn't do something just made her work harder to prove the person wrong. So she became valedictorian of her class, excelled in sports, and learned to speak English better than any other student at the State Deaf School. It was all part of her plan to go to college, then vet school, to reach her dream.

"What do you think I should do, Jacob?"

"Well, I'd check out the ads, see what's available. Remember, you have a college degree from Huron Junior College, the first in your family. So even though you're deaf, that should give you an advantage over most people applying for jobs."

"I don't know about that. You know how hearing people are about us Deafies."

The reminder of junior college brought back bad memories. She'd chosen Huron rather than Gallaudet University to show the vet schools that she could succeed in a hearing environment. But it had turned out to be more difficult than she'd anticipated. Many professors were difficult to speech read, and classmates avoided her because they had trouble understanding her. Some of the students even made fun of her when they thought she wasn't looking. But Sandra persisted, and by dedicating herself to studying long hours, did well academically.

Jacob checked his watch again. "If I don't go now, I'm going to miss my train."

They embraced, savoring this final moment with each other for sixty days.

"I'll write you every day," he said.

"You better."

After another look into Sandra's eyes, Jacob signed, "I love you" and headed down the driveway.

She watched him walk to the street, then along the sidewalk. He was somewhat overweight, perhaps two inches taller than her five and a half feet, and had unruly hair. But he was the kindest person she'd ever met. So what if he was shy, or didn't have a lot of friends? Her dates with him had sustained her during those two awful years of junior college. He treated her well, loved baseball as much as she, and perhaps most important in these difficult times, had a steady job. He was the son of a family that owned a successful company. What more could she really want in a man? She felt her eyes misting when he looked back from the corner one last time and blew a kiss before disappearing from sight.

When she finally dried her eyes and went back into the house, she wandered it aimlessly, trying to decide what to do. Everything seemed so mundane. Sandra went upstairs to straighten her room, walked to the living room to stare out the front window, and checked the pantry before finally plopping on the den couch. Her dog sat down at her feet, and she petted him.

Two months without Jacob. Two long months. How was she going to make it? He'd been the only bright spot in her life lately. She shook her head. After all the time and effort she'd put in, it was hard to believe that her life had come down to this. Not at all like she had dreamed.

The mutt rolled on his back, and she chuckled. Dogs were so straightforward. So unlike humans. Always trusting, always on your side. And never holding a grudge. She knelt on the floor and scratched his chest. Although Sandra couldn't hear his moans of pleasure, she clearly saw his joy.

She wiped away beads of sweat on her brow. It sure was hot. The fans, running full blast, barely dented the oppressive humidity. Sandra scratched behind the dog's ears, remembering her friends telling her, "No one's going to give you a chance no matter how well you do—because you're deaf." Some had ridiculed her for setting such high goals. But back then she had believed in justice, that she'd be given a chance to become a veterinarian because of her successes.

Sandra Horowitz had loved animals for as long as she could remember. She even liked the house mice that drove her mother crazy, and got upset when she saw them dead in traps.

"Why do we have to kill them?" she'd asked the first time. "They're not hurting us."

"You should only be so kind to your brother," her mother had replied. "The answer is because they're mice. They're dirty. And they don't belong in houses."

"Then let's trap them in cages and put them outside instead of killing them."

"Are you *meshugga*? They'd just find their way back inside. If only we could get rid of them all!"

Sandra cried herself to sleep that night, and any other night after seeing an animal dead. To be a vet who cared for creatures! Who helped keep them happy and healthy. There was nothing else she'd rather do. She had applied to Michigan State, after getting honors at Huron Junior College, but was turned down within a month. She then applied to other universities over the next year, with the same result. None put it in writing, but a family acquaintance had learned it was because she was deaf.

And now, after two weeks of celebrating her college graduation, reality was closing in. It was time to find work, and she wasn't excited by the possibilities she'd found so far.

Sandra startled out of her reverie as the vibrations from the pounding on the wall reached her. Her mother, all fifty-nine inches of her, immaculate as usual, dark hair neatly coiffed in a bun, signed from the doorway across the room. "You've been sitting here for an hour since Jacob left. Is something wrong? You two break up?"

Sandra shook her head as she rubbed her dog behind the ears.

"Then what's the problem?"

"Oh, nothing much, Mom. Just trying to decide what I'm going to do now."

"About Jacob?"

Sandra shook her head again.

"Why don't you two go get married already? You've been going out now for, what, two years?"

"He wants to, but I want to be totally sure before making a commitment."

"What? A nice successful Jewish man like him, and you're not sure? He's the only man you've gone out with who makes it a point to sign to me when he comes over. What's wrong with him? He not rich enough for you?"

Sandra lifted her eyebrows and gave her mom a look.

"God willing, he'll do well and you'll have a big family, a roof over your head and plenty to eat. And some money to go to those Tigers baseball games you both like so much."

"I'm just not sure I love him, Mom. I mean, he's wonderful and I really like being with him and all that, but it's not... well, not quite what I thought love would be. But I'll have some time to think about it while he's in New York for the next couple of months."

Her mother walked over and sat down next to her on the couch. "Look, honey, I understand exactly what you're thinking. When I was your age, I was just like you. Looking for that perfect man. Took me awhile to learn he doesn't exist, or at least not a deaf Jewish one that I could find. Luckily, your father didn't give up on me, because if he had, heaven knows whom I might've had to marry. The moral of the story is, Sandra, if a decent deaf Jewish man comes by, grab him. Save yourself some grief. Jacob Winter may not be the most handsome man in the world, but he's a caring person with a good job who can put food on the table. And that's more important than you realize. Take my word for it. Grab him before you lose him."

"Thanks for the advice, Mom." Sandra gave the dog a last pat before standing up. "I think I'll go over to Gabby's for a while."

"Again? You've been either there or at a Tigers game every day this week. Don't you remember there's a war going on? You know we barely get enough food coupons to cover the meals, so you should only be out looking for a job instead. There are lots of other jobs besides being a vet, you know."

"I won't bowl today. Promise. I just need to walk around awhile, think a few things through. Then I'll start looking for work."

Mrs. Horowitz stood and looked into her daughter's eyes. "I don't understand your generation. Jobs don't just wait for you, you know." She leaned over to inspect her daughter's blouse. "If you must go, then go, but first iron those wrinkles out."

"I'm just going for a walk. It's not like I'm meeting someone important."

"Oy" the older women signed. "Okay, okay. If you want to go looking like a slob, then go looking like a slob. Just make sure you're back by two-thirty, when Mrs. Goldberg comes over. I know you hate her speech therapy lessons, but God willing, they'll help you get a decent job. She told me your speech is at the point now where most people can understand you."

"I'll be back in time, Mom. Promise."

Two

Sandra walked into the bright sun and squinted, glad she had changed to a loose cotton dress. It was even hotter outside than in the house. There was no breeze, and the sun beating from the cloud-less sky was relentless. The temperature had been over ninety for almost a week now, and there seemed to be no end in sight. Definitely unusual for September in Michigan.

She donned her sunglasses and slowly walked the three blocks to Gabby's. Springville was populated by working couples who couldn't afford to live in or close to Detroit. The houses, mostly ranches except a few two-stories, were modest and wooden, with concrete front porches. Quite a few of them had star decals in their windows, showing that someone in the house was in the service. The well-maintained yards were small, and some had trees. There were few driveways. Most of the homes were built before the age of the automobile, so cars were parked on the street or in nearby garages. The styling of the cars was boxy, with spoke wheels and heavy fenders. Some of the older ones had radiators in front. Almost every vehicle had a gas coupon label on the windshield, another reminder that the country was at war.

Several people were outside today, despite the heat and its being a weekday. But Sandra was so absorbed in her thoughts, she didn't notice them, the cars, or the children playing kick the can. It wasn't fair, she mused, the way hearing people discriminated against deaf people. It just wasn't fair. Deaf people were just as smart and capable. Like at her senior year high school state track meet. The officials had tried to keep her from running, stating they worried she wouldn't hear if someone was passing her and might trip them and cause an injury. It was only due to the strong protest by her father's hearing parents that she'd been allowed to participate. But she'd been forced to start at the back because she couldn't hear the starting gun. At the back so "she wouldn't interfere with other runners." Sandra had finished third, two seconds behind the winner. She'd always wondered if she would've won had she started closer to the front.

A familiar flood of hate against hearing people rose inside her. They were the reason she couldn't become a vet. Tears came before she managed to get control of herself. Blaming them wouldn't make things better. Still, she wondered whether deaf people would ever have an equal chance in life.

The bowling alley was in an older building, run by Mr. Krause, the owner. It was solid, but showed its age. Its threadbare carpet, dim lighting, and worn furniture gave it a shabby look. Gabby's stayed in business for two reasons: it was cheaper than the new bowling alley in neighboring Jefferson, and it had a contingent of loyal customers who'd been coming there for decades.

Sandra entered Gabby's and looked around. There were twenty lanes, a small soda fountain, and three pool tables in the far corner. Big band music was playing in the background, though she couldn't hear it. People were bowling in two lanes, and one pool table was being used. The only person she recognized was Mr. Krause sitting behind the desk. The place was comfortably familiar. Since she was a young child, Sandra had gone there weekly with her parents for the Thursday night deaf bowling league. It was as much a part of her life as school had been.

She sauntered down the corridor, casually reading the wall posters. War posters were everywhere. One had a picture of a man yelling, "Come on, Gang! We're Building Arms for Victory." Another had a hand pointing and said, "Are YOU Doing All You

Can?" There were recruiting posters for women, as well as announcements about the upcoming fall bowling leagues and advertisements hawking used equipment for sale. In the center of the hallway, several plaques commemorated the bowlers who held the records at the alley. She noticed it had been over a year since someone bowled 300, although her uncle had come close two months ago with a 297, probably because so many men had signed up for the war.

As she reached the desk, she nodded at Mr. Krause.

"Bowling today?" She read his lips, comfortable doing so as she'd known him so long.

Sandra shook her head. "No money," she replied in her nasal voice, signing simultaneously as she talked. Used to the speech of deaf people, he nodded and resumed reading the front page of the *Detroit Free Press*. The headline said, "Marines Secure Guadalcanal Airfield."

She passed the desk, continuing to glance at the flyers. Soon she found herself by the three pool tables. The one in the middle, clearly much newer and nicer than the others, was the one being used. The man playing didn't seem to notice her, concentrating on his game. Sandra stopped to watch. He looked to be her age and was tall, perhaps two inches over six feet, and slender in build. Short-cropped light hair meshed nicely with clean-cut, dark features. His face was interesting, now set in concentration over his pool cue. And he was obviously a soldier, his Army khakis neatly pressed.

What struck her most, however, was an air of self-assuredness, a sense of confidence that she rarely saw in men her age. Perhaps it was because he was a soldier. None of her friends were in the service, their deafness keeping them out, so she didn't personally know anyone in the armed forces.

Sandra turned her attention back to the game. She'd never played pool. Her parents associated it with gambling and had prohibited her from trying it, despite her childhood pleas. But over the

15

years, she had come to understand the game. She leaned against the wall to watch. Soon she began anticipating the man's moves, vicariously enjoying his successes and suffering with his misses. It looked like fun. Very different from baseball, her favorite sport, but enticing nonetheless. She wished she had money to try it, for a moment debating whether to use the quarter she'd kept hidden in her top dresser drawer, but then nixed that idea. Money was too tight these days.

That was when the young solider looked up and saw her watching him. He smiled and resumed his game. Sandra felt her cheeks blush at being caught watching a hearing stranger, and was glad he hadn't said anything. Despite years of speech therapy and somewhat intelligible speech, she knew better than to talk with hearing people unless it was absolutely necessary. The man remained focused on the table, and she sighed inwardly with relief, deciding to watch a little longer.

When the last ball had been knocked into a corner pocket, he turned and smiled at her again before she could walk away. She saw his lips move, but didn't understand what he said. She just stood there, stunned by his unexpected greeting.

"Hi. My name's Rudy." She saw his lips move again, and this time she managed to understand what he was saying—though she could only guess that his name was Rudy, and not Trudy, or Ricky, or some other similar-looking name.

She nodded shyly, then realized he was waiting for a response. Panic flitted through her. As soon as she spoke, he would notice her speech.

"What's your name?" he asked again.

"Sandra," she enunciated as best she could.

She saw his face become more attentive. Like all deaf people, she was an expert at reading body language.

"Did you say Sandra?"

She nodded.

"Glad to meet you. You been here before?"

She nodded again, relieved his lips were so easy to speech read even though his face had the typical blankness of most hearing persons.

He waved his hand at the building. "Is the place always this quiet?"

"I'm sorry. What did you say?"

He repeated himself.

"No, not always." Her hands moved instinctively to sign the words. He was talking about the lack of sound and she the lack of activity, but the problem was the same.

He studied Sandra closely, intrigued by her unusual elocution. Her face, not overwhelmingly beautiful, was attractive enough with its cleft chin, cheek dimples and brunette hair flipped on her shoulders. It was the way she communicated that captivated him, particularly how she watched him so intently. And the charming way she illustrated her comments with her hands. He wondered what country she came from, being unable to place her accent.

"This is my first time in this part of town. I grew up ten miles east of here, near Cedarville, out by the Buick factory. You know where that is?"

She missed half of what he said but, like most deaf people who read lips do, filled in the blanks using the context from what she did understand. She took a guess at what he'd said and nodded.

"Left there two years ago when I graduated from East High and joined the Army. They sent me to Fort Bragg in North Carolina." He turned to gather the pool balls from the various pockets and put them in the triangle on the table. Fortunately, his lips remained in profile. "My parents decided they wanted a smaller house, and when they found one here, I decided to use my leave to come see their new digs."

Sandra continued to miss many of his words, but was confident that she had the gist of it. Regardless, she clearly was not going to ask him to repeat himself. That would only turn him off at best and create problems at worst. She decided to leave, but before she could, he turned back to her and caught her watching him closely. He felt self-conscious. Was something on his face? His hair messed up?

"Are you working?" Rudy smiled as he casually patted his hair, but Sandra easily noticed the telltale body signs of his discomfort. She shook her head, avoiding speaking unless necessary. She tried to figure out how best to get away before things went more downhill.

"In school?"

She shook her head again. "I just finished."

"Oh really? Where?"

"I'm sorry?"

He repeated himself and she replied, "Huron Junior College." He managed to understand it was a junior college.

"Looking for a job?"

"Pardon?"

"I'm sorry, what did you say?"

It was happening. Sandra wanted to get away before it got worse. She really focused on her enunciation. "You asked me a question, which I didn't understand."

His face again became more attentive when she spoke. "Oh. I just asked if you were looking for a job now that you're finished with college."

She nodded.

"It's hard to find a decent one these days, isn't it? That's why I joined the Army. Thought about junior college too, but figured the Army would be better for me in the long run. I'm hoping that by the time my stint's over, times won't be so bad. Guess I'll find out eventually, though it may be awhile. Depending on what happens with the war, I mean."

He picked up a cube of blue chalk and rubbed it on the tip of his cue. She couldn't see his face now, but it was obvious from his body language that he was talking. Sandra took a deep breath. Should she ignore whatever he had said, or tell him she couldn't hear and ask him to repeat himself? Or just take advantage of his not looking to walk away? She hated these moments of truth with hearing people, when they found out she was deaf. The result was always the same—they suddenly treated her differently, as if she were incompetent or dumb.

She decided to leave, but again he turned before she did so. Rudy gestured toward the pool table, his eyes questioning. "I'd really love to have you join me. Will you play?"

"Sure," she blurted without thinking, surprising herself. The lure of finally playing pool was just too great. Then Sandra remembered her promise. She looked at her watch. 2:25. She was going to be late for Mrs. Goldberg if she didn't leave right now.

"Oh, I can't! I have to go," she signed in frustration as she took a few steps in the direction of the door. Then realizing he wouldn't understand, she used her voice. "I can't. I mean, I'd love to play, but I'm late for an appointment with someone to help me with job interviews."

"Okay." He smiled hesitantly, his eyes warm. "I'm not sure I got all that. Can you say it again, a little more slowly?"

She did.

"Now that's definitely more important than pool. Well, I plan to be here tomorrow at the same time. Want to meet and play then? It'll be on me."

Her boldness surprised her again. "I'd like that."

"One o'clock work for you?"

She verified the time that she saw, knowing how common it was to get that wrong with lip-reading, then nodded.

"Good. See you then."

Rudy watched her dash down the hallway and out the door. After she left, he absent-mindedly shot a few more balls before gathering everything up and returning it to the desk.

"You know that girl who just left?" he asked Mr. Krause as he paid his bill.

"Yeah."

"What's her name?"

"Horowitz, Sandra Horowitz."

"Sandra Horowitz," Rudy repeated the name out loud. "What country is she from?"

"Oh, she's a home-grown American, young man. Grew up right here in this town. I've known her since she was a kid."

"She is? Interesting, because she has a strong accent. Any idea where she got it?"

"Oh that's no accent, soldier. It's because she's deaf," Mr. Krause said bluntly.

Rudy's eyes opened wide with surprise.

"And I mean stone deaf. She can't hear nothin'." Mr. Krause eyed the soldier a second, then leaned forward. "I know she ain't bad looking and has a pretty nice figure too, but you don't stand much of a chance with her. Her whole family's deaf. You know what that means, don't you?"

"No, tell me."

"You haven't had much contact with deaf mutes before, have you?"

"None at all."

"That's what I thought. Most people don't, but I know a bit about 'em, as a large group of 'em been coming here every Thursday night for years. Lemme tell ya. They're clearly a different breed. Nothin' like you and me. They tend to stick together and rarely do anything with the rest of us unless they have to. Most of 'em ain't too smart, either." Mr. Krause leaned even further toward Rudy. "And another thing, young man. They don't speak or understand English much, preferring to communicate in their primitive way, using signs. You familiar with that?"

"Nope."

"Then lemme give you some more advice, soldier. Don't waste your time with a deaf mute."

"She seemed to understand English just fine when I talked with her."

Mr. Krause grunted. "I'll warrant she's better'n most, but you still shouldn't waste your time."

"Why not?"

"Because it ain't gonna work, that's why. I've seen a few guys chase after some of the better-lookin' deaf chicks, and they all gave up real quick. Trust me, soldier. Deaf mutes are different from us. Save yourself some grief."

"Hmm," Rudy said after a short silence. "Thanks for the tip."

So that explained it all, he thought as he left the building. Why Sandra moved her hands so elegantly. And why she'd watched his face so intently. Interesting! He'd never spent time with a deaf person before and found himself looking forward to his date the following day.

Three

"Well, what kind of work are you going to do?" the elderly man asked Sandra.

"I don't know," she signed back. "I haven't been able to find a job yet."

She looked around the room where the Tuesday evening Deaf Club meeting was being held. After three frustrating hours with Mrs. Goldberg, trying to say sounds she couldn't hear, Sandra was bushed and looked forward to some relaxation. She'd always felt comfortable at Deaf Club gatherings, where everyone knew what it was like to be deaf in a hearing world. The area was a popular one for deaf people. There were auto plants nearby, one of the few industries that employed them. So the club was larger than many.

Tonight perhaps fifty people were in the large rented room. To a hearing person, it would've been strangely silent, except for the occasional grunt, thump or chair scraping the floor. But to a deaf person, the place was alive with conversation, camaraderie and movement.

The younger children ran around, chasing each other. Several teenagers in the far corner were playing a card game only they knew. Older adults were scattered throughout the room in different-sized groups. Three young deaf adults were present, all women, none of whom Sandra was close with. A hearing man, a child of deaf adults, intermingled with the three women. Like most hearing members of deaf families, he often associated with deaf people.

After all, he had been raised amongst them, and American Sign Language was his first language, so he felt equally at home in this setting and in the hearing world.

The elderly man waved his hand in front of Sandra's face to get her attention again. "Do I have it right? That even though you have a college degree, you can't find a job?"

She made a fist and flexed it down.

"It's because you're deaf, right?"

"Are you surprised?"

"Yes, I am. I thought things were changing, that society was beginning to understand that just because we're deaf, we aren't dumb. Especially someone like you who has a college degree." He put a hand on her shoulder and signed with his remaining hand as only deaf people can do well. "Don't give up, Sandra. Someone, somewhere, will give you a chance. Just be sure you make the most of it when you get it."

Sandra smiled at his encouragement, then saw a man her age come in. She excused herself and went over to him.

"Hey! Where've you been?" she signed.

Matthew smiled and gave her a bear hug. "I got off work late." He signed effortlessly even though he was hearing, for he was another CODA, child of deaf adults. "I have some big news."

She raised her eyebrows.

"I'm going into the Marines next month."

"Wow. Are you scared?"

He shook his head. "I'm looking forward to doing my part. What's more, they're excited that I know sign language and may put me with some other guys who know it to use as a secret language the Germans and Japanese can't understand."

"So you'll definitely be going overseas, then."

"It sure looks that way."

Just then, his mother got their attention from across the room. "Matt, don't forget the insurance man's coming over to the house at seven-thirty. You need to be there to interpret for your father."

He looked at his watch, then sighed. "I better go if I'm going to make it in time."

Sandra watched him leave, not surprised at the turn of events. Hearing members of deaf families often interpreted for them with hearing society. Even young hearing children would interpret for adults. She knew many CODAs disliked doing this, particularly when they were teenagers, but saw it as their obligation because they could hear.

Sandra went over to the three young women who were now alone. They were talking about another deaf woman who wasn't there that evening.

"Did you hear about Rosie?"

"Serves her right."

"What happened?" Sandra signed.

"You know how Rosie's been going out with a hearing man the past few months?"

Sandra nodded. That had been the talk of the deaf community.

"Well, she got mono and had to stay at home awhile, away from everyone else. Probably got it from her boyfriend, as no one else the family knows has it. Just the other day, the doctor finally said she wasn't contagious anymore, but when she went to the boyfriend's house, he had another girlfriend already."

One of the other women signed, "What did she expect? He's hearing."

Everyone nodded.

A new woman entered the room, someone Sandra didn't know. Sandra got everyone's attention and nodded at the newcomer. "Who's that?"

No one knew, so they walked over to introduce themselves. Sandra signed first. "Welcome."

The girl responded fluently, without an accent. Clearly a native signer.

"Where are you from?" Sandra followed the custom of first ascertaining whether someone was culturally deaf by where they lived and went to school, before asking their name.

"From Battle Creek. We just moved here recently."

"Where did you go to school?"

"The State Deaf School."

"Me too. When did you graduate?"

"Eight years ago. You?"

"Two years ago. My name's Sandra."

"I'm Ruth," the woman replied as the lights flicked on and off a few times. Everyone stopped signing and looked at the front of the room as the president of the club stepped up onto a chair. He made a few announcements, then introduced a man who had just moved into the area from Toledo. Next, he reminded everyone that although deaf people couldn't serve in the military, they could support the war effort. He encouraged people to buy war bonds or donate to the Red Cross, and passed out an announcement about job openings in the auto plants that were now making items for the military. There was then some talk about future social events, and a woman suggested they have a Halloween party in October. After discussion, this was voted upon favorably.

Then it was time for DINGO. Deaf Bingo. The older members eagerly got their bingo cards and sat at the tables, while most of the younger people left to go for a walk or play outside. Sandra lingered in the doorway a couple of moments to watch. Her parents were among those playing. The game started. Numbers were picked out of a basket and signed to the group. Sandra noticed the announcer scan the room after broadcasting each number to check if anyone was signaling DINGO. She also noted there was less conversation than there had been earlier. Deaf people can't watch someone else sign at the same time as they look at the announcer or their cards.

Sandra left the room and ventured outside into the warm evening. She looked around until she saw what she was looking for

—her little brother in the playground with his friends. She walked over to him. "Time to go home and get ready for bed, David."

"I don't want to go."

"David, come on. Don't make a big scene again. You know you have school tomorrow and what your bedtime is."

He made a face and reluctantly went with her. They signed as they walked, watching each other most of the time with only an occasional glance ahead to be sure they didn't run into something. David was trying to convince his sister to let him stay up later than usual. A block from home, they passed a group of teenagers talking in front of a house. The hearing people stopped and stared at the deaf people, their interest piqued by the signing. Sandra and David were aware of the scrutiny, as they always were around hearing people, and felt uncomfortable at being singled out.

Then she noticed one of the boys, a heavy one, mimicking their sign in a grotesque fashion and the others laughing. She tried to block the view of that from David, but was too late. Before she knew what had happened, David stopped, faced the boy who had been making fun of them, and signed, "What's so funny? You're the dumb one because you can't even understand what I'm saying."

The heavy man paused a second, surprised at the child's boldness, then mimicked David's signs again. His friends roared.

"You're the fat one, not me," David persisted.

Sandra pulled her brother away before something bad happened and herded him home, all the while burning inside, furious that hearing people could be so hateful. What kind of satisfaction did they get out of making fun of their signs? And why did they always have to stare at her? She found herself speculating on what they talked about. Was it the same things deaf people talked about? Other than the hearing members of deaf families, many of whom really were culturally deaf, and the teachers in the State Deaf School, who were also comfortable with deaf culture, Sandra's only experience with hearing people had been with the professors and students in junior college. And that had been a disaster from the beginning.

Ignoring the stares, yet wanting to appear normal, they stopped signing and walked the last block silently, pretending not to notice anything. It wasn't until they were inside their house that David resumed his pleas to stay up late. Life went on.

It took Sandra Horowitz a long time to fall asleep that night. She lay in bed, eyes open, ignoring the shadows cast by the small light most deaf people leave on at night so they can see. She pondered what she had done. She'd actually agreed to shoot pool with a soldier. The idea of that was quite alluring, in part because of the forbidden nature of it. That alone would have made the date unusual. But the fact that she was going to do it with a hearing stranger made the rendezvous momentous. The notion was both exciting and scary. Exciting because she'd really never been alone with a hearing man for more than a few minutes. And scary for the same reason.

That didn't matter, though, Sandra reminded herself. Because it gave her a chance to play pool. She had no interest in a long-term relationship with a hearing man. Even though they'd gotten along fine so far, they'd already had some trouble communicating. She knew what hearing people were like and how such a relationship would end up. But the opportunity to play pool made it worth doing. Especially since Rudy was relatively easy to understand. She hoped he found her easy enough to communicate with as well, so that he didn't cut her time at the game too early.

Sandra knew her parents would be furious if they knew about her plans. Playing pool would be bad enough in and of itself, especially since she'd be doing that rather than looking for a job. Much worse, though, would be her violation of the deaf taboo against dating a hearing person. She recalled her father telling her time and again the two reasons for this: the ever-present communication barrier, and hearing people's inability to understand what life was like for deaf people. Violating the tradition, he always warned, led to trouble.

She recalled the gossip at the Deaf Club about Rosie. That was different because Rosie had been actively dating a hearing man. Sandra was just using one to get a chance to play pool. Besides, Rosie's situation notwithstanding, Sandra believed the taboo was antiquated. The consequences may have been true in the past, but this was 1942. Times had changed. The whole world was in the upheaval of war. There was no way playing pool with a hearing man would impact her life. It wasn't as if she were planning to get serious with him. There was no reason not to have some fun until Jacob came back.

For a moment, she watched the quite shadows from her night light. She deserved it, too, she reflected, after spending half of yesterday afternoon and much of the evening practicing her speech, working on specific phrases until she could say them clearly. First, there had been the hours with Mrs. Goldberg earlier. Then, after putting David to bed, yet another hour in front of the mirror perfecting her tongue and lip placements. She hated it as much as any deaf person, but if she couldn't be a vet, she wanted another good job. Most deaf people had low-paying jobs because they couldn't communicate in English. She was determined to be different.

What to wear while shooting pool? Something loose enough to be comfortable, but not too casual. For a moment she wished her family could afford fancier clothes, especially those new sling-back platform pump shoes, the ones with the open toes, that so many women seemed to have. But there was no use wishing for that. They didn't have the money. She decided the red jumper with her white blouse and plain blue pumps would do just fine.

During the last half hour before falling asleep, she debated how to keep Rudy from learning about her deafness as long as possible. An image of him—kind eyes, smiling—came to her. And with that came the recollection of the air of confidence he projected. She wondered again whether it was because he was a soldier or because he could hear.

Then she found herself wondering how different life would be if she could hear. She'd for sure be in State now, getting ready to go to vet school. She closed her eyes and tried to imagine what different things might sound like, things she had read about or seen but never heard. Birds chirping. Music playing. Leaves rustling. Cars. Animals. Voices. Yes, especially voices. What did they sound like? Was Rudy's voice unique, she wondered, and how was it different from Mrs. Goldberg's? Was it deep? Soft? Or masculine-sounding, whatever that meant? And what did hers sound like? What was this nasal tone of hers that the speech therapists kept talking about? She wondered about the strange nature of the auditory sense. She'd read that dripping water makes noise, but had never read or seen anyone say that about tears. Did they? What about dripping ice cream?

Sandra sighed, then suddenly felt uneasy at the realization of what she was doing. Rudy was hearing, and he didn't look the least bit Jewish. Not the kind of man she should spend time with, even if it did enable her to play pool. Especially since she knew nothing about him. Once he found out she was deaf—and she knew that was going to happen despite any effort she made to hide it—who knew how he might try to take advantage of her?

She put her hands behind her head. There was no way to cancel their date, though. She could just not show up. But he was a soldier. It wouldn't be right to stand up someone who was defending their country. Besides, she really—REALLY—wanted to try the game of pool. So she decided to meet him, but only this once.

Around her the familiar shadows were comforting. Sandra turned on her side and closed her eyes.

Day Two

Four

Sandra spent the next morning applying for jobs in Springville and Jefferson. She didn't find anything, despite visiting numerous places with ads in the paper or "Help Wanted" signs in the window. Most of the businesses rejected her quickly in favor of other applicants. And everywhere there were the war posters, showing people gazing proudly at some far horizon or doing their bit. She just couldn't seem to fit in. By the time she returned home at noon, Sandra felt testy and irritable. Life seemed more and more unfair. Just because she couldn't hear.

She started to get ready to play pool and her spirits lightened. It was going to be so much fun. She would make it so. She brushed aside the fears from the previous night, determined to make the most of her experience. By the time she ate a quick lunch, got dressed, and applied her makeup, it was time to leave for Gabby's.

"Where are you going?" her mother signed as Sandra came into the kitchen.

"Oh, just out to meet someone."

"You should only dress so nice for your family. And you do this just for a friend?" The graying woman stood with her arms akimbo, head tilted, using her body language along with her hands to ask the question.

Sandra nodded.

"Who is it?"

"Someone you don't know."

"A man?"

"Mom, c'mon. Do you know any men besides Jacob who've asked me out lately?"

"If you ask me, you should spend the afternoon looking for a job. Don't you remember there's a war going on? You meet this friend, heaven forbid, you may miss a job opportunity."

"It's not like I haven't been trying. I spent the entire morning looking for work. And I'm not giving up. It's just that I'd already made plans to meet this person."

"You're as stubborn as your father. Look, it's hard enough for a hearing person to get a job these days, let alone a deaf one. You have to try harder because you can't hear. It's as simple as that. You've had your fun this summer, Sandra, what with all those parties, Tigers games and going out with Jacob. It's time to get serious about finding a job."

"I am serious, Mom. Just give me some time."

Mrs. Horowitz threw up her arms. "Okay, okay. You should only pray your children don't give you half as much trouble as you give me. Go meet your friend. Just remember, Yom Kippur starts tonight. We're eating dinner at six and leaving for the synagogue at seven. Don't be late."

Sandra nodded and left before her mother could ask any more questions. The sky was more overcast, but the day was just as hot as it had been, and the clouds were fluffy and white, not the kind that suggested the relief of rain. She walked toward Gabby's, her heart now racing in anticipation as she neared the building. What if Rudy wasn't there? She hoped he was. She really wanted to play pool. Sandra paused at the door. She took a couple of deep breaths, wiped a bead of sweat from her forehead, and patted her hair one last time.

The place was a little busier today. Strangers were bowling in several lanes. A young man was sitting on a stool at the soda fountain, sipping a Coke and listening to the big band music that Sandra was totally oblivious to. For a second, she didn't see Rudy, but then he stood up from where he had been leaning over the new pool table. He saw her, waved, and started to walk toward her. She waved back shyly.

"Hello." He smiled as they met in the middle of the corridor.

"Hi." She was glad she'd chosen the clothes she had. Although he was in his Army uniform again, Rudy somehow seemed to be dressed more nattily today.

"Hot day, eh?"

She nodded, conscious that her hands felt moist.

"Well," he pointed in the direction of the pool tables, "I got the good table again. Shall we go play?"

She nodded, ignoring Mr. Krause's look of surprise as they passed him.

"I'll tell you," Rudy looked at her as they walked, "it's much more comfortable here than at my parents'. Their house is so hot, it's like an oven. Here, at least, the big fans make it bearable."

Sandra felt thankful again that his lips were so easy to read. It was, of course, impossible to understand every word he said, but she was able to get the gist most of the time.

When there was a silence, she realized it was her turn to say something. She almost signed instinctively, but caught herself in time. Gathering up her resolve, and concentrating on each sound, she plunged ahead. "I'm looking forward to playing pool. My mother doesn't like it, though… well, you know how mothers can be." She raised her eyebrows.

He laughed heartily. "I sure do."

Sandra watched him, pleased. She had known his smile, and now she knew his laugh. And he really put his body into that. What was more, she had made him laugh. That had never happened with a hearing person before. It pleased her, and she felt a little glow inside.

There was another silence, though less awkward now, until they arrived at the tables. Rudy looked at the middle one, smiled and pointed. "Isn't she beautiful? It's a top-of-the-line Brunswick."

He leaned over and rubbed the felt, then the edge. "Must have cost a lot. Look at how nice the wood is." He nodded at the panels and legs.

Sandra didn't understand the words, but could tell from his body language that he was admiring the table. She looked at where he nodded. She knew nothing about pool tables, but could see that this one was solid and nicely made compared to the other two. Sandra ran her hand against the wood. It was smooth.

"Well, go pick out a cue stick, and we'll start a game."

Sandra had looked at him just in time to see him talk, but didn't understand. "What?"

"Your cue stick. Go pick it out."

She still had no idea what he meant. It looked like his lips said "kootik."

"Your cue stick." He held his up. "One of these."

"Oh." She then added sheepishly, this time signing and speaking simultaneously, "I never played before and didn't know what those were called."

"No problem. Everyone has a first time."

She wondered if it was spelled "kootik" or some other way, and vowed to look it up when she got back home. Like many deaf people, especially those who had some familiarity with English, knowing the spelling helped her better know the word. Sandra walked to the wall that held the rack of cues. They were of different lengths and she studied them, wondering how one knew which size to choose. Turning to Rudy again, she asked, "How do I know which one's right for me?"

He showed her, then demonstrated how to chalk the tip. After explaining the game of Stripes and Solids, he set the balls up in the standard triangular position. Facing Sandra, he gestured. "Ladies first."

She put the white ball on the table. Assuming the position she had seen Rudy use the day before, she moved the stick back and forth a few times, just as he had, before striking for the ball. Her stick barely glanced the left side, and the ball veered off slowly to the right, missing the pack of balls entirely. Sandra blushed, then sneaked a glance at Rudy.

"Well, we have at least one thing in common," she managed to understand from what she saw him say. "I did that my first time too." He picked up the white ball and put it back in its original place. "Try it again. This time, though, hold your cue like this." He showed her a different way to place her fingers on the stick. "And move your arm back and forth smoothly, concentrating on hitting the center of the ball." He kept his face and eyes on hers, not looking down at the cue and ball.

She tried again. This time, she did hit the pack of balls, though weakly, on the left side. As the game progressed, Sandra learned quickly that the sport was harder than it looked. Still, she found herself enjoying it immensely. Rudy was a good teacher, giving her frequent pointers, always keeping his mouth easy to see, his eyes friendly. So unlike every other hearing person she'd been with before. He often let her repeat shots. And she'd not had to ask him to repeat himself very often, because he would demonstrate so well. She felt surprisingly at ease with him, despite the fact that he was hearing and so different from deaf men. Even Jacob, who was very successful in what he did, didn't have Rudy's casual grace.

Near the end of the third game, when three balls remained on the green felt, Sandra faced a difficult shot. Rudy showed to her how to lean over the edge of the table and execute it with her stick held out on a bridge in front of her. As she tried to do this, he came over and picked up her arm to reposition it. It seemed to Sandra that his hand lingered a second longer than it needed to. She felt her breath catch, then gasped silently at her reaction. Sandra refrained from looking at him and focused on the shot. When she missed, Rudy hit the remaining balls into the same pocket.

He turned and made sure she was looking at him before he pointed at an ear and asked, "How long have you been deaf?"

The unexpected question hit Sandra hard. She felt her composure leaving her. Struggling to regain it, she first signed then spoke, "How did you know about that?"

He didn't understand her. She concentrated on her enunciation and repeated herself.

"Why? You aren't trying to keep it a secret, are you?"

"Pardon me?"

He repeated himself, and she shook her head for lack of a better answer.

"Good, because it's obvious pretty quickly when you don't respond to things I say." Rudy nodded at Mr. Krause. "He told me yesterday when I asked him what country you were from."

Sandra silently damned the owner for revealing her secret.

"So how long have you been deaf?"

"I was born that way."

"I'm very sorry to hear that. It must've been a shock for your family when they found out about it."

She shook her head firmly and looked him in the eyes as she wondered if this was when Rudy was going to start acting like a typical hearing person. But she didn't care anymore. They'd finished playing pool, and she was not going to let this putdown go unanswered. "There's nothing to be sorry about. And actually, my parents were happy about it."

"I'm sorry, what did you say?" He had become more comfortable with her speech, but he wasn't sure he'd heard her right, though he understood that she didn't like the fact that he'd said he was sorry.

She repeated herself.

"That's what I thought you said. What do you mean?"

"Both my parents are deaf. All our friends are deaf. So my not hearing meant that I'd fit right in. In fact, two of my friends who are pregnant want their kids to be deaf because they want their children to be like they are."

He looked at her, taking in her words, catching the angry edge to them. "Wanna go have a soda and talk some more?"

Sandra looked at her watch, then back at Rudy. Her mother expected her to help prepare the Yom Kippur dinner, and it had already been two hours since she'd left home. But Rudy's body language was friendly, despite her hard-edged answer. He was so unlike every other hearing person she'd met. And, in a different way, from every deaf male as well. She still hadn't figured out what made him different, though. "Sure."

They went over to the soda fountain, where Rudy ordered two cherry Cokes. He paid the ten-cent tab and they sat down. She felt so extravagant. Playing pool. Having Cokes. Talking to a hearing person. Things her family and friends never did. And Rudy himself. A hearing soldier, who actually made her feel good at times.

"You know, you're the first deaf person I've ever talked to," Sandra saw his lips say as she sipped on her straw. She was asking him to repeat himself less and less as she became familiar with his face and lips.

"How come?"

"Never met any others. There are none in my family, school or neighborhood. And there's none in the Army."

"I'm surprised, since there are so many of us around now. Because of all the auto plants here. A lot of deaf men were able to find jobs there when the war started, since so many of the regular autoworkers were drafted into the Army."

"Well, there may be a lot of you around," Rudy smiled, "but I haven't met them."

She smiled back. "I must admit, I haven't spent much time with hearing people either."

"Really? Now that's amazing, considering that most people hear."

He had to repeat himself so she understood. "I've had no need to do so. Most everyone I know is deaf."

"What about when you were in school?"

"You mean before junior college? I went to the State Deaf School, where everyone was deaf. And in college, I just showed up for classes. Most of my classmates didn't want to talk to me, so I didn't talk to anyone much unless I had to."

"Wow. That sounds like it was an awful experience. Where's the State Deaf School?"

"In Flint." The Coke was cold and fresh in her hand. Sandra explained how most deaf children in the state went there, and how the classes were taught in sign language. She could see Rudy was becoming accustomed to her speech and understood most of her words. "The kids who go there prefer being deaf; they're happy to not hear."

"Why wouldn't you want to hear?" Rudy stirred his Coke with his straw, swirling the ice.

"Why would I want to hear?"

"Because you're missing all the sounds."

"Why do you think I miss hearing sounds?"

When he didn't respond, she watched him. He looked boyish, caught up in thought. She spoke over her straw. "Hearing people have no idea what it's like being deaf. Hearing people think we're not happy living in silence, that we would rather have a lot of sound in our world. It's just not true. Look at me. I have no interest in hearing sounds." Her body language displayed a defiance. "I'm very happy with who I am."

"Wow. That's so different from what I would've thought you'd feel."

Sandra leaned toward him, encouraged. "In fact, nothing annoys me more than when a hearing person tells me they're sorry I'm deaf."

"Which is exactly what I said just ten minutes ago. I didn't know."

"Huh?"

He repeated himself.

"I'll forgive you," Sandra said, a smile tugging at her mouth, red with her best lipstick.

"I promise, I'll never do it again."

She watched him as he took a sip of Coke, absently tapping his fingers on the table, moving his head in unison with his finger motions. She wondered if that's what hearing people did when they were nervous. He caught her looking at his tapping fingers. "I love Glenn Miller, and especially 'Kalamazoo.'"

Sandra eyed him closely. There was no sign of comprehension. "Say that again."

"The song playing now. 'I've Got a Girl in Kalamazoo.'"

She shook her head, but before she could say anything, Rudy realized his mistake. "I'm so sorry, I wasn't thinking. You can't hear it, can you?"

"No," she said, again almost in defiance, proud of her deaf heritage, her deaf parents and community.

He stopped tapping. "Can I ask you a dumb question about sign language?"

"Sure."

"How old were you when you learned it?"

"How old? I'm not positive, but probably I started when I was around one. Why?"

"Okay. I guess my question then is, how did you learn it before you learned English?"

"What do you mean?"

"Well, if you're signing the English language when you use sign language, then it would seem that you'd need to know English before you can sign it. Right?"

She shook her head. "No. When I'm signing, I'm not signing English. I'm using sign language. They're totally different."

"Wait a minute. Are you saying now that sign language is not based on English?"

"Yes. That's what I'm saying." She saw his eyes, curious. "Actually, it's kind of interesting," she said. "I'm told that the sign language we use in America was brought here originally by a Frenchman. I don't know French, but I'm told that because he brought it here, American Sign Language is more similar to French than English."

Rudy then peppered Sandra with more questions, trying to learn more about deaf culture, quickly realizing how distinct a group this population was. He found himself surprised by some of their customs. But they made sense when Sandra explained the rationale behind them.

When he paused to drain his glass and order another cherry Coke for both of them, Sandra was able to change the subject away from deafness. "So how long are you in town from the Army?"

"Three more days. I'm due back at Fort Bragg Sunday at six p.m."

"Is it really bad being there? I mean, I've heard so many stories about how badly they treat soldiers in the Army."

She watched him ponder her words carefully. Respecting her, she thought. Respecting her thinking. And his body language remained warm, engaged.

"Well, like anything, it depends on who your boss is. For me, it's been pretty tolerable because my drill sergeant is a decent guy. Besides, it sure beats any job I could've found around here. And in a month my platoon will be going to Europe. I've always wanted to go there. Especially since they've been showing those pictures in the *Movie Time News* at the theaters. The country over there looks real interesting, with all the old buildings and stuff. Definitely different from what we have here."

"I'm sorry, I didn't get that." It was the first time Rudy had said more than a couple of sentences together, and she had lost him by the third sentence.

Rudy smiled. "I guess that was a mouthful, wasn't it?" He repeated himself, a little more slowly. When Sandra still looked confused, he said, "Did you get that?"

She nodded, but seemed confused.

"You sure?"

"I think I did, but that movie thing you were talking about—"

"The *Movie Time News*? You know which one I'm talking about, don't you? The ones where they show the Germans and Hitler, that leader of theirs?"

Sandra hesitated before replying, wondering how Rudy would respond to her confession. "I've never seen the *Movie Time News*, because I don't go to the talking movies. I can't hear anything they say, so it makes little sense to me."

Rudy was embarrassed and cursed silently for not realizing the obvious again. "I'm sorry, Sandra. That was stupid of me."

Trying to keep her hearing loss from becoming the issue again, she quickly returned to their previous discussion. "But aren't you afraid that if you get involved in the fighting over there, you may get killed?"

"Sandra," he said, leaning forward with an earnest look on his face, "of course I don't want to die. But if we did go to war, I'd be fighting for my country, for the preservation of freedom. What nobler way is there to die than that?"

She thought for a second, then said, "Dying to save the life of someone you love."

He smiled and hit the table with his palm before pointing at her. "You're right. You win that one." Rudy looked at her appreciatively. She might be deaf, but she sure was smart. And so different from any woman he'd ever met. It was exciting to be with her, because he never knew what she was going to say next. Mr. Krause was right. She did come from a unique world. His eyes took her in, noticing the abundant curls of her shoulder-length dark hair, the contours of her breasts and good muscle tone of her arms. This was one fine woman.

Sandra engaged his look boldly. Rudy realized she had watched what he'd done, and he blushed. Her eyes never seemed to stop watching him. It had been disconcerting at first, but now he rather liked it. She really paid attention to what he said. In a way, it made her sexy. Another refreshing thing was the lack of the usual flirting that most hearing women displayed. And he'd already become so used to her speech that he didn't even notice it was different unless he thought about it.

"You have any brothers or sisters?"

She nodded. "A younger brother. What about you?"

"An older brother. He's married, lives in Tennessee. We hear from him every few weeks or so. What kind of work does your father do?"

"He's a tailor. He learned the trade from his father, who came over here from Russia. And yours?"

"He was the manager at the Ford plant in Flint, but with the war, they sent him to Willow Run to help figure out how to make that place faster at making parts for the airplanes for the war. They're really trying to speed up production. Mom told me he's been working long hours."

"I'm sorry. What's he doing?" Sandra felt comfortable asking now. Rudy told her again. "Wow," she answered. "Sounds like he's an important man."

Rudy shrugged. "I don't know how important he is, but a lot of people do ask for his help. Some of that comes from people in our church. He's real active there."

"What church?"

"St. Patrick's Catholic Church. You know that one?"

She nodded. "It's a beautiful building. Are you religious?"

"No. I mean, I believe in God and all that, but I just don't get anything from going to church every week. I think religion should be more than that."

"What do you think it should be?"

He was silent for a moment, slowly rotating his Coke glass. "Something that brings mankind together. Something that gives people hope and teaches them to appreciate other people, not attack them. When I look around the world, though, I see the opposite." He watched her, making sure she understood. "Religion seems to be responsible for a lot of the wars. I mean, people actually kill each other over religion. Or over people being different. It's so sad. And what makes it really a tragedy is that religious leaders often support this behavior. Like now, in Europe. Where Hitler is picking on the Jews and all the other groups who aren't part of his Aryan race. And the German churches there aren't protesting. In fact, many of them are rallying to his side. That's just the opposite of what religion should be." His eyes were dark in reflection.

For the first time, Sandra was able to keep up with Rudy's lips for more than three sentences. "I agree. It's now happening here too."

"What do you mean?"

"In California. In the relocation camps for the Japanese."

"But don't you think there's a difference? They're Japanese, and we're at war with Japan."

"No. Think about it. Those people were born here. They're just as American as you and I are."

"They may have been born here, Sandra, but they've tended to remain separate from everybody else. They haven't become integrated in America like the rest of us, when we came from Europe, I mean. For all we know, they're secretly helping the Japanese government."

She looked at him. His body language was sincere, not the ugly contours of a bigot. "I disagree. Look at deaf people. They've remained just as separate from society, if not more so. Are we dangerous?" She shook her head, answering her own question. "I don't think so. And tell me, if it is true that immigrants remain loyal to their old country, why are we doing that to the Japanese but not the Italians? I don't know any Italians, but from what I've read, many of them continue to speak Italian at home and tend to socialize together. Yet they're not being put into camps, even though Italy is fighting on Germany's side. No, I think it's happening to the Japanese because of prejudice. Either because of the way they look or for some other reason. It's pure prejudice, nothing more."

"You've got a point there." Rudy nodded. "In fact, you've got a very good point. It reminds me of one of my favorite poems from when I was young. It was in Robert Louis Stevenson's *A Child's Book of Verses*. At the time I didn't really appreciate what it was saying."

"What was it about?"

"Well, it basically tells how a child thinks his life is better than some child in another culture."

"Sorry, Rudy..."

"So you don't know it? That's okay."

Sandra shook her head. "I've never really enjoyed reading poetry. In fact, now that I think of it, I don't know any deaf person who reads it, though I'm sure there's one someplace who does. I mean, it's not like we don't know about poems. Of course we do. I had to read them in college. We just don't know how many of the words are pronounced, and we can't hear the rhythm. So we don't really see what hearing people see in them."

The soldier's eyes watched her intently, struck by yet another difference between deaf and hearing people. "Sandra, sometimes it's not just the rhythm that makes a poem so nice. It's what it says and how it makes its point. The poem I was talking about is a perfect example. It's called 'Foreign Children.' I still remember the words. Listen."

He began to recite, his eyes never leaving hers, but hers were on his mouth.

Little Indian, Sioux, or Crow,
Little frosty Eskimo,
Little Turk or Japanese,
Oh! don't you wish that you were me?

You have seen the scarlet trees
And the lions overseas;
You have eaten ostrich eggs,

46

And turned the turtle off their legs.

Such a life is very fine,
But it's not so nice as mine:
You must often as you trod,
Have wearied NOT to be abroad.

You have curious things to eat,
I am fed on proper meat;
You must dwell upon the foam,
But I am safe and live at home.

Little Indian, Sioux or Crow,
Little frosty Eskimo,
Little Turk or Japanese,
Oh! don't you wish that you were me?

Sandra watched his face recite the lines and noted the way he almost imperceptibly nodded his head with every other syllable as well as paused at the end of each line. In a way, it was like when he had been tapping earlier, presumably to the music beat. It was the first time she had ever sensed a rhythm in a poem, and it gave her some inkling of what music might be like. In a way, the lines were mesmerizing, even though she didn't get many of the words. But those she did get were just like Rudy had described—how a child would feel about another culture.

"I like that poem," she said slowly. "By putting it in the context of a child's mind, he's able to talk about how adults also think, without turning them off."

"Exactly."

"Are a lot of poems like that?"

"Oh yes. And each poet has a different way of doing it. I've always loved reading poetry."

They sat quietly, looking at each other, Rudy hearing the female vocalist being broadcast and Sandra in a familiar silence. Each tried to act casual. Each was aware of the other's movements. It wasn't that they were at a loss for something to say. They were more comfortable just sitting there with each other. Getting to know each other. Sandra found herself proud to be seen with a soldier, a symbol of prestige with a war going on. She'd never had the opportunity before. Rudy also felt content. Spending time with a deaf woman had opened up a new world to him, different and exciting.

Sandra looked at her watch and gasped. "It's five thirty-five! I have to go." She jumped up, their mood shattered.

Rudy got up too. "I enjoyed talking to you," he said awkwardly.

"Me too."

"Would you like to go out for ice cream later?"

"I'd love to, but I can't. Tonight's Yom Kippur."

"Tonight's what?"

She'd been so focused on the fact that he was hearing, she hadn't thought about his religion. Now she remembered he not only didn't look the least bit Jewish, he'd also told her he was Catholic. No wonder he was ignorant about Yom Kippur.

"Yom Kippur," she repeated her words carefully. "The holiest time of the year in the Jewish religion. I'm Jewish, so I'll be going to services."

"Really?" He paused, but only for a second. "I've never really known anyone Jewish before. I mean, I know some Jews, but you're the first one I've ever had a real conversation with."

A bit defensively, she studied his body language. Still nothing negative. Sandra looked back at his face just in time to see him say, "I'd love to hear more about this holy time and what it's about. How about we meet somewhere tomorrow morning, say around ten?"

She shook her head. "Yom Kippur lasts twenty-four hours, from sundown tonight until sundown tomorrow. Except when

I'm sleeping, I'll be at the temple. I won't even eat, because we fast the entire time as part of getting ourselves to think how we can do better in the coming year."

Rudy looked at her. He had only three more days before he returned to the base, and he had to see her again. "So the holiday's over at sundown tomorrow?"

"Yes."

"And then things are back to normal?"

She smiled. "If you mean I won't be at services in the temple or fasting, yes."

"Some high school friends of mine are having a party then. Will you come with me?"

Sandra saw his almost pleading eyes and body language, and she wanted to go. But she knew better, feeling uneasy with her growing attraction for him. He was hearing, and he was a goy. Two clear strikes against him. Moreover, she recalled the one time she had gone to a hearing party with some deaf friends. They weren't pleasant memories. It was best to end this relationship before something bad happened.

"No thanks, Rudy. It's been fun talking with you today, but even so, I've had to work hard to understand you, and you happen to be someone who's easy to lip-read. In a group of hearing people, it's impossible for me to do that. Every time I've been in that situation before, I've never been able to follow the conversation. I'm afraid I wouldn't be much fun. Thanks for inviting me, though. And thanks so much for the pool game, and the Cokes." She started to leave.

He touched her arm to get her attention. "I wouldn't worry about that. The people who'll be at the party are very easy to get along with."

She smiled at him again. "I'm sure they are, but I really don't think I should go. Thanks again."

He reached after her again. "I'd really, really like to see you tomorrow. I think you'll find this party fun, but if you won't go, would you be willing to get together with just me?"

The desire displayed by his body language practically shouted at her. As a deaf person, Sandra was more in tune with that than his speech, and she felt her own emotions get the better of her.

"Okay, I'll try it this one time. I'll go to the party."

"You will? Great! You'll like it. I'm sure of it. What time should I pick you up? Seven o'clock?"

"Better make it seven-thirty to be sure I'm back from temple."

"It's a deal. Now where's your house?"

Sandra told him, and they exchanged goodbyes. She started to walk out, but suddenly stopped. "You never did tell me your last name."

"Townsend."

As with anyone who depends on speech reading, Sandra often couldn't understand spoken names. "Can you spell that?"

He did so, then she left, stopping to wave before exiting through the side door. Rudy remained in place a long time, lost in thought, idly tapping to a new pop tune. Sandra was downright interesting. First deaf, and then Jewish. What would he learn about her next?

Rudy left Gabby's in time to get home to catch the end of the Tigers' victory over the Cleveland Indians on the radio. The rest of the day he spent with his parents, but time crawled. He went grocery shopping with his mother, Molly, who spent much of that time gushing about the movie she'd seen recently, *Casablanca*, and the bestseller she was reading, a book by Rachel Field called *And Now Tomorrow*.

His father was more interesting. George Townsend, a wiry, five-foot-ten-inch man with a Don Ameche mustache and slicked-back hair, was very enthusiastic about the war-related projects he was working on. He regaled his son with stories about the production changeover at the plant from cars to Army vehicles. But Rudy had heard much of this before. There was none of the freshness and insights that occurred with Sandra. And when the conversation shifted to people in the neighborhood, none of whom he knew, Rudy lost interest. Boredom began to creep in.

Dinnertime. Anticipating her son's departure, Mrs. Townsend had made one of Rudy's favorite dishes: fried trout, Brussels sprouts and rolls. After a brief prayer, they dug in.

"Rudy, remember Father Coughlin?" George Townsend asked. "The priest who gives those wonderful Sunday broadcasts about the state of the country?"

The soldier-son nodded, his mouth full. "The ones from the Shrine of the Little Flower?" Rudy recalled that his parents never missed hearing them.

"Father's show last week was one of the best I've heard in awhile."

"I didn't realize he was still around. I thought I heard he'd stopped his show."

"No, he's still doing it and is as good as ever," his mother said, glancing around the table, seeing if anyone needed more food. "I don't understand why so many people have stopped listening to him. I think he's right on target with the problems in this country."

Mr. Townsend waved a roll for emphasis. "Last week he talked about how corrupt the Federal Reserve is, how it's a conspiracy by international bankers to destroy our economy. He's been in touch with a professor from Ireland, Dublin, I think, who has proof that the Jews are behind it all. Honey, do you remember the name of that professor?"

"Dennis. . . I think the last name is Fahey or something like that."

Before George Townsend could continue, Rudy spoke. "In the Army, I've heard people say that Father Coughlin is actually pro-Hitler. A lot of people in the Army don't like him because of that."

His father sat still, the roll lowered to his plate. He looked right at his son. "Well then, they don't understand what the man is saying. He does agree with the Germans that we need to do something about the Jew problem, but he's not pro-Hitler. I myself, at least two different times, have heard him make it very clear that the good Father is against Nazism."

Mrs. Townsend played with her napkin, then changed the subject back to the book she was reading. The two men ate silently as the tension disappeared. It was a romance about a doctor, Mother explained, who was trying to find a cure for deafness.

Rudy reached for a roll. Sandra was Jewish and deaf. Now their conversation had gone from Jews to deafness. Weird. Just weird. "I've heard that some deaf people are perfectly happy being deaf."

"What?" His mother's eyes widened. "Who would ever want that? That just doesn't make any sense."

"Have you ever asked a deaf person?"

"Of course not. You know as well as I do that there's no way a deaf mute would understand what I said."

Rudy didn't respond. After another silence, the father glanced carefully at his son. "So how was bowling today?"

"Fine. Actually, I decided to play pool instead of bowl."

"Son, wish I could've taken off some time to play with you. I know it's not as much fun playing alone."

"Don't worry, Dad, it worked out fine. It turned out I wasn't alone. I ended up playing with a girl I met there."

His mother became instantly interested, her romance novel churning her own emotions. "Really? Who was that?"

Rudy scolded himself for mentioning Sandra in his mother's presence. He should've known she'd pester him for details. And after the conversation they'd just had, he had no desire to talk about that. He was pondering how to change the subject when he happened to glance at the kitchen clock. It was almost seven.

"Oh! 'The Little Theater off Times Square' will be on any moment. I've missed hearing that show since I've been in the Army, so if it's okay with you, I'm going to go listen."

He walked to the living room, where the radio sat on the floor. Almost four feet high and two wide, it was state of the art, bought just a month earlier. Rudy turned the radio on, watching the dial light up, and sat on the couch across from it. Just as his parents entered the room to join him, the voice familiar to millions of people across the country came on the air.

"Welcome to the Little Theater off Times Square. This is the First Nighter reporting from the theater, and the play is about to start. A hush has come over the audience, and the curtain is rising. Let's be quiet and listen to the show. . ."

The Townsends sat quietly, spellbound by the voice of the First Nighter as he described the play. By the time the show was over an hour later, Rudy's mother had forgotten about his date. Mr. Townsend changed the tuner to a different station so they could listen to the Eddie Cantor show. After that was the Amos and Andy comedy hour. Near the beginning of this show, Andy joked about not being able to hear someone. Suddenly, Rudy realized another way Sandra was different from him—she almost certainly had never listened to the radio, and probably had no familiarity with any of its shows. This thought lingered the rest of the evening. Somehow, it epitomized the difference between deaf and hearing people. The radio, a major means of communication and enjoyment for most Americans, was irrelevant to deaf people. He remembered Sandra explaining that deaf people like being deaf and wondered if, despite that, they ever missed not hearing the radio.

After Walter Winchell's nightly news report, the Townsends talked about the turmoil in Europe and debated how much the U.S. should get involved. Mr. Townsend wasn't convinced America should join the Allies in Europe, though he hated Japan, which had attacked America. His wife's main concern was for the safety of her son. Rudy argued the other side, advocating that Hitler had to be stopped before he got too powerful. If that happened, he asserted, democracy and tolerance could vanish from the earth.

It was almost midnight before they went to bed. Neither side had convinced the other. Rudy lay in the dark but couldn't sleep. He turned on the bedside light to read, only to find himself rereading the same page. He then lay back on his pillow, looking at the ceiling.

"Home is where the heart is," was the first thought that came to his mind. Who said that? He couldn't remember, but knew he didn't feel like he'd come back home. It was nice seeing his parents again, but their new house lacked the warm memories of the one he'd grown up in. At least they had a place, and a nice one at that. So many people didn't these days. That was something he'd realized from being in the Army, where stories of other recruits about their families driven into poverty had touched his heart.

The idea of a career in politics floated into Rudy's mind. That was how he could bring about change. He'd been thinking about that a lot. The potential to help people, particularly those who struggled to make ends meet, touched something inside him. He recalled his school experiences with politics, beginning as class representative in eighth grade. He'd found it fascinating, the way people with different ideas came together to discuss ways to make things better for everyone. In high school he was elected to Student Council as a freshman. He ran successfully for class president as a sophomore. That had been a rude awakening. Being president was more than just being senior to the representatives; too much time was spent resolving conflicts, placating those who didn't get their way, and encouraging those who were moving slower than one wanted. Rudy had preferred the role of representative, where he could focus on what was important to him.

The untried soldier wondered what it would be like to be a U.S. senator. He lay in the solitude of his room bathed in lamplight, his mind quickening. Senator seemed to be similar to representative, except the longer term was a plus. The fact that there were only two from each state also gave more clout. Either way, whether he was in the House of Representatives or the Senate, he'd have power to get things done. And he'd meet all kinds of people too. There were so many interesting folks out there.

Like Sandra. Rudy adjusted his pillows. Such a unique woman. So different, from not only him, but also anyone he'd ever dated. And those differences intrigued him. Her thoughts and ideas were so unique, a whole new world and way of thinking. He looked forward to learning more. About deaf culture. About Jewish customs. About other surprises she would reveal. And best of all, she was cute and fun to be with.

Rudy studied the ceiling. She was worried about the party. But he wasn't. His friends were an outgoing bunch. He was confident she wouldn't have problems communicating, and they were certain to find her as interesting as he did.

His parents, though, would be more problematic should they meet Sandra. They were overall good people: faithful members of their church, supporters of charitable causes, friends with many types of people, and tolerant of most things. But not some things. Like Jews. Rudy had no doubt how they'd be if they ever met her.

A fly buzzed against the lampshade. He watched it slowly gravitate to the light bulb. Life had seemed so straightforward a week ago when he got his leave from the Army, anticipating a lazy week at home. He glanced at the bedside clock, then switched off the light. Life was proving more complex than anticipated, but it was more exciting too. Rudy closed his eyes. Sandra's face conjured itself, her intelligent eyes watching, her curls tumbling. He couldn't wait to be with her again.

Day Three

Five

It was solemn in the temple, yet also serenely festive. It was the Day of Atonement, the holiest day of the year. The time all Jews ask for forgiveness for their sins, and a time when souls are refreshed. In this Yom Kippur service, the effects of the war were evident. When everyone prayed for a good year in the book of life, they were hoping for an end to war and the hardships it had imposed. And many were praying for the safe return of loved ones.

Sandra counted herself lucky. For the last few years, three hearing members of deaf families had taken turns interpreting the service. They even signed the songs. She knew what was happening, unlike in most synagogues where deaf Jews either sat through services understanding nothing or opted out of going. Over the years, she'd become comfortable with the rituals of the holiday. She had found comfort in the prayers offered. And she had always loved the mood of holiness, the feeling of communing with God that occurred on this special day. Still, starting with the three-hour Kol Nidre service the night before, the congregation would spend almost fourteen hours in the sanctuary. A long time. Especially for someone so eagerly looking forward to her date.

She counted the pages left in the prayer book before Yom Kippur services would be over. Sandra knew from prior years how much time they would take. Forty-five minutes. It seemed like forever. She fidgeted until her father shot her a glance, then forced herself to stop. Sandra tried to reflect, to concentrate on the needs of her soul. But with the end of the service in sight, she was having a hard time doing so. Her thoughts kept meandering to Rudy.

What attracted her, what drew her to him? It wasn't that he was taller or, in a different way, handsomer than Jacob. It was his interests, the things he talked about. Things never discussed by deaf people. Like music. Life in the Army. What people watched at talking movies. And the nobility of fighting for one's country. Furthermore, though Sandra preferred signing to speaking, she didn't mind talking with Rudy. He was easy to speech-read. He didn't seem to mind when he had to repeat himself. And he seemed to understand her just as well.

For the first time in her life, Sandra looked forward to spending time with a hearing person, in spite of her fears about going to a hearing party. Rudy was a breath of fresh air, an escape from the usual, a fairy tale. Maybe his friends were the same. Maybe there really were other nice hearing people. It promised to be even better than baseball. Like Cinderella meeting the prince without a fairy godmother. With midnight a long, long way away.

A nudge from her brother brought Sandra back. She found her place in the prayer book and ignored another glare from her father. She focused on the interpreters, mouthing words with the congregation as they sang the Sh'mah.

Sundown finally came. The shofar was blown, signaling the end of the High Holy Days. After joining the rest of the congregation in wishing each other L'Shanah Tovah—Happy New Year—Sandra left to get ready for her date. She had excused herself with great difficulty from the traditional break-the-fast celebration at her grandparents' house. But any regrets were outweighed by the anticipation of seeing Rudy. The fact that everyone else would be at the food fest was actually good; they wouldn't be home when the soldier came to get her.

Sandra grabbed a bite from the kitchen, then went to get dressed. She had decided to wear something dressier than she had at the bowling alley, her prized navy pleated dress with white trim, along with a matching pair of shoes. She felt fortunate to have a pleated dress with the fabric shortage. Although her mother had found it in a thrift shop, it looked new and fit her perfectly. Sandra got ready, thanking God again that she was home alone.

At exactly seven-thirty, just as she finished checking herself in the mirror, the lights in the house flashed on and off. She opened the door. It was Rudy, his uniform freshly cleaned and pressed. "Hi," he said. "You sure look nice tonight."

Sandra smiled and invited him into the foyer. He took in the living room and den with a glance. The place was clean, with a comfortable but simple ambience. The walls, covered with family pictures of solemn older faces, were faded. The carpet showed signs of wear. The furnishings were old, but well maintained, brightened with homey touches of pillows. It was clear to Rudy that although the Horowitzs didn't have much money, they took pride in their home.

"You here alone?"

Sandra nodded. "My family's at my grandparents' house for dinner. That's a Yom Kippur tradition we've had as long as I can remember."

"I'm so sorry. I didn't mean to take you away from a family tradition. If you want to—"

She cut him off with a wave of her hand. "Don't worry about that. I didn't want to go there this year anyway."

Rudy looked at the pictures on the wall near him. One in particular caught his attention. It was a group photo of around thirty people and looked like it spanned four generations. The older people looked solemn, none of them smiling. The younger generations had more smiles on their faces. "This your family?"

"Yes. That's my mother and father." Sandra pointed them out. "Those are my grandparents, the ones who are having everyone over for dinner tonight. And those are my grandfather's six brothers and sisters, and their families."

"They're the ones from Russia?"

She nodded.

"They look…" He hesitated, turning to look at her. "Kind of short."

"They are. My grandmother isn't even five feet. I think it's due to malnutrition when they were growing up."

Rudy put his finger over a younger woman with longer hair, smiling from the middle of the photo. "This is you, isn't it?"

Sandra smiled. "I was fifteen then."

A dog nudged Rudy's hand. He looked down and patted it on the head. "What's his name?"

"Speedy."

"He looks pretty old," Rudy said as he knelt and rubbed the mutt behind the ears, noticing the grizzled hair on the muzzle and the animal's stiff movements.

"He is. He turned thirteen last month. We've had him since he was a puppy, and he's a great dog. Unlike a lot of people I know, Speedy's always there for me. He never gives me a hard time. He accepts me unconditionally."

Rudy stood up, smiling. "That's what I like about dogs. No matter what happens, they love you, always happy to see you."

Sandra bent over to hug Speedy. "Shall we go?"

Rudy nodded. She retrieved her purse and locked the door as they exited the brownstone house into the balmy night. There was no one else on the street.

Rudy started to talk, then realized he wasn't looking at Sandra. He started over again. "My parents offered me the use of their car, but I thought we could talk better if we took the bus. Number 71, on Pratt and Kenneth, takes us to within a block of the party."

Sandra got enough to understand, despite the difficulty seeing his lips in the dark. "Gas rations are too scarce to waste on driving to a party, anyway."

"Actually, that's not a problem for my parents," Rudy said as they walked under a streetlight. "My father gets C coupons because he uses the car at work. So he never has any problems getting gas."

"You have C coupons? Wow! You're so lucky. That must be really nice. We only get A coupons and have to really be careful how much we drive so we can make the gas last for the month."

They walked side by side to the bus stop, the street dimly lit by the lights from the houses and an occasional streetlamp.

"So what kind of job are you looking for?"

Sandra didn't respond. She was looking straight ahead and hadn't seen his lips move. The soldier tapped her shoulder to get her attention, then repeated his question. They were in between two lights, so she still couldn't see him well enough to understand, even though she was comfortable speech-reading his face. It wasn't until they got closer to the next streetlamp that she got what he said. "What I'd really like is something to do with baseball or animals, even if it's an entry level job. But I'll take anything. One can't be too picky these days."

"That's for sure. If you could do whatever you wanted, though, what would you do?"

"I'd be a veterinarian," she replied, then added after a pause, "but I know that's impossible."

"Why?"

"Because I'm deaf."

Rudy was quiet a moment. He said carefully, "Are you sure it's impossible? Some people say you can do anything you really want to if you're willing to work for it."

"Not in my case."

They stood in the halo of a sidewalk lamp. "I'm not so sure."

"Look, Rudy. Just the fact I'm a woman makes it hard enough to become a vet. It's a fact. There are no women in most veterinary schools in this country. That's strike one. And it's no secret there's quotas for Jewish people as well. That's strike two. When you add

63

my deafness, well," she forced a smile, sad in the light, "that's a fast ball down the middle for strike three."

Under the streetlight, Rudy's eyes found hers. "I've only been in the Army four months so far. But I've already seen and heard about people doing things they didn't think possible. So, now I believe that if you think you can or can't do something, you're right. Maybe it is true, like some people say, nothing is impossible. You must never give up on your dreams. Miracles do happen."

They both were aware that he had instinctively held her arms. He let go slowly.

"Well," Sandra said, "maybe I'll give you that it's not impossible. But it's darned close. Actually, for most of my life I felt like you do now, that if I worked hard and did well, I'd get the chance. But then last spring, I got my last of several rejections from a university, even though I did better in junior college than the hearing people who did go on to a university. So, I'm more realistic now. Or whatever you want to call it. I'll probably go to Gallaudet University, though I'm not sure exactly what I'll end up doing."

He didn't quite get what she'd said, so he simply responded, "Tell me more." When she finished re-explaining about her rejections, Sandra could sense Rudy wasn't convinced. "Let's put it this way. No one that I know, or who I've ever talked to, knows of any deaf person who has ever become a vet, a doctor, a dentist, or even a lawyer. Not just in America, but in the world."

"Someone has to be the first one. Why can't it be you?"

She looked into his gaze, seeing his idealism there. "Do I ever wish that were possible! I'd love being a veterinarian so much. It's what I've dreamed about all my life."

"Where is this Galulaidet... how do you say it?"

She spelled it out for him.

"Gallaudet. Where is Gallaudet University located?"

"Washington, D.C. It was started by Congress for people who are deaf. They teach the classes in sign language."

"That's how you do it then. You get your degree there, then go to vet school."

She pressed his hand. "You don't understand, Rudy. No matter what I do, I won't ever get into vet school because I can't hear." She pointed to her ears and shook her head to emphasize the point. "It has nothing to do with how smart I am, or whether I'm capable of being a vet. It's because of this prejudice against us deaf people. This belief that we're dumb and can't do anything. Just like the prejudice America has against the Japanese we talked about yesterday. Even if I were to go to Gallaudet and do really well there, it wouldn't matter. I just don't see the vet schools changing their minds."

They walked the remaining block in silence, reaching the corner as the bus pulled up. When the driver saw Rudy's uniform, he insisted the soldier ride for free. They scooted down the aisle to the last seat on the right and sat down, she next to the window. Each was conscious of the other's closeness, trying to avoid too much contact while acting casual.

Sandra looked at the houses they passed. Most were wooden bungalows built around the same time period, with large cement front porches or verandas. Every once in awhile she saw a brick home; these were usually bigger too, and some even had a driveway next to the house. She noticed that many windows had small red frames with a blue star on a white background. Someone from that house was in the service. Several had two stars, and she saw one house with three. She wondered what it must be like to have three sons in the war, and turned to Rudy.

"Remember yesterday at the bowling alley, when you said you're going to Europe in a month?"

He nodded.

"When you joined the Army, did you think you'd end up getting sent to the war front?"

"Yeah, I did. Everyone's getting sent over there, so I figured I would too. Besides, that's the way politicians work." When he saw

Sandra's puzzled face, he turned to face her, repeating himself. "I'm not saying they deliberately want us to go to war. It's just that... well... take the President, for example. It's easy for him to justify our country getting involved. And it gives him something to distract people from how bad the economy is. You know how he does it, don't you? He'll go on the radio and give a big razzle-dazzle speech about how America needs to help our friends and save the world from a tyrant."

There was enough light on the bus for her to see the essence of what he had said. "A lot of people listen to those radio speeches?"

"Oh yes." Rudy nodded vigorously. "Just about everyone in the country who can hear will do so."

"What does it sound like?"

"What do you mean?"

"Well, does it sound like a live voice, like someone's in the room with you?"

"No. It sounds like a voice coming through a microphone. You know what I mean?"

Sandra shook her head. "I have no idea."

"It's got a metallic sound. That means it kind of grates and has a crackling noise to it, sounds like... you know, it's hard to explain what it sounds like to someone who's never heard it, but it's clearly different from a live voice."

Sandra paused to contemplate a metallic sound, and how that might differ from voices. "Can people understand everything that's said on the radio?"

"Usually. As long as there's good reception."

"Good. Because it's clear that Hitler is massacring thousands of Jews and other people. So if the President explains that to people, then everyone would agree that stopping Hitler would be the right thing to do, right?"

"Well, I don't know. I've heard rumors about the massacres too. But as far as I know, it hasn't been proven."

Sandra studied Rudy's face. It looked as sincere as ever. "It seems pretty clear to me. Just look at the facts, the way they're removing Jewish people from all the countries they control. It's so scary. They're separating mothers and fathers from their children, and no one knows where they take people, although there are some terrible rumors. Just imagine what that would be like if it happened to you."

There was no response from the soldier. Sandra thought about the windows with the stars she had seen from the bus. "A lot of people are going to die in this war. I'm thinking about all the families in the country who have sons in the war, and all the other countries in Europe and Asia as well. Too many of them will find themselves trying to cope with the death of their loved ones. And the longer the war goes on, the greater the number of families who will suffer." She watched him, her eyes wet.

"You're right, you're right," Rudy said, pulling out a folded handkerchief and giving it to her. "That's exactly what'll happen. But to most politicians, it doesn't matter. They'd justify it as a necessary tradeoff for the good of the country." He gave her the handkerchief. "Sometimes I think people in power don't really care. They don't care what happens to those who suffer as a result of political decisions. It's that kind of attitude I want to change.

"Sandra, I'm going to tell you a secret. Something I've told only a couple of other people. My life goal is to become a member of Congress, probably as a United States senator. And when I get there, I'm going to do my best to make Congress more responsive and less political."

"How would you change things, Rudy?" She pressed the handkerchief into her hand.

"I'd make sure my fellow congressmen thought more about the impact of our decisions on the people of this country." He gently touched her arm. "If America had to go to war, for example, Congress should at least be doing what it could to minimize the impact on the home front. And we need to be sure that everyone is

67

treated the same when the armed forces are deciding whether or not to draft them. Not like the way it is now. You know what I mean, don't you? How a lot of congressmen will vote for war and be all rah-rah-rah about it, but then do everything they can to keep their own sons out of the Army? That really irks me."

A man two rows ahead turned and stared at them a second before turning away. "I better stop talking before I get in trouble," he mouthed silently at her, figuring she'd be able to read his lips. "Being in the Army, I'm not supposed to say things like that. At least not in public."

She nodded. In a way she was glad for the pause, because she was quickly becoming fatigued trying to understand Rudy. Speech-reading was always exhausting, partly because at best only half the words are understood. The deaf person has to guess what the other words are.

The bus reached their stop and they got off. Rudy pointed in the direction they were going. As they walked, he began to tell her about his friends who would be at the party. The street was poorly lit, making it hard for Sandra. He had to repeat himself several times before her eyes became adjusted to the dimness so she could speech-read again.

"Most of the folks who'll be there I hung around with in high school. I haven't had much contact with them in the past year, so it'll be nice to see what they're up to, especially two of them. One is Mark, my best friend growing up. I haven't seen him since I left to join the Army. He was visiting family in Chicago and just got back today. He'll be leaving next week for the Navy, so this might be the last time we see each other for a long time. The other is Pam, one of two girls I dated seriously in high school." He made sure Sandra was looking at him and understanding his words. "I want you to know that I don't have the least bit of interest in Pam. I just want to see what's happened to her since we graduated."

"Will the other woman be there too?"

"No. Susan moved away after the first semester of our junior year. That was the last I ever saw her. She was my first real love." Rudy smiled self-consciously. "I was really upset at the time, but that was years ago. I haven't thought about her in quite a while."

He pointed to a house just ahead. "That's the place." They turned at the beige brick bungalow, and Rudy led the way to the front porch.

A tall young man answered the doorbell. "Well, look who's here!" The man gave Rudy a bear hug.

"Mark, you haven't changed a bit."

"Neither have you, old man. Come on in."

As they did so, Mark nodded approvingly at Sandra and said as he turned to close the door, "And who's your friend?"

Sandra didn't see the question, nor Rudy's reply. She'd been scanning the inside of the house.

"Welcome, Sandra. Nice to meet you."

She looked at him after he had finished and smiled, still not realizing he had spoken to her.

"The gang's in the back," Mark said, "in the family room."

They followed him and found a roomful of people. Rudy recognized "Chattanooga Choo Choo," the hit song of the year, playing on the record player, then everyone milled around the new arrivals to greet their former classmate. Sandra noted immediately that the lights were dimmed much more than they would have been in any deaf household. That made it even harder than dealing with the usual difficulties speech-reading a group. It seemed to her, from what she could see of the body language and demeanor of most of the crowd, that they almost seemed to be awed by Rudy. She knew soldiers were held in high regard and wondered if that were the reason, or if it was their experiences with him in high school. Several of the women had unfamiliar perfume fragrances. It must be a hearing thing, she decided. Most of her friends and family didn't use perfumes. Aside from the cost, they simply weren't part of deaf culture.

Rudy introduced Sandra, but other than cursory greetings, people were more interested in Rudy. She understood very few of the names, and even less of the discussion. One appeared to be about Greer Garson and Walter Pidgeon in *Mrs. Miniver.* She remembered seeing the title in the newspaper, allowing her to identify it when she saw it on lips. From their body language, people seemed very enthusiastic about the film. Sandra remembered seeing posters of Garson and Pidgeon at the downtown theater. She wondered what it was like to watch a movie where one could understand what was being said, as well as hear all the other non-verbal sounds. ·

She focused hard on three men near her. One of them had somewhat intelligible facial movements. He was discussing his draft status, and she thought she saw him say he had been classified as 4F and was telling the others about it, but she wasn't sure. This was all new and unfamiliar to her. Deaf people never discussed the talking movies or the draft. And, of course, they also used sign language so she could see everything they were communicating.

On the other side of her, a young man was talking to two women. She couldn't understand either of the women's faces despite a shaft of light illuminating all of them, but was able to make out the man saying, "Want to hear a joke?"

The women nodded.

"Did you… cannibal… passed his mother… path…?"

All three of them laughed. Sandra looked away before she was caught watching them, and wondered what was so funny about walking by one's mother in the jungle. Either she had missed too much of what he had said, or it must be a hearing thing, something related to hearing culture.

Rudy nudged her arm. She looked up. "I want you to meet Jim, who played baseball in high school with me," Rudy said.

"Nice to meet you," Sandra said. Jim had a handlebar mustache that covered his lips. Fortunately, Rudy then asked Jim a question and took the pressure off. A few others came up, and they were part of a larger group.

As she had feared, Sandra found herself lost, unable to follow the conversation as it moved around. The dim lighting worked against her, as did her unfamiliarity with most of the places and topics discussed, many of which centered around their high school days. But even if she had been familiar with the talk and the lighting had been perfect, she still would have had a major problem. Aside from the fact that the best lip reader gets at best fifty percent—and more commonly only twenty percent—of a conversation with someone who is easy to speech read, Sandra was dealing with multiple people, some with unintelligible lip movements. Moreover, as soon as she figured out who was speaking and looked at his or her face, someone else started talking. And no one looked in her direction when they spoke. She glanced at Rudy. He was clearly enjoying himself. So every time he looked at her, which was quite often, she would smile, pretending all was okay.

She scanned the room, amazed at how easily people communicated by sound. It didn't seem to matter whether they looked at each other. They seemed to understand just as well when spoken to from behind. And because no one used their hands or body to communicate, the atmosphere was calm compared to what she was used to. Everyone here was so expressionless. No one used their faces or bodies much. And the few hand gestures she saw didn't seem to have any meaning. If she hadn't had the ability to tell from their body language that they were enjoying themselves, she could have been convinced the party was a bust.

Everyone started swaying, slightly at first, then more vigorously. Sandra knew about dancing, but had never seen it in a party setting like this. A few began bouncing jauntily, smiling at each other, their movements in perfect unison. Everyone's swaying became more and more pronounced. A woman went over to the record player and turned the volume up. Two guys grabbed one of the women next to them and started dancing. Others around them clapped to some beat, and she could see everyone's lips moving. A song, a beat. All of it beyond her. She turned to Rudy, who had clearly gotten into it. Sandra got his attention and nodded at the activity in the room, a quizzical expression on her face.

"A special song?"

"Yes. It just came on the record player. It's the one I told you about at Gabby's. 'I've Got a Girl in Kalamazoo.' It's really popular around here because Kalamazoo is in Michigan." He paused. "Can you feel the sound? It's really loud."

She shook her head and looked back to watch everyone dance. After about three minutes, everyone stopped and started talking again. Someone turned the volume back down. Song over. For her, unknown, gone into the ethos.

Sandra again found herself pondering what life would be like if she could hear. She saw someone put a new record on the player and wondered what kind of music was filling the room. What did it sound like? She told Rudy she'd be back and walked over to the record player. The needle tracked the spinning disk. It was somehow pulling out sound that hearing people found enjoyable. She put her hand on the speaker and felt vibrations. Then Sandra looked at the record jacket. "This is the Army, Mr. Jones." Did the words in the song tell a story about Army life, or were they something different?

Sandra scanned the crowd again. The music didn't seem to distract anyone. Everyone she looked at took in the sounds effortlessly. In some strange way, they were able to hear the music without it interfering with their ability to talk to each other. That concept seemed incredible. But when she thought more about it, she realized that with her eyes she could be aware of more than one object at a time. Maybe it worked like that. But she couldn't focus on two things at the same time with her eyes, like hearing people seemed to do with sound.

She walked back to Rudy. "Everything okay?" she saw him say. She lied again, not wanting to take him away from the party.

He introduced her to another friend, put an arm around her shoulder, then resumed conversation.

Sandra felt boredom, fed by exclusion, edging in. She tried not to daydream as she usually did when cut off from her familiar life. She wanted to be alert when the inevitable question came her way. Above everything, she mustn't embarrass Rudy.

Sandra found herself stealing glances at a woman in the group next to her, the one Rudy had said was Pam. She was very pretty. Her eyes were attractive and skillfully enhanced with makeup. There always seemed to be a crowd around her. Sandra wondered why Rudy had broken up with her. Or whether she had been the one to dump him. Or perhaps she still cared for him… Sandra felt her already anxious heart skip a beat.

She walked over to the refreshment table. From there she made her way back to Rudy. Aimless walking, adrift in a sea of movement. She stood next to him quietly, trying to keep track of even a fragment of conversation. It was another ten minutes before what she had feared happened. A man to her left asked, "Sandra, that's your name, right? Where are you from?"

Sandra wasn't looking at the man who'd spoken. A woman said something then. Sandra didn't respond. Rudy saw what had happened and nudged her. "Julie asked you a question," he said, smiling, pointing at the speaker.

Sandra looked at Julie, concentrating her hardest on the placement of her tongue and lips. "I'm sorry. I didn't hear what you said."

It was the first time she had spoken a complete sentence, and the change in body language around her was instantly obvious.

"I just asked where you're from?" Julie repeated.

She wasn't easy to lip-read, but Sandra guessed correctly.

"Springville, about five miles west of here."

Then someone from the other direction wondered out loud, "What country are you from originally?"

Sandra had no idea the question had been asked, but did notice everyone staring at her. She felt increasingly uncomfortable. It was a mistake to have come. She just shouldn't have come to a hearing party. She'd been naive to let Rudy convince her it could be different. That Rudy's friends would be easier to communicate with than other hearing persons she'd experienced. Now she was embarrassing him, and she was sure Rudy was sorry he had brought her. She glanced at him just in time to see him answer the second question.

"She was born in Michigan, Tyler, but she didn't hear you ask because she's deaf. That's why her speech is different."

So now they knew. She hung in her silent world, normally a world of beauty and love and intellect, but now a frightful cocoon that kept her from understanding these staring people. She didn't know whether to be mad at Rudy, then realized he had to tell people. She'd been missing too much of what they were asking her.

The group's body language toward her changed from that of curiosity to uneasy rejection. She looked at Rudy, as if to say, "I told you so," then realized he was hearing and couldn't sense this change, though it would have been overwhelmingly clear to any deaf person. Sandra felt like she was on display, like some circus freak. She scanned the room. Mark was the only one who seemed unaffected by the revelation.

A woman next to Mark came up to Sandra and, putting her head in front of Sandra's, spoke very slowly, over-enunciating each word. "I am very sorry to hear about that. Can you read lips?"

Sandra felt her hackles rise and signed back immediately, "No. Can you read my hands?" She kept herself from repeating it verbally.

She saw Rudy answer instead. "There's no need to be sorry, Melissa. She's fine with who she is. And yes, she reads lips."

A man came up to Sandra and over-enunciated very slowly as well. "Where do you live?"

74

It was difficult for Sandra to understand the distorted lip placements. Her speech-reading skill had been developed for normal speech, not exaggerated movements. She instinctively answered in sign, guessing at the question. She then realized her mistake and spoke, trying hard to articulate sounds distinctly as she explained she had just finished junior college.

"Oh," the man drawled, nodding as slowly as he had spoken. His face held a puzzled look. She had guessed wrong. She felt even smaller and more freakish. *I've got to get out of here!*

Soon, everyone except Mark and Rudy ignored her, though Sandra caught many sidelong glances when people thought she wouldn't notice. She broke away from Rudy and went to the far corner of the room, by the snack table. Rudy came by and gently brought her back to the group. She stood next to him, trying without success to follow the conversation. She had to get out of there and soon. She was positive now that Rudy was wishing he hadn't brought her. He hadn't said anything, of course. In fact, she was surprised his body language remained so positive.

She watched the group meld into song and dance, swaying a lot slower this time. "What song is this, Rudy?"

" 'The White Cliffs of Dover.' " He explained what that song was about.

Time dragged. People moving, records turning, refreshments appearing. And lips churning in the never-ending communication by sound alone. While she debated with herself when to ask Rudy to take her home, she happened to glance again at Pam. She was talking to another woman nearby. Sandra managed to see Pam's lips, haloed in lamplight, and got the gist of what the woman was saying. "It doesn't make sense. Why would Rudy want to be with her? I mean, she's deaf, can't speak intelligibly, and can't even understand anyone. The only reason I can think of is that she must be putting out."

Sandra lost it. She stormed over to Pam and thrust herself in front of the woman. "That's not true," she signed and spoke at the

75

same time. Having no way to judge the intensity of her voice, she didn't realize she was shouting. Everyone in the room stared at her, especially the way she moved her hands, but Sandra was too upset to care. "Just because you don't understand deaf people doesn't mean there's something wrong with us."

"What? What are you talking about?"

"I read your lips and saw what you just said about Rudy and me, and it's not true. We're together because we enjoy each other's company, not for any other reason."

Pam went pale in the lamplight. She shook her head and mumbled subconsciously, forgetting that Sandra was the one person who could understand her voiceless words. "I didn't know you could read my lips from that far away." Then she said out loud, "I don't think you understood me right."

Even if Sandra hadn't known Pam was lying, the faint blush now staining the woman's face and her body language gave it away. She glared at Pam. Rudy came up. "What happened?"

"Take me home."

"Tell me what she said."

"Just get me out of here!"

He turned stiffly to Pam, but she avoided eye contact with him. "What did you say to her?"

"Nothing. She thinks I said something I didn't and doesn't believe me when I tell her she misunderstood me."

Rudy looked at the other woman standing there. "What did Pam say that upset Sandra?"

"I didn't hear anything," she said. Her lie fell into the tense room.

Rudy watched both hearing women. He took his time, making sure they read his look. Someone turned off the record player. People stood still, in groups of twos and threes.

Sandra had never seen Rudy like this before, deeply angry, coiled like a snake. She wondered what hearing people did in situations like this. They seemed uncomfortable in the stillness, their bodies stiff. No one made eye contact, but looked away. So different than deaf people. She watched as Rudy looked back at the people he'd thought were his friends. Angry at the destruction of what had been an enjoyable evening for him. Angry at Pam.

"I don't believe you, Pam."

She shrugged uneasily. "What do you want me to say?"

Mark came up. "Hey, why don't you two come over and talk with us?"

Rudy shook his head, putting his arm around Sandra. "Thanks, Mark, but I think we're going to leave."

"Are you sure? The party's just started. There's still a lot of catching up to do." Sandra caught the pain in Mark's eyes and body.

"Yes, I'm sure, Mark. Now's just not a good time to do that."

"Okay. We'll catch up on things later."

Rudy shot Pam one more glare, shook Mark's hand, then guided Sandra out the door.

The evening was still warm, the humidity instantly cloying. They walked in silence down the steps and onto the sidewalk. Sandra stared straight ahead, her jaw tight, her forehead furrowed. Rudy stared ahead too.

When they reached a streetlamp, he stopped. She looked at up him, waiting. "I'm so sorry for making you go there."

She burst into tears. He pulled her to him and held her tight, bathed in gentle light. She sobbed uncontrollably against his chest. Tears ran hot. Finally free of the frustrations, the condescension, the insults, she clung weeping to Rudy. Then she pulled back, keeping her arms around his waist, and spoke haltingly about how she'd felt in the room, ending with what Pam had said.

"Sounds like Pam hasn't changed a bit. You can see why I broke up with her. She's so closed-minded and opinionated." He stopped a second, then added, "Not at all like you." They looked at each other intently. "I shouldn't have pushed you to come to the party when you hadn't met my friends ahead of time. I had no idea it would turn out the way it did. I thought they'd be more accepting."

"I tried to explain yesterday. . ."

"I know. You did. I'm afraid I just didn't realize how hard it would be for hearing people to accept a deaf person, and for a deaf person to understand hearing people. It's my fault totally."

"I forgive you." She felt his arms tighten around her.

"Some senator I'll make."

"You'll make a wonderful senator." Sandra felt her mood lighten. "It was so different, Rudy, even right from the beginning. I mean, the first thing hearing people always seem to do when they meet you is ask you what your name is. Then—"

"Wait, wait. Help me to understand this. What's wrong with asking you for your name?"

"Asking me my name? Nothing. But as the first thing when they meet me? No deaf person I know does that. We'll find out where the person is from, where they went to school, things like that. Then, after you know something about them, you can ask them what their name is." Sandra wiped some makeup from Rudy's shirt. "But not the very first thing. And then it went downhill from there, and finally it just got to me when I saw what Pam said."

"Sandra, I had no idea deaf people wait awhile before asking someone their name. And I'm sure no one else knew either. For hearing people, it's very common to ask someone their name when you first meet them."

He had to repeat himself once before she understood.

"This may sound stupid," she said, "but I saw someone tell a joke at the party and didn't understand it at all. But everyone thought it was hilarious. I want to know if it's another hearing thing."

"What was it?"

"I probably missed the key part of the joke, but what I saw went like this. 'Did you... cannibal... passed his mother... path?' "

The soldier chuckled, his eyes bright under the lamplight. "I've heard that one before. It goes like this. 'Did you hear about the cannibal who passed his mother on the jungle path?' "

"Okay. What's so funny about that?"

"Do you know what passed means?"

"Yes, to go by something."

"That's one meaning. It can also mean to go to the bathroom. You know…" He motioned with his hand behind his buttock.

Sandra grinned sheepishly. "English is so strange. It's so weird the way the same word said the same way means different things. I remember several times in college when the professor said something that didn't make sense to me, but did to everyone else. In sign language, a sign can have more than one meaning. But it's how you do the sign, and the way your face and body language are, that tell people which meaning you're using."

She sighed. "Rudy, I'm so sorry I ruined your evening. I can find my way home if you want to go back to the party."

"Naw. I have no interest in going back."

"Really, I won't be upset. I'd totally understand. You haven't seen your friends for a long time."

He looked at her eyes, then brushed the remains of a tear with his thumb. "First, after tonight, I don't consider most of them friends anymore. And second, I'd much rather be with you." He moved his face closer to hers. "You were right when you said we're together because we enjoy being with each other."

Sandra felt herself gathered up in his arms, his mouth gently on hers. No words. No signs. Only feelings.

Six

"My parents got a new car last week," Rudy said as they walked in the warm evening. "A Studebaker. It's really neat. Want to see it?"

"I'd love to."

The short bus ride took them to Rudy's parents' home. The house was a block from where they got off, and the car was parked under a streetlamp. It was a white convertible, with white leather seats to match the body. The headlights were glittering chrome, perfectly positioned behind the fender. Running boards ran along the car's length, making it seem substantial and elegant. In the windshield was the C gasoline ration sticker.

"Nice, eh?"

Sandra nodded approvingly.

"Look at the front hood. It's the new style that is one piece and opens from the front rather than the split hood that opens from the side."

She walked around the car to check out the hood.

"They made a good choice," he said. "It's almost as nice as my favorite car of all time."

"What's that?"

"A 1938 Cord convertible. Especially the one with a bright yellow finish and white chrome. That looks great against a black top and black wheels."

"Tell me again what your favorite car looks like? I missed that."

He did so, and she said as she ran her hand along the gleaming white Studebaker hood, "I've never seen a yellow Cord."

"They didn't make many of them, but they're just... just beautiful." He rapped on the Studebaker. "Want to go for a ride? My parents said I could borrow it."

"Really? I'd like that."

Rudy got the keys from the house, then folded the car top down. He helped Sandra into the passenger seat, then got in. He was reaching for the ignition when he said, "Wait, let me get something else," and ran back into the house.

A minute later, he came out with a book and handed it to Sandra. "You asked me yesterday whether there were other good poems. Here's a whole book of them, Sandra, and each one is different." They sat in the quiet of the car and its new leather smell. "I want to show you an example of one that tells a story." Rudy opened the book to "The Highwayman," then looked right at Sandra. "This is one of my favorites. It has so much power, provokes so many images, and although different lines do rhyme, it's really how the words are put together more than the rhyme."

Sandra had started to read it when the soldier put his hand over the page. She looked at him. "This has a different cadence than 'Foreign Children,' the poem I told you before. I mean, you read it differently. Instead of an emphasis on every other syllable, each line is broken into two parts, and you should pause between them. Let me read you the first part to show you what I mean."

The opening words to "The Highwayman" passed into the night. Then Rudy let Sandra read silently. She quickly got the cadence and read the entire poem. Rudy sat quietly, the car keys warming in his hand.

"This is a love story," she said, her eyes tearing for the second time that night. "One with a sad ending."

"It grabs you, doesn't it?"

81

"It sure does."

She looked carefully through the pages of the book, then handed it to him.

"It's yours, a gift from me."

Sandra looked at him, startled. "Are you sure? I can get a copy from the library."

"I would be honored if you kept it."

"Thank you." She kissed him. "This is very nice. I'm looking forward to reading it."

"Let's go for our drive." Rudy started the engine, its surge of power shattering the quiet of the evening.

At the stoplight, he turned to Sandra. "Do you drive?"

She shook her head, watching the red traffic light reflect on the Studebaker's hood.

"Ever think about going for a license?"

"Yes, but they always make it so hard for deaf people."

"What do you mean?"

"I'm not sure, but I think they believe we're more likely to have an accident. I don't agree with them, though. Driving's not that hard. And I've never heard of a deaf person who's had an accident. Besides, I know how to help watch the road. I do it all the time when I ride with my father."

The light changed to green and Rudy accelerated through the intersection. "You mean he lets you drive part of the time?"

"No. I mean I help him watch the road when he's driving and signing to me."

"Wait a minute. If he's driving, why isn't he watching the road?"

"How's he going to see what I'm signing if he's looking at the road all the time?"

"Then how does he avoid hitting another car?"

"Because I'm helping to watch the road for him."

"I'm sorry, I don't understand."

Sandra realized how foreign this must sound. "Okay, this is how it works. When two deaf people are riding together, and they're signing, it means the driver has to look at the passenger to see what she's signing, right? So, the driver goes back and forth between watching the road and watching the passenger sign. The driver keeps looking back at the road to make sure all is okay. But the passenger helps him by also watching the road in case something's coming."

"I gotta say, Sandra, that sounds dangerous to me. No wonder they are so worried about letting deaf people drive."

"Now wait a minute." Sandra put her hand up to her hair as the wind caught at it. "Are you saying we're not capable of driving? Remember, I've never heard of a deaf person having an accident, and I know a lot of them. I remember three hearing people in junior college who had an accident, and I only know a few hearing people."

It got too dark for further conversation until they stopped at a gas station. They sat quietly as the attendant put gas in the tank. They watched him check the water and oil. The man smiled as he washed the glass. "About deaf people driving," Rudy said, "I didn't say they aren't capable of it. It just seems so risky to not watch the road and depend on the passenger."

"That's because you're coming from the perspective of a hearing person. If it's so risky, why aren't we having accidents?"

He shrugged as he gave the attendant a $1 C coupon plus a nickel to cover the $1.05 charge. "I guess you're right. I need to be more open-minded."

Once out of the city, the gleaming Studebaker took them smoothly along the two-lane, gravel country roads. A full moon hung above them, a breeze caressing their faces over the windshield. It hadn't rained for well over a week, and the dirt roads were firm. Everything was open and peaceful. Sandra slid along the bench seat until she was next to Rudy and leaned against him. Farmhouse lights punctuated the darkness. Moonlight bathed the swaying corn.

After awhile, they came upon a small lake, and Rudy parked. The handbrake rasped in the silence, which only he heard. They got out and leaned against the driver's door, looking up at the stars cascading across the night sky. The temperature had cooled to a pleasant seventy. No one else was around. Even Sandra sensed the quietness to the night. The lake was still, the reflection of the moon in the water almost as bright as the moon itself.

"It's beautiful," she said.

"Watch the lake," he said. "A fish will jump soon."

Rudy pointed at the stars, naming some constellations. His arm roved around Sandra's shoulder, drawing her to him.

"Know what's odd?" he said, kissing her cheek.

"What?"

"Most girls wear perfume, but you don't."

"You mean most hearing girls wear perfume. I noticed that at the party. Most of my deaf friends don't."

He looked at her, eyebrows raised.

"I hope you like the smell of soap."

He pulled her down onto the soft grass. "I do. I do."

He kissed her again then, exploring, not holding back, and she gave to him, feeling safe and loved. Rudy pulled his head back so she could see his lips in the moonglow. After two days, she knew his lips intimately. She now asked him to repeat his words only occasionally.

"I wish tomorrow wasn't my last day here," he said. "Now that I found you, I don't want to leave."

Sandra studied him in the penumbral light. "Rudy, will you come to my house for dinner tomorrow? It's Shabbat, the Jewish Sabbath. We'll be having a special dinner to celebrate."

"Shouldn't you ask your parents first?"

"I don't have to. On Shabbat, it's traditional to have others over. Besides, I won't accept no for an answer."

He swept a curl from her eye. "From who? Me or them?"

"Both of you."

They laughed.

"Then teach me some sign language so I can talk to them."

"That'll take awhile, a long while. A very, very long while."

"No problem. We've got the whole night."

"I'm talking years, Rudy, not hours. It took me fifteen years to learn to speak English as well as I do. Hearing people don't realize it, but signing is just as complex a language. So you can't learn it in an hour. If you want, though, I can teach you how to finger-spell the alphabet."

It took him just fifteen minutes to master that, so she taught him a few signs as well.

"You sure are a fast learner."

"That's because I have a great teacher."

Sandra gave him a playful jab. Then her face turned serious. "I'm going to teach you a special sign. Every deaf person has a specific sign name. We use that to identify each other rather than spelling our entire name out every time. We call it the person's sign name. Each one is unique, designed just for that person. Mine is this." She made a fist with her right hand and covered it with her left palm in front of her body.

"I can see you're making the letter S, which I guess stands for Sandra, but why are you covering it like that?"

She didn't understand. He repeated himself.

"Someone gave me that sign because I'm so crazy about baseball. That sign's supposed to be like a ball in the glove, as well as an S for Sandra."

He chuckled and then practiced her sign name until he had it down pat.

"Now what sign name should we give you?" Sandra thought awhile. "Okay. I've got it. I've got a great one." She crossed her second and third finger on her right hand, making the letter R, then put that rigidly next to her temple.

He copied her, then asked, "How did you come up with that sign?"

"The R, of course, stands for Rudy, and the sign is like a salute, because now you're in the Army, and also because in the future people will salute you because of all the good you'll do as a U.S. senator."

He did his sign name, and she nodded her approval. Then she taught him how to say, "My name is Rudy."

He repeated it, using his sign name appropriately. She nodded, then cautioned, "People don't use their sign name with everyone. They usually spell out their name with most people and save their sign names for friends and family. So when you meet my parents, be sure to spell out your name."

He nodded. "Let's try it again." The soldier stood up, backed slowly into the moonlight, and then walked up to Sandra. "Hi, my name is Rudy. How are you?"

"Not bad, not bad. You need to have more expression, though. Signing with a blank face and your body limp is very hard to understand. It's like writing English and misspelling each word. When speaking sign language, the face movements and body positions are almost as important as the hands."

"How would I do that? Show me."

"Okay, watch me." Sandra got up and faced Rudy. "Hi, my name is Sandra. How are you?" She used her face and body the way a native signer would. "Now, I'll do it like you did without any expression." She repeated the sentence, this time with a deadpan face and limp body. "See the difference?"

"Wow. I sure do." Rudy tried it again, this time trying so hard to be expressive that he looked comical. Sandra burst out laughing. He grabbed her. "I'm that bad, eh?"

Lying back on the grass, they looked again at the stars. After awhile, Rudy nudged Sandra. "I'm sure my parents are going to want me home tomorrow. It's my last night, the last time they'll see me for who knows how long. They've already complained I haven't spent enough time with them the past couple of days." He got up on one elbow and kissed her brow. "If you'll come back to my house tomorrow, after we have dinner at yours, I'm okay with telling them why I can't be there earlier."

She spelled out, "O-K."

He replied "good" in sign, and they laughed and Rudy gathered her into his arms. Sandra snuggled against him, inhaling his scent and relishing the warm sensation of his skin. Sometimes a gust of wind blew over them, causing their hair and clothes to ruffle. When that happened, Sandra could detect a fragrance of flowers, though she couldn't tell what kind they were. The moon was now a lustrous orb at the horizon. More stars were visible. The outline of the Milky Way spilled toward the horizon. All was serene. There was only the two of them.

She felt Rudy's arm and looked at him. There was still enough moonlight to easily see his lips. "The crickets are especially loud tonight. You can't hear them, can you?"

She shook her head. "What do they sound like?"

"It's like... um... like a high-pitched buzz. But it's not steady, like the noise a machine would make. It's kind of... I guess sing-song would be the best way to describe it, as it keeps changing."

"Sin-sin? What's that?"

"Sing-song." He spelled the word out.

"Sing-song. Does sing-song mean it's like someone singing?"

"No, not really."

"Is it like the rhythm when you read the poem?"

"No, it's not like that either. It's the crickets' way of singing, but it's different, more like... I don't know how to describe it."

"Do the crickets make it hard to hear me?"

"No. I know the sound is there, but I just tune it out when you talk."

Sandra contemplated how differently the two of them perceived the surroundings. "It's interesting that you say that. I was just thinking how peaceful it was around here, and just assumed it was quiet. I had no idea there were crickets all around, singing their songs, making a lot of noise. I guess it's not peaceful to you."

"Oh, it is, it is. The crickets don't bother me at all." He swept his hand at lake and sky. "This is just incredible. Nature is so beautiful."

They lay awhile next to each other, enjoying the night, thinking how different their lives were, because one could hear and one couldn't. And yet, truth be told, they were drawing together.

Sandra turned onto her side. Supporting her head with her elbow, she faced Rudy. "What do you think the world will be like fifty years from now?"

His face turned serious in the fading light. He took his time answering. "I don't know, but I've wondered that myself. I bet it'll be a lot different. I mean, look how different we are now from fifty years ago. They didn't have cars, airplanes, radio or telephones. Or even movies. Imagine not having those."

"I have no problem imagining life without radio, telephones or movies."

He smiled and nodded. "I guess those weren't the best choices, eh? I probably should have picked other things, like electricity and toilets in every home." Rudy put his arms behind his head. Sandra marveled at how it was so easy now to understand Rudy, even in the moonlight. She didn't get fatigued from speech-reading him anymore. "It's fun to think about what we might have in the future. I wouldn't be surprised if everyone had anti-gravity devices that let them fly places rather than drive. Or maybe there'll be robots that would wait on you and do whatever you wanted. I'll bet there will be other things we haven't even the foggiest notion of now."

"That would be something. Having a robot to do the dishes and laundry, and then cook dinner. I could definitely go for that." Sandra propped a hand under her chin. "I like to think there'll be a change in the way society is too. In fifty years, I hope deaf people will have an equal opportunity to become professionals or whatever they want. Like a doctor. Or a veterinarian, or a lawyer. And Jewish people, and colored people, and all types of people won't be discriminated against either. Just imagine what it could be like if everyone had the chance to be what they want, regardless of race, religion or whatever they were, just as long as they worked hard for it. Maybe there'll even be a woman President."

"Now that would be a huge change, wouldn't it?"

Sandra sighed and started to lie down when she suddenly rose up on her elbows again, powered by her thoughts. "I also predict that in fifty years the Tigers will have won a dozen more pennants and eight World Series, and that, if not Hank Greenberg, some other Tiger will have broken Ruth's record of sixty home runs in a season."

"The Tigers winning that many pennants and World Series? Wow. Now that would be something, wouldn't it? I'd love to see that."

"It'll happen, and it's going to be great when it does. And that reminds me of one thing that won't change in fifty years."

"What's that?"

"The game of baseball."

"I wouldn't bet on that, Sandra. I suspect there'll be some things about it that change."

"What would they change?"

"I don't know. But I'm sure there'll be something that'll be different about the game. Maybe they'll change how far the pitching mound is from the plate or the distance between the bases. Or maybe even add another inning to make the game an even ten innings."

Sandra's eyes roved among the stars, searching for their secrets, before looking back at Rudy. "Well, I beg to differ. There'll certainly be new records, but I don't think there'll ever be any changes in the game."

"You're pretty sure about that, huh?"

"I am."

She put her arms behind her head, and Rudy started tickling her. She got up and ran around the car. He chased after her and caught her. They fell on the ground and rolled around on the far side of the car, laughing hysterically. When they finally calmed down, they snuggled, arms and legs entwined, studying each other's faces. In their faces was everything. Trust, a first prelude to deeper knowing.

Sandra lay still, breathing lightly, her eyes bright. Feeling content. Rudy had connected with her as no one ever had. She was amazed it had happened with a hearing person, but really didn't care anymore. She felt so close to him, despite knowing him only days, and wanted to get to know him even better.

"I don't want tonight to end, Rudy," she murmured.

"Me neither."

Out here in the countryside, under a warm, bejeweled night sky, it was just the two of them. No one was putting up barriers. No rejection. Out here, it wasn't important that he wasn't Jewish. Or that she wasn't hearing. Or that he wanted to be a senator. And she a deaf veterinarian. All that mattered was how they felt for each other, and how much they wanted to be with each other. She could tell Rudy felt the same from his body language, especially the tautness of his muscles, the gentleness of his hands, and the expressions on his face. Suddenly she wanted him more than she'd ever realized it was possible to want anyone.

That realization shocked her, and she hugged him so he couldn't see her face, not knowing if hearing people could read even a little body language. She felt torn inside, confused as to how she had ended up getting so attracted to someone like Rudy. He was so different. Someone hearing. A goy. Doing anything more than they had already would be contrary to the basic principles her parents had raised her on. She should get up, stop this cuddling by the lake, before it got to the point where they did something they'd both regret.

But she couldn't move. She couldn't let go of him, especially when they only had one more day left to be together. And who knew? That could be their last day ever. Rudy was headed for the war in Europe. If he died over there…

Sandra forced herself to stop those thoughts. She couldn't do anything about that. Only God knew what would happen in the future. This was now.

She pressed against him, again surprised at her inability to get up. Maybe some things were meant to be. Maybe a force greater than either of them or her parents or society was working on them. A spiritual force. It certainly felt that way. If so, who was she to resist? Since he would be going to Europe, it might be years before they could get back together again. Thoughts about what war could mean weaseled into her consciousness. She remembered her father talking about his experiences in the Great War and knew how nasty war really was on the front lines. If Rudy were to end up there, he could get injured. Or worse. The thought of his dying hit her hard again. Even assuming he lived, the idea of waiting for his return to know him, and for them to know each other, seemed like an unbearable length of time. Yet it was the morally right thing to do.

They kissed, even more passionately this time. Sandra felt Rudy's feelings pour out of his body, inundating hers. He worked his mouth down her chin and explored her neck. It was heaven, and Sandra lay there, her hands rubbing the back of his neck, caressing his head, playing with his hair. She felt his body quiver, and his excitement heightened hers even more. She wondered whether either of them would get up before they got too far.

Then the sound of another car approaching, which only Rudy heard. Soon after she saw the flash of headlights. Rudy heard a door slam, then another, followed by loud voices. He pulled back and mouthed to Sandra that people were nearby, jerking his thumb in their direction. They separated clumsily, remaining out of sight behind the Studebaker as they patted their hair and straightened their clothes.

They got up, acting casually. Thirty feet away, two couples were leaning against a car, laughing at some joke. Rudy and Sandra nodded at the foursome. They got into their Studebaker's front seat, she in the middle next to him, and drove into the night.

The moon was crossing the horizon now, and the Milky Way was visible across most of the sky. Sandra looked at Rudy as the engine ran smoothly and the evening air wafted pleasantly over the convertible. His slight slouch forward told her he was as flustered as she. She snuggled next to him, put her hand around his shoulder and smiled when he glanced at her.

"I was thinking how lucky it is that you hear. Imagine how it would've been if you were deaf like me and neither of us had seen the headlights because we had our eyes closed. Boy, would we have been embarrassed."

He chuckled at first, and then pulled over to the side of the road as they burst into laughter. When they calmed down, Sandra rested her head on his shoulder. The engine burled in the quiet, instrument panel aglow, lights probing ahead. He waved his hand in front of her eyes.

"I have a dumb question."

"Go ahead."

"What happens when deaf parents have a hearing child? Do you know any who raised one who turned out okay?"

Sandra made a face. "Why are you asking me this? Why would deaf parents do any worse than hearing parents?"

"Well, when I was in, oh, it must've been fifth grade, I became friends with this kid in my class. His name was Steven. Steven Belanger. We got to be pretty good friends. But what I remember most was that his parents were deaf. They only spoke sign language and couldn't talk with me. Or anyone who didn't sign, for that matter."

He paused, but Sandra continued to concentrate on his face. "Steven could sign as well as talk, but always seemed embarrassed and upset with his parents. The next year, we went to middle school, and I remember he got into drugs. He tried to get me to do that too, but I wouldn't, and we drifted apart. Within a year, he was sent to reform school. I remember hearing that the reason they sent him there was because they couldn't talk with the parents and show them how to help their son. So they finally decided to send him away so someone could help Steven get better."

"So are you thinking that deaf parents are not capable of raising hearing children?"

"Well, let's say you had a hearing child. How would you communicate with society, with the schools, other adults, all the institutions that you'd have to interact with as part of raising your child?"

She turned on the white leather seat so that she was directly facing him. "I know lots of deaf parents who have hearing children. Every one of them has turned out okay. Remember, the hearing kids know sign language and can talk with their parents just fine. And they can talk to hearing people without any problems too. I'm sure this Steven you knew had other issues. Like an emotional or psychiatric problem that had nothing to do with his parents."

"So what do these hearing kids end up doing?"

"All kinds of things. One man I know owns a hardware store. Another works for one of the car companies. A woman down the block is a secretary for a lawyer." Impatience flickered in her. "But why are you asking me this?"

"I don't know. I guess that after what happened to Steven, I just wondered." He noticed the baseball glove in the back seat and retrieved it, putting on the mitt. He pounded the pocket with his right fist. "How long have you liked baseball?"

"Ever since I was a kid," she said, glad that the topic had changed to something more enjoyable. Her irritation melted. "My father took me to a game maybe fifteen years ago. I've been a diehard Tigers fan since."

"You have a favorite player?"

"Hank Greenberg."

Rudy nodded. "He's a great hitter, probably one of the best to ever play the game." He flashed a smile. "You know, I like baseball a lot as well."

"I really love the game, Rudy. If I was a man, I'm sure that's what I'd want to do for a living. Play for the Tigers."

"Lotsa guys around here want to play for the Tigers. Anywhere in the majors, really. When I was younger, I too wanted to play in the big leagues. But I wasn't good enough. I do listen to the games on the radio whenever I can, though."

"What's that like?"

"What do you mean?"

"What's it like to listen to a game? I mean, when you do that, what do you hear?"

Rudy thought about and chose his words carefully. "The sportscaster. He's calling the game, play by play, telling you what's happening." She waited, eyes glistening in the glow from the instrument panel. "Here, I'll show you. It goes something like this." He put on a businesslike face and, making his right hand into a fist, pretended to be speaking into a microphone.

"We're in the bottom of the ninth here at Tiger Stadium on a beautiful summer afternoon, and the Yankees are leading 2 to 1." Sandra pushed his hand down a little so she could see his face better. "Hank Greenberg's at the plate, with a man on second, and two outs. The count's two and two. The crowd's on the edge of their seats and not a single person has left the park. The pitcher drops the resin bag, looks around the infield and then straddles the rubber. He looks a bit tired out there, and his arm doesn't have quite the zip on it he had earlier. He nods at the catcher's sign. Here's the windup... he looks the runner back to second base... and now here's the pitch... it's a curveball low and outside for ball three."

Rudy glanced at Sandra. She was watching him avidly, smiling at the play-action, clearly understanding what he was saying even if she did miss some words. "The pitcher walks off the mound, picks up the resin bag again and rubs his hands on it as he looks around. The crowd's into it now. Everyone's standing and yelling. Now he's back on the mound and looks at the catcher again. The count's 3 and 2. Two out, a man on second. The pitcher doesn't want to put the winning run on base and is going to throw this ball in the corner of the strike zone. The man on second edges off the bag, trying to distract the pitcher. Greenberg takes a couple of practice swings and waits for the pitch. Here it comes. . . he swings and hits a line drive, deep into left center field." Rudy became more animated as his voice got louder. "The outfielder is going back, back, back to the warning track. It's out of here! It's a home run for Hank Greenberg! His forty-third of the season, and the Tigers win the game, 3-2. The crowd is going wild."

Rudy stopped and looked at Sandra.

"Wow. So it's almost like being there. When they hit the ball, can you hear that on the radio too?"

"Not usually. You can sometimes hear the crowd in the background, but you can't hear anything on the field."

"What about if you're at a game? Can you hear the bat hit the ball?"

Rudy nodded. "Oh, yeah. You can also hear it when a fastball hits the catcher's mitt. It sounds like a thud."

"What's a thud?"

"It's like this." Rudy slammed his right fist into his left palm and made a clucking sound with his tongue.

Sandra held out her hands turned up while raising her eyebrows, then pointed at her ears. "I didn't hear a thing."

Rudy realized there was no easy way to explain sound. "There's a distinctive sound when the ball hits leather," he said patiently. "It's different than when the bat hits the ball, for example."

"Make the sound again." Sandra put her hand on Rudy's throat and jaw, and this time, she felt the vibrations when he made the sound of the thud.

"This may sound stupid," she asked, "but does it sound different when different players hit the ball?"

He almost laughed, but caught himself. From her point of view it was an astute question. "No, it's pretty much the same. I guess that's because the bats are all made of the same type of wood."

"Oh. So you've been to Tiger Stadium a lot?"

"I always go to several games a year. Or at least I did when I lived in Michigan."

"Me too. I just love it, Rudy. No two games are ever alike. And there are so many different things that can happen in nine innings. That's what makes baseball so neat. It's impossible to predict. And I love discussing strategy with whoever I'm with."

"It's a complex game, isn't it?" Rudy checked the mirrors and pulled out onto the road, the convertible accelerating away over its shifting gears.

Sandra looked at him a long moment. "Yeah, kind of like our lives are now, eh?"

"No," Rudy said firmly. He waited until she gave him a look. He was starting to appreciate the silences and rhythms in talking with her. "Sandra, in the past couple of days, our lives have become far more complicated than baseball ever will be."

He waited, more comfortable with the pause than he'd ever have been before. They drove in silence until the houses became more frequent as they approached the city.

"Rudy, yesterday you talked about your thoughts about religion, but I couldn't tell if you are religious. Are you?"

The soldier shook his head. "If you had asked me a few years ago, I might've said yes, but not anymore."

"What happened?"

He didn't answer immediately. Sandra waited, comfortable in her world of silence as all deaf people are.

"When I was sixteen or so, I really got into religion. I loved the way it preached treating people nicely and how it forgave them when they made mistakes. And religion seemed to have an answer for everything—what to do and what to say for every situation. If you didn't know what to do, it was so easy to pray. Just leave everything up to an all-knowing God. The priest seemed so holy too. For awhile, it was like he couldn't do anything wrong." He glanced at the speedometer and slowed down.

"Slowly, though, I began to realize that there was more to it than I first realized. It probably started when I saw how poorly the priest treated some of the altar boys. Just the opposite of what he preached. Then I read about evolution, and realized there were other explanations for how things are, and that maybe the Bible wasn't always right. But the clincher was when I thought how, throughout the centuries, so many people and the church have justified killing or hurting others in the name of God. That was when I decided that religion wasn't for me."

Sandra ran a hand through her hair as the convertible sped through the night. "Just because some people abuse religion doesn't make an underlying faith wrong."

Rudy nodded, pulling the convertible nimbly around a slow-moving car. "Good point. I still occasionally go to confession—but it has nothing to do with my being religious, you understand. It just makes me feel better getting things off my chest. On the other hand, think about all the never-ending conflicts in the world. Like the Catholics and Protestants in Ireland. Or what's going on in Europe. Most of the conflicts exist because of religion."

"And because people are intolerant of those with different views," Sandra interjected.

"Right. If only folks would follow the dictates of their respective religions, war would be the last thing they'd do. I can't believe that if there was a benevolent God, he'd let all this war go on like it has." He glanced at her. "Sorry, I'm making speeches."

"No, you're not. I asked, remember?"

"Okay, now it's my turn to ask. Are you religious?"

"Well, I'm as Jewish as they come."

"So are you saying that you are religious?"

Sandra looked at the city lights that were brightening against the night sky. "No, not necessarily. Judaism is more than a religion —it's a culture, a tradition, a way of doing things. Yes, I believe in God. But I also believe that religion shouldn't control one's life. So, I'm not sure if that makes me religious or not."

"So there are different kinds of Jewish people, right?"

"What do you mean?"

"Well, I hear all kinds of things, most of which I don't believe. I know a lot of people who don't like Jews and seem to think they're all alike."

"Give me an example of how we'd be considered all alike."

"That you all hate Christ. Or spend all your time figuring out how to control all the world's money."

Sandra's face became more expressive than usual, even for a deaf person, showing bemusement but also a world weariness beyond her years. "By definition, Jews don't believe that Christ is the son of God. But hate him? Why would we do that? He was a Jew! Even if he did have different beliefs. And you're Catholic, right? Wasn't it the Pope who started anti-Semitism by claiming Jews killed Jesus?"

"I know, I know." They waited for a stoplight to turn green, looking at each other in the ambient light.

"What's more," Sandra said, "the myth of Jews controlling all the money is just as ridiculous. My family barely has enough to live on, let alone control what other people have. Half my Jewish friends also have no money." Her body assumed an angry pose. "Why can't people just let us be? We're not hurting anyone, and we're trying to make it in life just like anyone else."

Rudy's hand found hers. "It's crazy, Sandra, it really is. It's a prejudice that comes from people not thinking or talking with each other. But I think it's changing. It's going away. I think it's going to be different soon."

"No, Rudy, it isn't. You mentioned Europe. Look what's happening there with the Nazis. They're murdering Jews. In large numbers, I hear. Is your Pope taking a stand against it? I don't think so. Even our President doesn't seem to think it's a big problem. And what about that priest on the radio? I think his name is Father Coffin or something-"

"Coughlin."

"How do you spell that?"

He told her.

"Coughlin. Just a couple of years ago, it was really bad because it was like every hearing person in Michigan listened to his radio shows. I, of course, have no idea what he says, but I do know a lot of hearing Jewish people were afraid to go out after the broadcasts. They feared what might happen. And that's in America."

"Wow." Rudy sent the Studebaker forward. "I didn't realize the extent of the difference between just thinking about it and living with the consequences. You're right. It is a problem. But I don't know how true the reports are of the mass murdering of Jews. It may just be a rumor, somebody's propaganda."

"No Jew would even think, let alone say that, Rudy. And you wouldn't be saying it if it was Catholics being murdered."

"Sandra, I hope it isn't true, I really do. If it is, it's horrifying. And when I get to Congress, I promise you I'll do everything I can to make this prejudice go away."

They turned onto Sandra's street, headlights scribing an arc. It was long after midnight. The streets were deserted. Rudy parked on the street in front of the Horowitzes' house, only he hearing the handbrake rasping in the sudden stillness. Through the window shade, the silhouette of someone pacing the living room was clearly visible.

Rudy touched Sandra to get her attention and inclined his head at the house. "Looks like someone's waiting for you. You know, your folks need to cover the windows at night, or the air raid warden will be after them."

"It's my mom, I'm sure. And I'm sure the blinds are open because she's worried and looking for me."

"Maybe I should come in and apologize for keeping you out so late."

"No, no, no," she signed animatedly, knowing he could now understand that, then added vocally, "That would make it worse, because she'll find out you hear and aren't Jewish."

Rudy pulled a face, trying to lighten the mood. "A double-whammy, eh? I can see how they'd know I hear, but how would they know I'm not Jewish?"

Sandra leaned forward until her face was close to his. "If there's anyone who looks like a goy, it's you, Rudy Townsend."

"It's a cross I have to bear, Sandra," he deadpanned.

She pinched him, smiling in spite of herself.

"So what's a goy?"

"Someone who isn't Jewish."

"Does it really matter?"

"To them, it may be the most important thing in my choice of a husband. Maybe even more important than the fact you're not deaf."

"So then, you haven't told your parents about me?"

"No. I just told them I was going out with a friend."

He checked his watch. "They're going to find out anyway when I come over for supper tomorrow—I mean later today."

"That gives me some time to break the news to them, Rudy." She moved her face even closer to his and looked into his eyes. "Please try to understand. Deaf people are a close-knit group who socialize mainly with each other. Dating a hearing person, especially getting serious with one, is a big deal. A huge deal. It's like discarding your roots and leaving everything you and your kin stand for. It's strongly looked down upon. And it's perhaps even more for a Jew becoming involved with a goy, especially since my parents are so religious. So you have two strikes against you."

"But I haven't struck out yet, eh? Remember, Greenberg hit that home run and won the game with two strikes on him." He put his arms around her, making sure she could still see his lips.

"It's no different from the people I grew up with. Look at what happened at the party tonight. They're just as narrow-minded. You know, I once read that opposites attract. I can't think of two people who could be any more opposite than us."

"But it's one thing to attract, and quite another to cope with the consequences of the attraction."

"Yeah, you're so right. You are so right." He leaned forward and kissed her on the lips.

Sandra looked back at the house and saw her mother peering out the window. "I better go in before Mom sees us."

"Can we meet for lunch tomorrow?"

"Oh, I'd love to so much, Rudy, I really would. But I promised Mom I'd look for a job. I've put that off for so long I really can't get out of it, even just for one more day."

"We're still on for dinner though, right?"

"Absolutely. Be here at six."

As soon as Sandra entered the foyer, her mother confronted her. Mrs. Horowitz's hands moved furiously. "Where have you been? It's three in the morning, and we've been worried sick about you."

"I'm okay, Mom. I was just out having a good time."

"Who were you with out there?"

Her father came into the foyer from the living room. They might as well learn about it now, Sandra decided. "His name is Rudy Townsend." She finger-spelled his name.

"Ah! A man! I should've guessed." Her mother threw up her hands, a gesture hearing mothers would have empathized with.

"He's very nice. He's home on leave from the Army, and tomorrow's his last day before he goes back."

Mr. Horowitz finger-spelled T-O-W-N-S-E-N-D and looked at her questioningly. "Not a typical Jewish name, is it?"

They looked at Sandra closely, expecting her to reassure them. She felt her stomach turn with guilt. "That's because he's not."

"A goy!" Sandra's mother put her head in her hands. "God help us. We should only die before anything more happens."

"Does this mean you and Jacob have broken up?" her father signed.

"No. I just decided to see other people for now while Jacob is gone."

"Sandra," he started, then stopped. Something in her face convinced him this wasn't the time to lecture. "Please, think carefully about what you're doing here before you do anything you'll later regret."

"I will." She headed for the stairs, then paused at the bottom to gather her courage before turning and plunging ahead. "Mom, I invited him over for Shabbat dinner tomorrow."

"You what?"

Sandra nodded that her mother had seen correctly.

"Did he accept?"

Sandra shook her fist up and down. "Like I said earlier, it's his last day before he goes back to the Army camp, and I thought you'd like to meet him."

"What time did you tell him?"

"Six."

"Does he know what Shabbat is about?" her father asked.

"I explained that to him. Oh, and one more thing."

Her parents watched expectantly. Sandra was sure they'd guessed it anyway, because Rudy was in the Army. But she wanted to be very clear about it. Might as well get all of it out at once.

"He's hearing. I just wanted you to know ahead of time."

Sandra didn't wait for their response. She turned and bounded up the stairs for her room. So she missed seeing her mother's face turn white and her father's scrunch in pain.

Day Four

Seven

She was astride a large bay horse, on a dirt trail that ran through the woods, under a bright blue sky. Through the trees she could see small lakes on both sides, often with ducks and geese swimming, or a muskrat clawing along the edge. It all looked so peaceful. A stark contrast to the sense of urgency she felt inside.

Sandra glanced behind her. Gray rain clouds, ominous and closing in quickly. She inched up a little more on the horse. He was galloping as fast as he could, his sides heaving from the effort. There was no time to stop, though. Where she was going and why, she couldn't recall. But she did know that unless she got there in time, it would be too late and she'd regret it forever. And she knew she had to get there before it rained.

Horse and rider emerged from the woods into a large meadow. It stretched out as far as she could see, filled with flowers and grasses of different colors and heights. There was no sign here of other life. Just them. Up and down they dashed, over hills and gullies, leaping small streams in their race against time.

They were getting closer, but time was running down, a relentless beat. They were in danger of not making it. Behind her, the gray rain clouds were now almost overhead. Lightning daggered across the sky. She sensed the vibrations of thunder. Sandra dug her heels into the bay's sweating side, urging him on. She knew he was about done. He was beginning to foam at the mouth.

Then she saw it, up ahead, through the mist at the end of the meadow. A large house with a fence around it. Like a castle that weary travelers in times gone by must have headed for. Seeing it brought back memories of where she was going and what had happened each time before. She had gotten so close to it, only to have the rain come just before she reached the gate. And then the ground had given way, disappearing under them. She vowed this time would be different. She only had to get there a couple of seconds sooner. Just a little fraction more effort. She would push the horse harder this time. They'd make it.

The bay slowed, a first hesitancy from exhaustion. Just a slight change, but discernable to someone skilled at reading non-verbal clues. He'd done this the last time. She closed her eyes and held her breath as she leaned forward some more, putting her weight up as far as possible to help her mount. She whispered encouragement in his ear. Then she felt the first drops of rain. But the house was closer. Only a hundred yards away now, no more. The front gate was wide open. It could be reached. She squinted her eyes. Then she saw him framed by the open window, watching her. If she looked really hard, she could imagine seeing him pleading with her to hurry.

"Don't give up now. We're almost there!" she spoke to the horse. "I can see it now. Give me fifteen seconds."

Fifty yards, but the rain was coming down harder. He was still in the window, now waving wildly, trying to tell her something. She scanned the area but didn't see anything amiss, then looked back. His face blurred because of the distance and rain. He was shouting at her. Forty yards now. The horse's legs began to wobble. Sandra looked down. The ground was less firm now. It was starting to soften. Rain came down in torrents, causing her clothes to stick to her skin, blinding horse and rider. Her hair was plastered against her back, but she didn't care. The gate. The gate.

Twenty-five yards. She glanced back up at the face in the window. He was quite distinct now, despite the rain. Clean shaven, with long black hair that reached the collar of a beautifully tailored red shirt. Handsome as a prince. Eyes as dark as his hair. But he was agitated even more, trying to tell her something. But she couldn't see his lips clearly enough. Maybe he thought she could hear him. That was okay, though. She didn't see anything in the way, and whatever he was trying to tell her, she'd find out soon enough.

Ten yards to the gate. Just two seconds more. The horse stumbled, but didn't go down. She looked under his hoofs. The ground was disintegrating. The gate was just a few feet ahead now. She glanced up at the man in the window. Like before, his head bowed in grief. Like before, she saw a tear fall from his eye. Then, as the horse dropped through the turf into the gaping maw, she lunged for the gate with an outstretched hand. . .

Sandra woke up with a start, covered with sweat, the sheets sticking to her. That dream again.

The banging on the door was loud now. And this time, the sound penetrated Chuck Winter's consciousness, bringing him back to the present. He'd been so into his mother's story, he hadn't perceived the noise before.

"Mom." He waved his hand, getting her attention. "Someone's knocking at the door."

Frail, grateful for the chance to rest her arthritic joints, Sandra gestured for him to let the person in.

Chuck got up and unlocked the door. His sisters charged into the room. Lisa pointed at her watch, then signed to both of them, "How much longer are you guys going to be? It's been over two hours, and we want to see you too."

"I'm sorry it's taking so long, honey," their mother said. "I didn't expect it to take this much time. But it's really important that your brother and I finish our talk. Please, try to understand and give us a little longer."

"How much longer?"

"Maybe an hour or so."

"An hour or so! What's the secrecy for?" Judy's movements conveyed her intense feelings as much as the signs themselves. "I mean, what are you discussing that's so secret only Chuck can see it? He's not the one who lives around here or takes care of you, and besides, he's hearing. Why can't we see it too?"

"Judy, please, trust me. It's something I have to put to rest with him. We'll let you know as soon as we're done."

"You look tired, Mom," Lisa said. "Maybe you should take a break. How about if I got you something to eat or drink?"

Mrs. Winter shook her head. "Thanks for the offer, but not now. Please, let us finish now, okay? And close the door when you leave."

Judy stalked out of the room while Lisa, as usual much calmer, followed her and shut the door quietly behind them.

Chuck waited until he heard the door latch click shut, then nodded at his mother.

"Where were we now?" she asked. He reminded her. "Oh yes." She sat quietly a moment, her face thoughtful as she gathered her strength. Then her arthritic hands began to move with renewed vigor.

The day Rudy was to come for Shabbat dinner began with a torrential thunderstorm. The first rain in almost two weeks, it dissipated the oppressive heat, leaving freshness in the air.

Sandra Horowitz didn't get out of bed until after ten, despite her intention to spend the day looking for a job. She pretended to sleep, but had slept little since coming home early that morning. Her mind had been overloaded with thoughts and emotions—about the events of the previous night, about the turmoil her relationship with Rudy was already generating in her family, about how different their lives were. But mostly she dwelled on Rudy himself.

Today was his last before he returned to Fort Bragg. That thought weighed on her more than the others. Who knew when she'd be able to see him again? Or even if? Once he left for Europe, anything could happen. And now that America was becoming more involved in the war over there, reports of casualties were starting to come in...

The tears pressed hot in her eyes. Maybe dying for one's country was a noble thing. But she couldn't bear the notion that, should it happen to Rudy, she'd never see him again after today. Somehow, some way, she had to figure out a way to see him again after today, before he left for Europe.

She sighed, wiping her eyes as she got up to check the wooden splint on the broken bathtub leg. It was secure. She turned on the water. She wasn't sure what to say to her parents about Rudy. At least her father had long since left for work, so for now she'd only have to deal with her mother. Sandra took her bath, feeling the hot water ease her tenseness. She got dressed, looking at herself in the mirror, gathering her courage, before venturing downstairs.

The first person she met was her brother, David. He gestured toward the kitchen where Mrs. Horowitz was and signed, "Mom's really upset. She's been crying all morning. What happened?"

"Oh, just that she doesn't like the guy I'm seeing."

"I know. Because he's a hearing *goyim* who you invited over for Shabbat. And you know Mom. She won't stop bugging you until you give him up."

"It's my life. I'm not going to do that just to make her happy." Sandra started for the kitchen.

He grabbed her arm. "You know Mom won't stop until you do. Remember how she kept after me about my room until I finally cleaned it to get her off my back?"

When Sandra didn't answer, he continued, "It's just like the joke I heard yesterday from my friends. 'What's the difference between a Jewish mother and a pit bull?'"

"I don't know, David, and I don't care."

"The pit bull eventually lets go."

Sandra gave him a look. "David. You're still just a teenager. So you have to do what she tells you. I, on the other hand, am now an adult. I'm old enough to make my own decisions, and she knows it."

"Doesn't matter, Sandra. You know Mom."

But Sandra stopped looking at him. She walked into the kitchen and acknowledged her mother with a nod. Mrs. Horowitz gestured, "Good morning." Sandra responded, then made a mayonnaise and cheese sandwich on white, grabbed a peeled carrot, and poured a glass of milk before sitting down to eat. Her mother sat down at the table across from her. The elder woman's body language exuded sadness, with a hint of despair.

At first the conversation was general, but slowly turned to relationships, with Mrs. Horowitz doing most of the signing. She told her daughter once again that, when she was Sandra's age, she had also been serious about a non-Jewish man. And how it was only after she'd been married and had children that she realized the problems that relationship would have had, even though he was deaf. There are fundamental differences between Jews and Christians, she pointed out, that make it hard for interfaith marriages to succeed. Could you imagine, she asked, your son not having a bris or a Bar Mitzvah? Or a husband who wanted a Christmas tree?

Sandra watched politely. She had seen this story many times. The older woman paused and rested her hands on the table as she studied her daughter's demeanor. Whatever she saw was apparently not reassuring, because she began to expound on their deafness, and how that made them members of another very different group. She listed numerous benefits their deaf community provided. She emphasized that those who married into the hearing world lost this "family," finding themselves misunderstood and ignored by hearing persons, yet no longer accepted by deaf people. "Don't end up like that," her mother pleaded. "Tradition and culture may seem confining, but there's a good reason they exist."

Sandra had seen all that too. But never with such emotional signs. It was clear her mother felt her daughter was making a mistake.

When Mrs. Horowitz finally got up, Sandra remained at the table. She watched her mother lift the latch to the ice box and check inside, then set the card in the kitchen window for the ice man. Sandra knew they wanted 75 pounds of ice that day rather than the usual 25. Next, Mrs. Horowitz cleaned the oven and counters before making a grocery list for the upcoming Shabbat dinner.

They didn't discuss the topic anymore. Sandra left to go job hunting and this time came back at five o'clock, smiling broadly, with good news. Huron Kennels, just north of Springville, had hired her to help care for the dogs they boarded. It wasn't the best paying job, but it did involve helping animals and would provide an income until she found something better.

After signing the details to her parents, Sandra changed quickly so she could help her mother prepare for their special dinner guest. Mrs. Horowitz had used the extra wartime food coupons they had saved to buy higher quality meat. This Sabbath meal was going to be fancier than most.

Mrs. Horowitz was born in 1898 in rural Russia. Her family knew before she was even a year old that she was deaf. In the Russian countryside at that time, most deaf people were born to hearing families, and very few ever met another deaf person. As a group they did poorly, ending up mute, penniless and ostracized. Luckily for Lillian, deafness ran in the Uzlavsky family. Multiple people in every generation were deaf, and so many knew Yiddish Sign Language. Lillian, despite having hearing parents, could sign fluently by the time she was fifteen months old. She felt as much a part of her community as her hearing siblings. Public school wasn't an issue either. Even hearing Jewish children weren't allowed to attend local schools, so her education came from the extended family and the synagogue. Nor was there concern for her future. The deaf Uzlav-skys, because they had a language, learned trades as tailors and farmers; some were even taught Hebrew and were able to study the Torah.

Lillian's parents emigrated to America when she was seven to escape the pogroms of tsarist Russia. The only person they knew in the United States was her uncle who had settled in Detroit, so they joined him in Michigan. There, her father opened a shop repairing shoes. Even though he never learned to speak English, he was able to establish a customer base because of the high quality of his work.

His wife also had a hard time with English. But she eventually learned to get by in it after several years. Their hearing children, however, picked up the new tongue quickly. Lillian's hearing siblings were fluent within a year, while she, with the help of a small deaf community, became fluent in American Sign Language, retaining only a slight Yiddish accent.

The rudimentary schools for deaf children in America in those days were of poor quality. Lillian did attend one, but was never educated in the book sense. She couldn't read much, and could only write her name. Her experiences with the hearing world, during shopping or other public activities, exposed her for the first time to putdowns and negative attitudes from hearing persons. This was something she had never experienced in the old country. Soon, she developed the same mistrust of hearing society that most deaf people had.

Lillian was eighteen when she met her husband. Benjamin Horowitz was also short, a stocky five and a half feet at best. He had returned two years earlier from WWI, where he had been discharged after losing his hearing on the Western front. Like many deaf people, he could never learn to read lips well no matter how hard he tried. Thus, he communicated mainly by writing. This became increasingly frustrating both at home and work. He had learned the tailoring business from his father as well, but it was so hard to know what customers wanted, especially when they had special requests. And with family or friends, writing notes, besides being slow, was useless in group conversations. Ben became increasingly isolated, unable to communicate and increasingly depressed. He began to rail at society's lack of understanding at how devastating a hearing loss was. But his anger caused people to avoid him. His isolation worsened.

One day, while wandering his neighborhood, he saw Lillian signing to one of her friends. In what he later admitted had been an act of desperation, he went up to the two strangers and waved his hand. They smiled back.

"I'm deaf too."

When they didn't respond, he realized they didn't understand speech. He pointed to his chest, then his ears and shook his head.

"You sign?" one of them asked.

His answer was a blank face.

"Can you teach me how to talk with my hands?" He asked this by pointing at them, then himself, followed by moving his hands around each other, not realizing that latter motion was the sign for "sign language."

"Sure." They nodded as well, allowing him to understand.

They taught him signs for a few common objects, followed by some simple sentences. But what really allowed him to learn American Sign Language was their willingness to meet with him daily, often bringing other deaf persons, repeating themselves as often as necessary. Benjamin was surprised at how quickly he learned, and loved, the language. For the first time in years he was able to communicate without writing, even at the beginning, when he knew just a few signs. He immersed himself in the language, becoming conversational within a couple of months.

His family, however, refused to even think about learning to sign. This caused conflicts, which came to a head one evening when he was asked why he didn't continue trying to learn to read lips. "Dad, I've tried, and I just can't do it with most people."

"You do it pretty good with us."

"I guess I'm used to all of you, having been with you so much over the years."

"Well, if you can't do it with other people, you can at least write with them."

"That takes forever. I can't carry on a conversation that way. When I sign, though, I can. Just like I used to when I could hear."

"Ben, that's for deaf mutes, not you. You know a real language. You don't need to use sign."

"I disagree, Dad. In many ways, sign language is just as rich as English."

"Give me a break," his brother had interjected. "That isn't a language, it's just gestures."

"You're wrong, Danny."

"Okay, give me one example how it's as rich as English."

"Well, I've noticed that the word order can vary depending on the context. In fact, by using one's body, one can change the entire meaning of a sentence. You can't even do that with English."

"Name me one famous author in sign language," his mother said.

"Mom, it's a sign language. There aren't going to be any authors."

"Exactly my point."

Her son ran from the table in frustration. The friction built steadily, until Ben rarely communicated with his family.

They did come to his wedding. But it took years before they accepted his marriage to Lillian Uzlavsky, instead continuing to push him to "return to the real world." So Ben, despite having grown up hearing, developed the same cynicism of hearing society that other deaf persons had. He realized that not only did they not understand the impact of deafness, they didn't even want to try. Lillian was equally disillusioned, as her in-laws confirmed her own experiences with hearing Americans. The couple socialized with other deaf people, and when both their children were born deaf, the result of the Uzlavsky gene, they too became part of the deaf community, embracing its unique beliefs and distrust of the hearing world.

So Sandra's revelations about Rudy were a huge shock to her parents. Especially since she had invited him over for dinner that night. Ben and Lillian were deeply frightened of what would happen next.

Eight

Rudy was due any moment. Sandra kept glancing at the clock as she scurried around helping to get things ready. Her mother's parents sat on the couch signing with Mr. Horowitz as he opened the mail. He was telling them about something that had happened at work that day.

"This man came in to have his suit let out. He's a long-time customer of mine and has gained a lot of weight in the past year or two. So I measured him. Then he wrote a note asking when I could have it done. I told him two days by showing him two fingers. We've always managed to understand each other before, so I didn't write it down, and he nodded and left. I figured he understood. Two hours later, he came back. He thought I'd said two hours, not two days. I then wrote down 'two days' on paper, but he wrote that he needed the suit tonight for some special event. Like I said, he's one of my regulars, so I had to take care of him. I dropped everything else and got it done." His in-laws nodded their approval.

Sandra's father opened another envelope and made a face when he saw the contents. He got his wife's attention with a wave and held up a sheet of paper. "This bill is from when you went to the emergency room last month," he signed.

Mrs. Horowitz grabbed the counter and held her breath. Everyone looked at her. "I'm still so upset about that. Remember what the doctor did..." She squeezed her eyes tight.

When she finally opened her eyes again, her father signed, "What happened?"

"It was so embarrassing, although probably not anything worse than a lot of other deaf people have gone through. But in the past I've always been able to see Dr. Stein when I needed a doctor, so I never had any trouble before.

"I had this really bad stomach pain last month and didn't feel I could wait until the morning to see Dr. Stein. We couldn't find anyone who could call him for us, so Ben took me to the emergency room. The doctor there, when he found out I was deaf, just started examining me. He didn't even try to talk to me at all. He put his hands all over my body without telling me what he was doing. It was so humiliating! I kept trying to ask him to tell me what he was doing, and when I tried to sit up, he kept pushing me back down and telling me to relax. I just wanted to know what he was doing, what was going to happen."

A tear started. "Finally, he left and the nurse came in. I was shaking so bad, she couldn't take my blood. I felt like I was going to throw up. She was nice, though, and stayed with me until I finally calmed down a bit."

"That's awful, Lillian," her mother signed. "I had no idea."

"We hadn't told anyone else about it until now."

In the difficult silence, before anyone could reply, the lights flashed on and off. Rudy was at the front door. The mood turned to one of anticipation as Sandra walked over to let the soldier in. For the first time since they had met, he wasn't in his uniform. Instead he wore a beige cardigan sweater and dark gray pants. He towered over the short Horowitzes as Sandra introduced him to everybody in the room. As she did so, he signed to each person, "Nice to meet you," exactly as she had taught him the evening before. After that, however, he was unable to understand anything. Sandra acted as his interpreter, telling him what others said and signing his replies to her family. They marveled among themselves at how little she had to have Rudy repeat himself, and Sandra felt an odd pride.

"So you're in the Army?" Mr. Horowitz asked.

"Yes." Rudy answered this question himself, using the sign he had been taught.

"Where are you stationed?"

"Fort Bragg, in North Carolina."

"What do you think of the war in Europe?"

"It looks like it's going to be a long fight." His face became grimmer. "And unfortunately, a lot of people are going to get killed."

"Don't you agree we should be going there, though, to help stop Hitler?" Sandra's grandfather signed.

Rudy chose his words carefully. "That's a difficult question. I must say that I don't like at all what Hitler is about. But then, I'm not the one who makes the decision whether or not we go to war in Europe. That's up to the President, who has more information than I do about what's going on there."

"So you think we should go, right?"

"Again, that's difficult to answer."

"Let me tell you something," Mr. Horowitz signed again. Even though he retained some ability to speak, he refused to do so unless absolutely necessary. "I was in the Great War. I remember quite well what it was like. Horrible. Just horrible. I was only seventeen when I went. I'd gotten caught up in the excitement of the times and lied, saying I was eighteen so I could go. I was sent to the western front, and a month after I got there, we got in a terrific fight with the Germans. People were dying left and right. Blood was everywhere. Besides all the shooting, you could hear people screaming or moaning in pain. It was terrible. I'll never forget it. Then my closest buddy got hit in the arm. I was helping him in the trench, putting a blanket over him until we could get him to the medics, when suddenly there was this big explosion right behind me."

He paused, watching Rudy carefully.

"Sounds bad. What happened next?" the soldier asked.

"The next thing I knew, I was waking up. I'd been knocked out. That's when I realized I couldn't hear a thing, and from that time on, I've been deaf. The doctors think I damaged the hearing part of my brain when I hit my head on a rock, though they don't know for sure that's what happened. They told me I was lucky just to be alive. In fact, everyone who made it home felt lucky to come back."

"Wow. What happened then?"

"People who haven't been in a real war don't know how bad it is. If it was up to me, we'd never go back to Europe to fight unless we have a real good reason. Too many people get killed or crippled." He paused again, examining a fingernail as if it could offer answers. "But now, we have a very good reason to go back. It's that German leader, that Hitler. He's out of control. We have to stop him before he takes over Europe and kills everyone else he doesn't like. So, I believe we have no choice this time but to go back to war over there."

The grandfather spoke again, looking right at Rudy. "So, then we all agree then that America should go to war in Europe, to fight Hitler, right?"

Sandra watched Rudy. Despite the slightly tense muscles, he sat quietly, almost courtly. Like a future senator.

"Like I said before, I'm sure the President has more information about what's going on there than we do. That's why he's the one who makes that decision."

"Are you saying you don't think Hitler has been sending Jews and others into special camps to be killed?"

"I've heard that is happening." Rudy's eyes darkened.

"Well, my family hears normally like you. They've told me a couple of times that there's no doubt it's happening. So, I think we should go. Besides, if we don't go now, the way the war is going we'll probably end up fighting Germany anyway when they attack us here. So I'd go now. Keep them out of the States and save the Jews over there."

Rudy felt uncertain how to reply, a guest in their home on a religious occasion, but Sandra's brother saved him. David got the soldier's attention with a wave, then signed, "What's it like in the Army?"

Sandra translated, and Rudy relaxed a bit. "Well, it's not exactly the most exciting life, but it's tolerable."

"What do you do all day at Fort Bragg? Do you practice shooting a lot? Do you march around a lot?"

"Lots of marching, David. The Army loves marching." Everyone smiled when Sandra translated.

Rudy spent the next ten minutes satisfying the youngster's curiosity about Army life while Mrs. Horowitz worked on dinner and Sandra's father signed with his in-laws. When David was called to set the table, Rudy nodded at him as he left. "A fine young man, Sandra. So he's deaf too?"

"Yes, but unlike me, he's just a little hard of hearing."

"Then why didn't he talk to me instead of having you interpret?"

She shook her head. "Other than my father, who can do it a little, I'm the only one of us who is deaf that can speak."

"Sorry, I still don't understand. If he's only a little hard of hearing, how come he can't talk but you can?" He opened the top button on his cardigan, which Sandra realized was a sign he was relaxing more.

"Because I hear more sounds than he can, so I can say those sounds."

Rudy's face went blank, and she couldn't help smiling at him. "Now you have me totally confused. What do you mean you hear more sounds? If you're deaf and he's just a little hard of hearing, then he should hear much better than you."

She shook her head. "No, it's just the opposite. I'm not totally deaf, but I'm more hard of hearing than he is." When she saw

Rudy's look of incomprehension persist, she said hurriedly, "Let me show you." She got out a piece of paper and a pencil. On the left margin of the paper she wrote Deaf, on the right side she wrote Hearing, and between them she wrote Hard of Hearing. She glanced in the kitchen and saw her grandparents watching.

"Okay. Let's say we have someone who's totally deaf, then she would be here." She pointed the pencil at the word Deaf. "Now, let's say something happens so she can hear a few sounds. That would move her a little toward the hearing section." She moved her pencil to the right a little. "But because she hears only a few sounds, she's just a short way towards the hard of hearing section, like my pencil is, right here. Right? So she's just a little hard of hearing. Now let's say she can hear more. Then she moves more to the middle section," Sandra moved her pencil farther to the right, "sooooo, she's now more hard of hearing. Right?"

Rudy nodded, slowly understanding how Sandra perceived it.

"So since David's just a little hard of hearing, he's right here because he can't hear many sounds." She put her pencil near the word Deaf. "Me, I hear more sounds than he does, so I'm more hard of hearing. So I'm farther over to the middle here." She put her pencil closer to the middle of the paper. "Because I'm more hard of hearing, I hear more sounds, which is why I'm able to talk a little whereas he can't."

The logic was clear, but totally opposite of how a hearing person would describe it. Rudy was astonished again how it was like a totally different world. And so refreshing too, the way it challenged how he looked at things. He explained to Sandra, using the same paper, how hearing people would define hard of hearing.

Rudy looked up and noticed the grandparents were signing to each other even though they could hear. Their old wise faces that had witnessed too much changed facial expressions as their hands moved. He'd never seen hearing people that expressive. Rudy suddenly realized how easy it could be to eavesdrop on conversations. He nudged Sandra. Nodding at her grandparents, he asked, "How

121

would deaf people keep secrets from others if anyone looking at them can see what they are signing?"

Sandra nudged him back. "Spoken like a true senator! Actually, that's not a problem. You can use your body or a hand to hide what you're saying. Or you sign when no one else is looking. But it's not considered polite to watch another conversation if they don't want you to see them."

Speedy came up and nuzzled Rudy. He petted the dog's head, then looked back at Sandra. "So, if I learned to sign, I'd be able to understand all that?"

She moved her fist up and down. "And thanks for not pointing at them. That's also considered rude."

"And they'd understand me?"

"Yes, especially once they got used to your accent."

"Accent?"

"Sure. People who learn sign language later in life don't speak it the same as native signers. The way they move their hands is different. Some people can be difficult to understand. For example, my mother grew up speaking Yiddish Sign Language. So she signs with a Yiddish accent, though it's not bad. I have no problem understanding her since I grew up with her. But any deaf person will tell you that she doesn't speak like someone who grew up here. From what I've read, the same thing happens with people who learn to speak a new language later in life. They have an accent too that's different from native speakers. Right?"

Rudy nodded.

Sandra and Rudy talked together as family members drifted into the kitchen. Conversation between the visitor and rest of the family had ceased. None of the deaf people could understand him without Sandra interpreting, and her hearing grandparents were content to remain in the background. The Horowitzes settled into their pre-dinner routine, with Mrs. Horowitz finishing her cooking, her husband and parents reading the paper, and David helping his mother. They signed to each other occasionally, tapping or waving to get the person's attention. Rudy watched them, trying not to be rude about it, trying not to appear conspicuous yet finding the signing fascinating.

The soldier felt a tap and glanced back at Sandra. "I have big news," she said.

"What is it?"

"I have a job!"

"You do? Where?"

She told him about it.

"That's wonderful! You'll get some experience caring for animals, which should help you when you apply again next year to vet school."

Sandra pulled a face. He grimaced. "Even I know what that face means."

"Rudy, we've been through this already. They're not going to take me at vet school, no matter how much experience I get."

"Remember what I said before? About not giving up? If you think you can't do something, you're right. And if you think you can do it, you're right again."

"I remember very well, but it's not that simple," she said a little primly. "Let me tell you what happened earlier to give you an example of what I'm talking about. I was at Hudson's, applying for an opening they had. The lady I talked to, when she heard my speech, asked me if I was deaf. When I said yes, she wrote on a piece of paper, 'Do you know how to write in English?' I was blown away by that. I totally lost control. So I wrote, 'No, I can't read or write in English at all.' She then looked at me sadly and said, 'Oh, that's too bad.' " Sandra shook her head. "Amazing, isn't it? She was so sure that just because I am deaf, I am also dumb. And she didn't even realize that I had written her back in English."

Rudy's eyes showed a quiet bemusement. "Welcome to the human race, Sandra."

"What?"

"The world is full of people like that. But they're not typical of most hearing people."

She looked at him, watching for ridicule, but it wasn't there. "Okay, I'll give you that. But stuff like that happens all the time to deaf people. Well, maybe not quite that bad all of the time."

"Did you tell your parents about that?"

"Yes."

"What did they say?"

"They're deaf. They've been there too. My mom was upset with me, though, for losing my composure and ruining any possibility of getting that job. But no way would I have worked there even if I had gotten that job. Not for someone like that."

Before Rudy could reply, the lights flicked on and off. Mrs. Horowitz was pushing the white and black switches to let everyone know dinner was ready to be served.

Everyone sat at the dining room table, Rudy next to Sandra in the middle. Mrs. Horowitz lit the Sabbath candles and signed the blessing over them. Then her husband recited the Kiddush, his hands singing the prayer. Rudy watched intently, impressed by the religious mood created, again finding himself amazed at how beautiful hands could appear moving through the air, capturing love and kindness and goodwill. The movements were so varied, smooth yet purposeful, similar yet different. Sandra and her family understood effortlessly what was being communicated. He wondered what the words were, and how they compared to Catholic prayers.

A blessing followed over the food and red wine. A braided bread was passed around, and Rudy was surprised when people tore off pieces. When it came to him, he started to cut a piece with his knife, but Sandra explained it was traditional to tear off a piece of the challah. He did so, hesitantly, not used to eating bread that way. It had a succulent taste, different.

After the prayer over the wine, they each took a sip. It was the sweetest-tasting wine he'd ever had. He looked at the bottle label. Manischevitz. A name he'd never heard of before.

Then dinner was served. Three kinds of vegetables were put out first, two green and one yellow, then Mrs. Horowitz came by with the main dishes, beef brisket and chicken. She went around the table, stopping to give each person a choice of meat. When Rudy chose chicken, she turned to Sandra and signed, "What's the matter? He doesn't like my beef?"

"Mom, you asked him which he wanted."

"Tell him to put some beef on his plate too. No guest in my house is going to starve, even if he is a hearing goy."

Rudy was amazed when everyone started to eat and continued signing. He tried to follow as they got each other's attention by waving in the air and hitting the table. Definitely not what the etiquette books would encourage. And unlike hearing people, the Horowitzes could chew and "talk" at the same time. He had no idea what was being discussed, though. Even when people spelled out words, it was done so quickly he couldn't even begin to keep up. He looked at Sandra and found her smiling at him as she plucked at her vegetables with her fork. He got her message, unspoken: *Welcome to my world.* He smiled back.

But Rudy felt isolated. People were deep in conversation all around him, and he was unable to participate. It was an uneasy feeling, almost as if he were less fit than they. Sandra tried to interpret for him, but would get distracted by the discussion. He found himself daydreaming and stopped with a start, worried someone would notice. He recalled Sandra telling him deaf people were experts at reading body language. Could they tell how uncomfortable he was? Sandra must have felt this way at the party the night before. How naive he'd been to think she'd fit in easily. As he watched the family sign, he vowed to learn more of the language. He wanted to interact with them better the next time.

Sandra touched his shoulder. "David wants to tell a joke. I'll interpret it for you."

Rudy nodded and looked at David, who smiled and started to sign excitedly. The soldier looked back at Sandra. "There was this hearing timber man who was cutting big trees in the forest. One by one they were falling down. Then he saw this really, really big tree and decided to cut it down. He chopped and chopped and chopped until it was about ready to fall."

David paused until he could see his sister had caught up with the interpretation. "He pushed on the tree and yelled, 'Timber!' Nothing happened. He took another nick out of the trunk, then pushed and yelled 'Timber!' again. Still, nothing happened. A tree doctor just happened to be passing by, so the timber man hailed the doctor and told him what happened. The tree doctor took one look at the tree and knew exactly what the problem was. He pushed on the tree, fingerspelled "T-I-M-B-E-R," and stepped back as the tree fell. The doctor then turned to the timber man and said, "Tree Deaf."

Everyone around the table laughed, hearty joyous movements along with the sound, and David looked proud of himself. Rudy gave a fake laugh, all the while surprised at how funny everyone else, Sandra included, seemed to think the joke was. Maybe he had missed something in the translation.

People started signing, and Rudy felt himself an outcast again. Then he noticed the loud smacking noises made when they chewed their food. It was particularly noticeable because there was otherwise little sound in the air. At first he associated the smacking with being a Jewish custom. Then he realized it was happening because the deaf people couldn't hear it and had no idea they were doing it.

He felt thirsty and nudged Sandra. "Would it be possible for me to have a glass of milk?"

She shook her head. "We keep kosher."

"So, even though I don't keep kosher, I can't have milk?"

"That's right."

"Are you saying that milk isn't allowed if one keeps kosher?"

"It is, but it's not allowed at a meal at the same time as meat."

He looked back around the table and noticed the Horowitzes were engrossed with their conversation. He began to wonder what deaf people talked about. Were they the same things as hearing people? And did deaf Jewish people talk about the same things hearing Jewish people talked about? He remembered Sandra's description of hard of hearing and wondered how many other surprises there'd be if only he could understand the discussion.

Rudy glanced at Sandra next to him. As she signed to her grandfather, he tried his best to assess her body language, but had no idea what it said. He hoped she was content. In these precious few days they had been together, he realized his feelings had gone deep. At the same time, he was confused. About going back to the Army. About fighting in a war. About the possibility of dying. About his dreams, and how he felt driven to become a senator and help Americans. And about Sandra, and her deafness, and religion. And whether she would be part of his future. Tonight would be his last time with her for months, perhaps years. He wanted to make it a memorable one, a memory that could sustain him for however long and during whatever might happen to him in Europe.

He became bored, even impatient, and started discreetly checking his watch. Time dragged. Finally the clock hit eight, the hour they had agreed to go to his parents' house. Then he felt self-conscious interrupting what seemed to be a heated discussion, so he waited ten more minutes before nudging Sandra and pointing under the table at the time. She nodded, then explained to her family they had to leave.

As everyone stood, Rudy asked where the telephone was so he could tell his parents they'd be a little late. "We don't have one," Sandra told him, for some reason feeling a little embarrassed. "None of us who live here can use it."

Rudy berated himself. How stupid could he be? Of course they wouldn't have a phone. What would the family say about him now? Trying to look relaxed, he thanked the Horowitzes for their hospitality.

Outside, they remained silent until they were in the white Studebaker. "Well," Sandra asked, "what did you think?"

"I had a nice time. Your family is very nice."

She tilted her head. "You don't have to lie to me, Rudy. I could tell you weren't very comfortable in there. Right from the beginning, when Grandpa and Dad started asking you about the war."

"I thought you'd notice that."

"I'm sure everyone did. It practically jumped out of you. And also the way you kept checking your watch."

"I was that obvious?"

"You were. And because you're hearing, I'm sure my parents enjoyed seeing you uncomfortable."

"It was just so different from what I'm used to. I mean, it was a weird feeling I had. I couldn't..."

"Couldn't understand what we were saying and felt out of it?" she finished for him.

He nodded.

She moved closer to him. "Awful feeling, isn't it?"

"Sure is. And the way they kept bringing up the war and about Hitler sending the Jews to concentration camps. It really put me on the spot. I mean, they didn't even ask any general questions—they got right to it."

"That's another thing I noticed in college, Rudy. About how hearing people are different from deaf people. Hearing people tend to take their time working their way up to the main point. It annoys me sometimes. How long they can take to do that, I mean. Deaf people get right to the point. They don't waste time. They spend their time signing about the main point, not working up to it."

"That joke your brother told," Rudy said slowly. "It was kind of cute, but, at least from what I got, not that funny. Everyone else practically died laughing, though. Did I miss something there?"

"It was probably my fault because I didn't translate well. Part of what makes a joke so good in sign language is often the way the signs and hands are used. Sometimes it's the order of the words, or how the person signs a particular word, that makes the joke so good."

He gripped the steering wheel. "Wait a minute. You mean in sign language, you don't sign a word the same way each time?"

"That's right. How you sign it depends on what you are trying to say."

"Give me an example."

She thought for a second. "Okay." She put her right wrist on top of her left one, and brought them together and apart lightly. "This is the sign for work. Now, watch my whole body and face as well as my signs." She made a stern face, furrowed her brow, and looked intently at her wrists as she hit them together several times crisply and harder. "That means more than just the word for work, it means I'm working *hard.*" She then changed her demeanor and made a casual face, looked away into space, and lazily flexed her wrists against each other. "This is the sign for work again, but the way I'm doing it means I'm goofing off."

"Wow. That's so neat. We can't do that in English. We can change how we say a word, but it doesn't change the meaning that much."

Sandra spoke into the lengthening silence. "Rudy?

"What."

"Before you came, I had quite a debate with my parents about my seeing you. They're very upset about it."

"Because I'm not Jewish and deaf?"

"That's it exactly."

Suddenly, he hit the steering wheel in anger. "I don't understand the problem! Don't your parents realize the vast majority of people in the world hear? I mean, your father especially should know that. He used to hear for seventeen years of his life. Why do deaf people hate hearing people so much? What's so special about being deaf? I'd never want to be like that. So much of what the world offers has to do with sound. Music. Plays. Telephone. Radio. And even things as simple as talking to other people on the street.

Almost anywhere you go, just about everyone hears and talks. Why would they want you to limit yourself to deaf men?"

Sandra had never seen him upset before. She recalled the numerous times she'd felt similarly annoyed about hearing people. Reaching for his hand, she held it silently between both of hers until he calmed down, slumping back in the white leather seat.

"I'm sorry I got carried away," he apologized. "It's just that people can be so intolerant. I'm just so frustrated."

"I know. I've been there. Many times."

He let out a long sigh and turned to her.

"We better go." He started the car. Sandra felt its now familiar vibrations while Rudy heard the familiar rumble of its engine.

"Rudy, deaf people aren't dumb. We're aware of everything you just said. We know we're different and that there aren't that many of us in this world. That's the very reason we stick together. Because hearing people just don't understand what life is like for us. What's more, most don't even seem to care. Instead, they try to make us be like them. Such as trying to get us to talk instead of sign, even though to us, signing is so much easier and so much richer. If you really think about it, you have to admit it does make a lot of sense that we favor being with each other, doesn't it? Just like people of the same religious faith do?"

Rudy checked the rearview mirror and pulled away from the curb. "What you say makes sense, Sandra. But I still don't see why deaf people can't at least learn to read lips. And speak, like you do, so they can talk to hearing people when they have to. The immigrants who came to this country around the turn of the century also didn't know English. But they learned it so they could become part of American society. That's what America is about. Being a great melting pot."

"That's easier said than done, Rudy. Many deaf people can't learn to speak even when they want to. Look at my father. After losing his hearing, he tried for two years to communicate by reading lips. He never could. And he used to hear and speak normally.

Most deaf people don't want to even try. Why should they? It takes years and years of practice and aggravation to maybe be able to communicate some. Keep in mind, there's a huge difference between the immigrants and us. Because we can't hear the sounds, we have to do more than just learn new words. We have to memorize where to put our tongue for each sound. How to shape our lips. And which sounds to make in the throat and which in the mouth. It's hard. Really hard, Rudy. Even those who are so-called successful at speech reading—like me—still feel uncomfortable talking in most situations. I miss over half of what most hearing people say. So, we miss things that we don't miss when signing. And we have to practice constantly, or our enunciation gets bad again because we can't hear when we say something wrong and so end up putting our tongue in the wrong places. The difference between the right sound and the wrong sound can be a slight difference in where one's tongue is. My mother once compared learning to speak to asking blind people to learn to identify colors by feeling them. No one expects that of blind people, yet people expect us to speak."

Rudy's eyes were dark with concern. "Are you saying that you miss half of what I tell you?"

"Not anymore. You're an exception. Not only are you easy to lip-read, but I've been with you so long it's become second nature to me now. I get most, though not all, of what you say."

He nodded, aware of her steady gaze, her warm eyes bright and caring.

"You mentioned my father and his experience with the hearing world," she continued. "The only reason I've had as much speech therapy and speak as well as I do is because of him. Since he grew up hearing, he's aware of the benefits of being able to speak, and he insisted that his children learn to speak if possible, so we could communicate with the rest of the world when we had to. Yet I was the only one who was able to do this. David has never learned to do it, although he's certainly tried hard enough."

"How come he can't learn to do it?"

"No one knows. Some people can do it, and some can't. It doesn't seem to have anything to do with how smart they are. A lot of the smartest deaf people I know can't lip-read, while some who are kinda... well, not so smart, lip-read very well."

The Studebaker made its way down the street, its gleaming nose probing ahead. They drove in silence for some time before Rudy asked suddenly, "Do you have another dog besides Speedy? Or did you?"

"No. Why do you ask?"

"Oh, I saw the name DINGO written down on a piece of paper in the kitchen. Figured it was the name of another dog. I just didn't know if it was one of yours."

Sandra chuckled. "That's not a dog. It's the BINGO night our Deaf Club has once a month. My parents like to go."

"Why call it DINGO rather than BINGO?"

She shrugged. "For as long as I can remember, that's what they call it. It's short for Deaf BINGO, but it's basically the same thing."

Rudy leaned his head back against the headrest, then sighed. "We come from such different backgrounds and belief systems, sometimes the thought of us being together scares me."

The statement struck home. It was the first time either had openly mentioned a possible future together. She found his hand and held it tight.

He geared down as a family crossed the street. "They should use the traffic light," he said. "Anyway, there's one thing I better tell you now before we go to my house. My parents are practicing Catholics. Although I gave up religion, as you know, they're still quite devout."

"May I ask how you think they will react to me?"

He waited to answer until he came to a full stop at a red light. "To Mom and Dad, our two religions mix like oil and water."

Sandra had a world weary smile. "Sounds like our parents have a lot in common. Have you told them about me?"

"Sure, but not about your being Jewish. Just the deafness. I was afraid if I told them everything, they'd be against you before they even met you. I don't want that. This way, they'll give you a chance, and once they meet you, I'm hoping they'll like you. How couldn't they?"

"What did they say when you told them about me?"

"They weren't happy. But I think most of it had nothing to do with you. They just wanted me to spend more time with them today because I'm due back at Bragg tomorrow."

"I see. Well, I might as well be up front about being Jewish," she said firmly. "It's my turn at the plate to take a swing at the spitball, and I can't miss any worse than what you just did."

"That's for sure. Shall we go to their house then?"

She nodded as the light changed to green. Rudy turned right and headed for his parents' place.

133

Nine

On the way, Rudy and Sandra came upon a carnival. They were almost past it when he abruptly swerved into the last entrance to the parking lot and pulled to a stop near the main gate.

"What are you doing?" Sandra was holding on to the door handle.

"Well, Sandra, if I remember from when I was here a few years ago, they have a booth where we can have our picture taken. What do you say? Shall we?"

"Oh, I'd love that."

"You can let go of the door now."

"That was some sharp turn, soldier."

He laughed, helping her out.

They strolled to the area where he remembered the picture stand was located, and they were lucky. Not only was the booth there again, but there was no line. Rudy arranged for two pictures to be taken. They tidied up and walked into the camera alcove. The photographer was chatty, but had a bushy mustache, so Sandra couldn't understand a thing he said. Rudy interpreted for her, telling her where to sit and what pose to assume. She still felt uncomfortable being there. It just wasn't the type of setting deaf people would normally seek out.

Rudy paid for the pictures. As they started back to the car, he said, "The man said they'll be ready Wednesday. Since I'll be gone, can you pick them up?"

"I'll be happy to."

"Good." He gave her the receipt. "Keep the one you like best and send me the other."

It had been years since Sandra had been to a carnival. Tight money kept her from going. They passed a group of men banging a sledgehammer on a lever to see who could send a ball higher. Across the way were a brightly lit Ferris wheel and carousel. At five cents a ride, Sandra almost asked Rudy to take her, but then saw how long the lines were. They had to get to Rudy's parents' house.

Open tents were everywhere, held up by poles. Bare light bulbs hung in their lonely existence, illuminating the area. Several booths had prizes. Cloth toys dangled from beams—bears, rabbits, dogs. The fair was very busy, people moving around, kids animated. Workers' lips were in constant motion as they hawked their product, yelling jingles. Sandra read, "Three tries for a nickel." One tent had flaps blocking an entrance, and a man in front hoisting a sign that said, "SEE THE STRONG MAN BEND STEEL BARS WITH HIS BARE HANDS." Men in front were waving tickets at passersby.

She turned to Rudy. "I see a lot of people moving around and talking. Is it really noisy?"

"It's loud, but not too bad. There are so many different voices and sounds, it's kind of interesting."

"What kind of sounds do you hear?"

He listened to them for a second. "Over there people are yelling. They're selling tickets for the Strong Man. And someone behind us is shouting 'Three darts for two cents.' I hear other voices too but can't tell what they're saying. I hear the Ferris wheel out there," he pointed to its rotating, lighted circle, "but it's hard to be sure because there's all kinds of music coming from the booths around us. And I just heard the carousel music start up; that ride must be going again."

"Wow. I'm amazed you can tell all those sounds apart, yet hear them at the same time."

"I never thought about it like that, but I guess you're right. Do you hear any of it?"

"Not really, just a little noise. I can sure smell the food, though."

"Want something?"

"No. I'm still pretty full from dinner. Besides, I can't eat the meat here because it's not kosher."

He kissed her on the brow. "You'll have to fill me in sometime on what is and isn't allowed when one keeps kosher."

"Glad to."

A vendor was selling cotton candy. "Is that allowed if you're keeping kosher?"

She nodded. "But I'll pass on that right now, too."

"Just as well. Knowing my mother, I'm sure she'll have food galore when we get there. If we don't eat anything here, we'll have more room for it."

Two attractive women were passing them, going the other direction, when one of them suddenly grabbed Rudy's arm. "Rudy?"

"Susan? Susan Oakley?"

"That's me!" she beamed.

"I can't believe it." He hugged her close.

"I thought it might be you by your walk," Susan said, "then I heard your voice. I'd recognize that anywhere."

"The Army has me marching now. I've got little chance to walk."

"Well, it hasn't changed a bit."

"What are you doing here, Susan? I thought you moved to Ohio years ago."

"I did, but moved back last month. Never liked it down there, though my parents do. Oh, Rudy, it's so good to see you again!"

"You too. You haven't changed a bit! Still a knockout."

She beamed. "The first thing I did after coming back to Michigan was to look you up. That's when I found you had moved. The people who bought your old house didn't know where your parents had moved to. After asking around, I learned you had joined the Army, and I was so disappointed. I mean, I'm glad you're serving our country and all that, but I wanted so much to see you." She smiled warmly at him, then glanced at Sandra, who had missed much of the conversation.

"Oh, I'm sorry. Susan, this is Sandra. Sandra, Susan."

"Nice to meet you," Sandra said.

Interest flitted across Susan's face as she nodded politely. "You too." The woman introduced her friend, Elise, then turned back to Rudy. "So tell me, what's it like in the Army?"

"Well, marching, like I said. Getting in shape, learning to work together, use the weapons, stuff like that."

"Is it awful?"

He shrugged. "It's okay. Nothing really bad to this point. But we'll be heading to Europe before long. I imagine things will be anything but routine there."

Sandra found herself in difficulty. Conversation so fast, distorted by quick smiles and turning heads, even though only two people were talking. Her stomach felt queasy. It often did when she had to interact with hearing strangers for very long. Susan was difficult to lip-read for some reason. Sandra strained to piece together the conversation mostly from what she saw Rudy say.

And she felt herself becoming jealous. Susan's interest in Rudy was obvious—she was coming on to him in the strongest way. What bothered her more was how strongly Rudy's body showed an interest in Susan. The woman was good looking, Sandra had to admit. And she recalled Rudy saying that Susan had been his first love before she'd moved away. He hadn't said anything negative about her like he had about Pam.

Sandra struggled to project calm and was deciding whether to say something when Elise got her attention. "You from around here?"

The woman barely moved her lips. The kind of hearing person dreaded by anyone who depends on speech reading. And to make it worse, she wore sunglasses even though it was night, making it difficult to get any clues from her face. Sandra guessed and nodded.

Elise continued, "I don't remember you in school. Did you go to East High?"

"Pardon?" Sandra steeled herself. This would get worse. The woman repeated herself.

"I still didn't get that." She felt Susan eyeing her in that special, horrible way.

Elise said the question one more time.

"I live on the west side of Springville, near Coral Drive."

From their looks, she knew immediately she had guessed wrong again. Just like at the party. God, would this never end? Maybe she should just tell them she was deaf.

Then Rudy spoke up. "Well, we need to go. We're late for an engagement."

"Here, let me give you my name and number." Susan lunged into her purse. She handed the scrap of paper to him. Sandra caught a whiff of pungent perfume. "Do call me tomorrow, Rudy. I'd really like to get together."

"I can't, Susan. I leave early in the morning to go back to the base."

Susan telegraphed her disappointment so vividly, it had to be evident even to a hearing person like Rudy. Sandra watched with gathering anger as Susan moved closer to Rudy. *I can't believe she's actually doing that*, Sandra thought.

"What time do you leave?" Susan asked.

"Early, real early. Like seven a.m."

Susan pressed his arm. "I'll come by around six and see you off."

"You'll waste your time if you do that," Rudy said, smiling, head shaking. "I already promised my parents I'd be with them. But give me your address and I'll write you when I can."

She did that, then kissed him on the cheek. Again the heavy perfume wafted.

Rudy and Sandra walked off. Sandra grabbed Rudy's arm and felt Susan's gaze drill into her back. They got the rest of the way back to the car, but the tension was palpable. Sandra looked at Rudy. He seemed pensive, lost in thought. Even when they reached the Studebaker, he didn't say a word. Her nerves were screaming as they got into the car.

When he looked at her, Sandra forced herself to sound casual. "What did Susan's friend ask me?"

"If you went to East High School."

"Darn. She was impossible to lip read. So I guessed, and I guessed wrong."

"You sure did."

"Well, thanks a lot. Your support is just wonderful!"

"Hey, easy. She came up so sudden, I—"

"It was like your party friends all over again."

"Now that's not fair, Sandra."

She hesitated, wondering if this was where it ended. "No, it wasn't. I'm sorry. She seems like a nice person."

"She is."

"What did she mean, she'd recognize your voice anywhere?"

"People tell me I have a southern twang, like I grew up in Texas. But I never lived anywhere south until I went to Fort Bragg."

A southern twang. Sandra wondered what that sounded like. Perhaps that was like signing with a Yiddish accent. And how different from other people's voices was it? Was there anything else about Rudy's voice that hearing people would call distinctive?

Rudy broke in on her thoughts. "Well, shall we go on over to my parents' house?"

Sandra nodded. She decided not to say anything more about Susan Oakley. After all, she had only known Rudy for three days, and they hadn't made any firm commitments to each other. Her concern lingered, however. Rudy hadn't told the two women that she was deaf. He hadn't stepped in with Elise when he could have. That was different from what he had done at the party. Sandra wondered if it meant anything.

Ten

The Townsend house was six blocks past the carnival. It was a red brick, two-story Tudor that was bigger than most of the other bungalows on the street. The quarter acre lot was one of the few with a driveway. Light from the streetlamp in front of the house was bright, revealing the white window shutters and blue star proudly displayed in the window. A picket fence enclosed the back yard. The front yard was well manicured. In the neighbor's house, Sandra noticed a gold star in the front window, signifying that someone had died in the war. She pointed it out to Rudy.

"My parents told me his name was Jim Barnes. He was two years older than me and in the Navy. I never knew him, but from what they tell me, he was a nice guy. He was killed three weeks ago when his ship got torpedoed by a U-boat."

Rudy guided Sandra to the front porch. His father opened the door as they approached.

"Hello!" The older man smiled at them. His hand swept wide in a gesture of welcome. "Come on in."

They entered the brightly lit entry. It had a very different feel than the Horowitz house. The walls were wainscoted, with flowered wallpaper above the wood trim, so different from the plain white walls of Sandra's house. The furnishings were newer and of modern style, not colonial American. There was also a popcorn ceiling, a banister with art objects, and a mirror in the hallway. Waxed hardwood floors reflected the lights in the room.

"So you're the one Rudy told us about."

Sandra had been watching him and nodded, a first blush tinting her cheeks.

"I'm sorry. Rudy told me, but I forgot your name."

She answered, trying to enunciate well.

"Shandra," he said, savoring the sound. "That's certainly unique. What nationality—"

"It's Sandra, not Shandra," Rudy gently interrupted.

"Oh, pardon me, Sandra. And Rudy said you're from around here?"

She nodded as Mrs. Townsend came out.

"Molly," her husband said, "This is Sandra. Sandra, Molly Townsend."

"So nice to meet you." Rudy's mother smiled warmly as she took Sandra's hand in both of hers. "Come. Let's sit down in the living room." Fortunately Mrs. Townsend pointed the way, because Sandra had trouble lip-reading.

Sandra and Rudy walked ahead of his parents. Mrs. Townsend said, "Sandra, where did you say you lived?"

"Mom, remember I told you that she doesn't hear well?"

"Oh, that's right. You did. I forgot." Mrs. Townsend asked the question again, in a much louder voice.

Rudy tapped Sandra on the shoulder. "Mom just asked you a question."

"Rudy! She's a grown woman. She can take care of herself."

"Mom…"

Sandra finished for him, surprised at her sudden lack of modesty, wondering if it was leftover anger at Susan and Rudy's reaction to her. "I'm deaf. I read lips to communicate, Mrs. Townsend."

Mrs. Townsend looked a little flustered. "You're deaf and dumb? I thought you were just hard of hearing. Oh, I'm so sorry. That must be so hard to live with."

Sandra stopped walking, quite still on the polished wax floor. Rudy put his hand on her shoulder to keep her calm. "Mom, don't be sorry. She's doing just fine. It isn't a problem. And she's not dumb. She's got a junior college degree."

"I'm sorry. Rudy did tell me you didn't hear well, but I just didn't know you were deaf." The Townsends glanced at each other before Rudy's mother picked up the conversation. "I was just asking where you live."

The coolness in the woman's demeanor was inevitable. It hung between the bright lights and polished floor. "I'm sorry, can you say that again?"

Mrs. Townsend did. "Near Pratt Avenue, two blocks west of Gabby's Bowling Alley," Sandra replied.

"Pardon me?"

Sandra repeated her answer.

"Oh yes, I know the area." Sandra wasn't sure if the sense of disapproval was for her speech, her deafness or the neighborhood. "Are you working now?"

"Pardon?"

"Are you working now?"

"I just got a job, starting Monday."

"Where?"

"Huron Kennels."

The inevitable repeat. Was this all worthwhile?

"And what will you be doing there?" Mr. Townsend asked.

Sandra didn't see his lips. He realized this and was trying to decide how to get her attention when his wife helped out. She repeated her husband's question.

"Helping to care for the dogs being boarded."

The elder Townsends flashed each other another look. Sandra looked at Rudy. *See*, she telegraphed to him, *See how it is?*

They started walking again and passed the kitchen, where Sandra saw a real refrigerator rather than an icebox. No one she knew could afford one yet. The living room itself was expensively furnished and extraordinarily neat, even down to the magazine arrangement on the coffee table, but the focus was clearly the grand piano. Another difference from her home.

When Rudy and Sandra sat down, Mrs. Townsend asked, "Anyone want a drink?"

Rudy chose a beer, Sandra a Coke, and Mr. Townsend went over to make himself a martini. When everyone was served, his mother said, "Rudy, since it's your last night home, I made a surprise snack for you. They gave me some extra ration coupons because you were coming home, so I figured I'd use them to get things you like. I'll be right back with it."

After she left, Rudy's father started talking about the Detroit Tigers' latest victory. He talked like Rudy, making him easier than usual for Sandra to understand. And baseball was something Sandra knew a lot about. So she held her own in the conversation, genuinely getting into it as Rudy smiled at his dad. She impressed Mr. Townsend with statistics he didn't know, as well as the fact that she'd been at the All Star game at Briggs Stadium when Ted Williams hit the game-winning home run. She was describing how excited the fans were when Mrs. Townsend came back and placed a tray of cut sandwiches on the table.

She smiled at Rudy. "Cold pork and Swiss with mayonnaise on wheat bread. Your favorite!"

"Cold pork and Swiss? Thanks so much."

"Mmm hmm." Mr. Townsend picked one up, along with a napkin, and took a big bite.

"I had a big dinner, Mom," he said, "but I appreciate your doing this." He took a half-sandwich. Sandra didn't.

"Don't you know there's a war going on and food is scarce?" Mrs. Townsend told Sandra, an insincere smile on her face. "Take one. Don't be bashful."

Sandra looked at the gleaming tray, napkins and neatly arranged sandwiches being pushed in front of her. "Thank you very much, but I'm not hungry. We just came from dinner, and I'm full."

"Try one. They're good." Rudy's mother moved the tray closer to Sandra.

"I really do appreciate that, but I think I'll pass this time."

Suddenly, Sandra saw Rudy stiffen in realization. Thank God. He could do something. "Mom, don't push her if she doesn't want any."

"All right. If you don't want to even try Rudy's favorite sandwich, that's up to you."

Sandra could feel the censure, felt her arms get goosebumps.

Rudy's father talked again about the war in Europe, worried about the probability that his son would be going there. He mentioned how devastated Jim Barnes' parents were when they found out their son had been killed, and wondered whether it was worth the lives of American men to fight Hitler. Sandra watched, getting much of it, but weary of the subject. She had her own worries about Rudy's safety. His opinion was that it was a disagreement between European countries that should be solved by them. Mrs. Townsend agreed, and a discussion followed about the merits of the conflict. Sandra tried to follow the conversation as it speeded up, but only got a small portion of it. No one looked at her when they spoke. She tired of it quickly, a genuine fatigue setting in from trying to follow.

Then she sensed Rudy's body become taut, and she looked at his face in time to see him say, "I'm not sure I agree with that."

"C'mon, Rudy," his father said, after dabbing at his mouth with a napkin. "You're being too idealistic again. Remember last year when you had the crazy idea of the government making sure that poor children had a more equal chance in life? This is like that."

"What if it's true?" The son faced the father.

Sandra looked at Mr. Townsend and managed to see him mouth, "I mean, there's been no proof, has there? I think it's all a hoax that's part of an attempt to justify the war. But even if it's true and Hitler really is killing all those kikes in Europe, is that really something we should get involved in? Let's be realistic here. Get our priorities straight. Does anyone think it's worth sacrificing the lives of our American boys to save Jews?"

Sandra felt the blood rush to her cheeks. She kept silent. *Focus. Focus.* These were Rudy's parents. His last night home. She mustn't ruin that for him. And maybe she hadn't speech-read him right. Still, even though she had been forewarned, his father's anti-semitic comments bit deep and ugly. She was drawn to the discussion now. She focused as hard as she could, ignoring the damned sandwiches. Rudy debated the issue with both his parents. Neither side gave in, and he finally changed the subject to the economy. After another debate on whether more public work projects were needed to provide more jobs now that there was a war going on, Mr. Townsend picked up another sandwich and bit into it. Sandra thought he bit into a sandwich as savagely as he bit into his prejudices.

He looked at Sandra. "You're missing something really good here." He waved the sandwich. "Rudy's mother is famous for these. C'mon. Just try one. You'll like it. It's the best pork in town."

Sandra's anger escaped her. She uttered her truth simply, speaking for her people. "Thank you for offering, but I think I'll pass. I'm Jewish. I don't eat pork."

A vicious satisfaction took her as she read the change in Rudy's parents' body language. But then she glanced at Rudy, at his tension. She wished she hadn't been so combative and had kept her mouth shut. An odd thought mixed with her distress, her feeling of abandonment. Susan Oakley would've eaten the sandwiches.

An unpleasant quiet filled the living room. Sandra frantically tried to think of what to say to make things better, to salvage things, yet thinking too that she was right. It was they who were wrong.

Rudy finally broke the silence when he asked his parents about some of their friends. They talked about that for a few minutes, but the tension remained. Sandra stared at the magazines on the coffee table, smiling faces and Rockwell covers about Liberty and Peace.

Then Mr. Townsend stood up and asked Rudy if they could talk privately for a moment in the kitchen. Alone with Sandra, Mrs. Townsend tried to make small talk but never looked directly at her, clearly unhappy. Avoiding eye contact is considered extremely rude in deaf culture; it made Sandra even more upset. She felt like a stranger in a strange land. Especially when Rudy's mother got up and poured herself a shot of whiskey without offering some to Sandra. She watched the silent cascade of ice and flow of amber liquid. She was glad when Rudy returned a few minutes later, until she read his anger. She waited. What had happened in the kitchen? Whose side would Rudy take? The questions went unanswered.

The time dragged. The Townsends left Rudy to include her in the discussion periodically. It took all her focus to give an appearance of paying attention. She wondered how much longer she could continue the façade.

Finally, Rudy stood up, attracting Sandra's attention by his movement. She looked up in time to see him say, "Sandra and I would like some time alone, so we're going to leave now."

"You'll be back in a half-hour or so, right?" said his father. "It's your last night home for a long time, boy, and your mother and I would like to be with you."

"It'll probably be late when I return," Rudy said, positioning himself so Sandra could read him. "Don't wait up for me. I'll see you both in the morning."

The Townsends protested, but Rudy held firm. He and Sandra got into the car and drove away, away from prejudice, anger, humiliation. Neither spoke. They sat, watching the scenery as Rudy drove around town, each rehashing the events of the evening in their minds.

It was almost ten minutes later, at a stoplight, when Sandra felt his hand on her shoulder. "I'm sorry my parents were so rude. No matter how upset they may have been at finding out you were Jewish, they should've treated you more civilly."

"It's partly my fault, Rudy. I shouldn't have said that to your father, especially since you had warned me what he thought about Jewish people. It's just that after your mother said she was sorry I was deaf, and then your father used the word *kike*, it got to me." Her smile was bitter. "Odd, isn't it? I could easily read 'kike.' I wished I couldn't. Anyway, they were no different from how my family treated you."

"No, they were worse, much more obvious. They, of all people, should know how to be better hosts since they consider themselves leaders in this community. But after what he said to me in the kitchen, I'm embarrassed at how some of the so-called leaders in this country are so closed-minded. They just don't think. I mean, my father is someone who is well read, intelligent."

Sandra's eyes watched him. More ugliness was coming, but she could take it. She'd been taking the blows all her life. She would take it now, not just for herself but for her people, and who she was.

"What did he say?"

"Do you really want to know?"

"Yes."

"It isn't pleasant."

"I've already figured that out."

He paused again as the light turned green. He stepped on the gas, sending the Studebaker through the intersection. "My father wanted to know why I was with you. I tried to tell him how much I enjoy being with you, then he asked... if I was in debt to you or something."

Sandra's laugh was bitter, knowing what was coming.

"When I told him no, he asked me why I would have any interest in a deaf mute when there were so many better and more fitting—those are exactly the words he used—women in the world. I asked him what he meant by that. He said a woman who... um... was not a... um... he used that 'kike' word again... but a normal human being."

148

In spite of her efforts, Sandra felt the tear roll down her cheek. Then another, and another. She began to sob, softly at first. Rudy pulled over and held her tight. When she looked up at him, she asked, "Do you ever weep for your people, Rudy?"

He had tears too. He got it, he understood, and she rejoiced.

"Not the way you can for your people, Sandra." They held each other quietly awhile.

"You have such a different background than me, Rudy, in every way." She sat up suddenly. "Before you met me, what did you think about deaf people?"

"I don't know. I guess I never really thought about it."

"Really? No thoughts about it? None at all?"

"Well, maybe I did a little bit."

"Okay. Let me guess. You thought we were dumb. And were lousy workers. And that we couldn't be good parents."

"That's because I didn't know much about deaf people. I did hear those things, but I'm not sure I really believed all that. I guess I really didn't think about it much before."

Sandra sighed. "So people really do say that about us, eh?"

"Yeah."

"Why? What is it that makes hearing people have all these stereotypes about deaf people that just aren't true? And then, because they do have those distorted ideas, it affects how they interact with us, which makes it all even more difficult. It's just plain wrong."

He nodded.

"You know, Rudy, last week I was in the grocery store buying some tomato sauce. I was looking at the different brands, trying to decide which to buy. Then someone tapped me on the shoulder lightly, and when I turned around, there was a whole line of people with carts who were trying to get by my cart that was in the middle. I apologized and got it out of their way. But it's so weird. I'm sure people had called out to me several times and I hadn't heard them. Still, despite all these hearing people waiting, it was like they had been afraid to touch me until one finally became brave enough to do so. Almost like I would break if they did."

"I don't know that they were afraid to touch you."

"Maybe not. It just seemed so weird, that's all. That they'd wait so long when I wasn't responding. Deaf people would have gotten the person's attention much earlier. There are a lot of ways of doing that nicely."

Sandra dabbed at her drying eyes with Rudy's handkerchief. "I've noticed a lot of other ways hearing people do things differently."

"Such as?"

"Like when we took the buses yesterday. You asked the drivers what the fare was. I mean, you just took for granted that you'd understand what they said. I would've found out the fare ahead of time. I would have had the exact change so I didn't have to worry about communicating with him."

"Sounds like you plan your activities with the outside world before you go out there."

She nodded.

"Wow. I never do."

"I have to. It makes things go a lot smoother. You've seen what can happen when a deaf person tries to talk with hearing people."

"Yeah." Rudy smiled and squeezed her hand. "But I've also noticed you and I rarely have to ask each other to repeat anymore. It gets easier with time. Maybe if you did it more, you'd find it easier."

She pulled her hand free. "You really don't understand what it's like, do you?"

"I guess not yet, but I will, Sandra. I'm planning on learning."

She looked at him a second, then lay her head back on his chest for awhile. Suddenly, she had to ask him the question. She just had to know after everything that had gone on tonight. "Rudy, do you wish you were with Susan now instead of me?"

150

He kissed her lips. She turned away.

"Rudy, answer my question. Do you?"

He looked into her eyes. "No, I don't."

She searched his eyes. Warm, inviting. Not at all deceitful. "You didn't say that very convincingly."

"I was just so shocked to see her again after all this time."

"You seemed so interested in her, and I… okay, I'll admit it. I was jealous."

"I can understand that. I would have been jealous if it had been your former boyfriend who'd come up to you."

She pursued her worries. "Rudy, do I embarrass you when I don't hear other people?"

"No, not at all."

"Tell me the truth."

"You really don't."

"I just… just couldn't understand Susan's friend because she doesn't move her lips at all. And I didn't want to upset everyone by asking her to keep repeating herself. So I thought it was better to guess what I thought she was asking and answer that."

"I know. Don't worry about it."

"Even though she doesn't move her lips, is her speech really just as easy for hearing people to understand as someone who does move their lips?"

"Usually it is." Rudy took her hands between his. "Sandra, believe me. I really don't get upset if you can't understand someone speaking. I think, though, it's better to admit it than to guess what they're saying. Otherwise, it could cause a real big problem someday. Like if someone says something very important, and you miss it."

"You're right, but it's just so embarrassing. Making people repeat themselves again and again and again. And then the way they treat you after awhile when you do that… I guess most of us deaf people would rather just not ask."

He sighed and ran his hand through his hair. "I still can't believe my father said what he did. I mean, he's my father."

"I'm sure our parents believe they're acting in our best interest. Considering their backgrounds and the way they were brought up, it does make sense why they do and say what they do. Still, that doesn't make it easier to deal with. I hope I can remember when I'm a parent not to be so stubborn and old-fashioned."

"Me too."

Sandra chose her words carefully. "Rudy, if we still know each other in the future, remind me if you ever see me doing that with my kids."

"It's a deal. And you do the same with me."

Sandra kissed him quickly, impulsively, her hands on his shoulders. "Rudy, I'm going to miss you so much." She pulled him against her, then pulled back. "It's hard to believe how fast one's life can change. Just a few days ago I didn't even know you existed. Now I don't know how I'm going to stand it when you're gone."

"It's like this for soldiers too. We talk about it in the barracks."

They looked deep into each other's eyes, savoring the moment. "How much time did you say you have in North Carolina? Before you go to Europe, I mean?"

"I'm not sure, but from what we can tell, it'll be around a month or two."

"And how much more in the Army?"

"I have over a year left officially. But who knows how long it'll really be once I get to Europe? It could be a lot longer if the war doesn't go well."

"At least you'll be part of something important when you're over there. You'll come back a big war hero."

"Well, I don't know about that."

"I do. When you get out of the Army, you're going to become a United States senator. Maybe you'll even run for President someday."

He shook his head vehemently. "No. No, I never want to become President. That's a thankless job, nothing but stress and people expecting the impossible from you. And the newspapers following every little thing you do. I know you've never seen the *Movie Time News*, Sandra, but it's obvious from President Roosevelt's voice and looks that the job is affecting him. You can see how much he's aged during his time in office. I once saw an article comparing pictures of Presidents Harding, Coolidge, and Roosevelt at the time they were elected and just a few months after they were in office. Every one of them had aged dramatically in that short period of time."

"You'll look distinguished," she said impishly.

He smiled. "Seriously, Sandra. I don't want to be President. I just want to be a representative or a senator. In Congress, one can do a lot of good and help a lot of people, yet avoid the overwhelming responsibility the President faces."

They remained on the side of the road another twenty minutes, embraced by the spacious leather seat, talking about little things, avoiding the big ones. Then Rudy brought up what he'd been thinking about. "Because this is our last night together, probably for many months or even years, I want to make it as memorable as possible. I mean, because despite what many others think of our relationship, you mean so much to me."

She studied his face and body language closely for clues, fairly certain what was going through his mind.

"How about if we go back out to the lake?"

Sandra shook her head and smiled inwardly at the look registering in his eyes. "No, Rudy. The roads and fields will be really muddy after last night's storm, and it'll not only be hard to get there, it'll probably also be a mess." She traced a sensual finger across the back of his hand. "Let's go somewhere more comfortable, someplace where we can have some privacy."

"Like where? Our parents are both home, so we can't go there."

Her finger made slow circles across his hand. "There's got to be someplace where we could be alone without worrying someone might show up. Although I don't know of such a place."

Rudy smiled. "I do."

Eleven

Lake's Motor Hotel was a small one-story building two miles west of Springville, with seven rooms for rent. Cars were parked in front of only two of them. The rest of the parking lot was empty. Rudy pulled up to the office and parked, then looked at Sandra.

"I thought we could rent a room here. That would give us total privacy, and we wouldn't have to worry about anyone interrupting us."

She was stunned. She looked at the motel and then back at Rudy again, not sure what to say. This was much more than she'd been thinking about when she had mentioned finding a private place —despite what she had felt last night. She shook her head subconsciously, wondering if Rudy's coming here was a hearing thing, something hearing people did. Or maybe it was worse. Maybe she had been wrong about him. Maybe he was just pretending he liked her, but planned to take advantage of her because she was deaf. She knew of deaf girls who had had that happen to them with hearing men.

Sandra noticed Rudy begin to fidget. His face turned a little red. His body language was not that of someone who was being deceitful. In fact, he seemed disconcerted.

"I'm sorry. I just thought it would give us the privacy we want," he floundered. "But it was a dumb thought. I didn't mean to make you uncomfortable—"

He turned the key in the ignition and started the motor. Sandra smiled inwardly and felt relieved. There was no way he could've faked that body language. And she realized he was right. A room would give them total privacy. Besides, she now trusted him totally.

She grabbed his arm. "This is a great idea, Rudy. We would be alone, and that's what we both want. Right?"

"Right."

"Is it very expensive?"

"No, the price is very reasonable."

She ran her finger along his cheek. "Let's get a room, then."

"Are you sure?"

"I'm positive."

He turned off the engine and went in to register. Sandra stayed in the car. Rudy requested the room farthest from the road—it would be more secluded there—and paid in cash.

"What name did you put on the form?" Sandra asked when he returned to the car.

"Mr. and Mrs. Townsend. Is that okay? The woman inside saw you through the window and asked if you were my wife. I didn't know what to say, so I just said yes."

Sandra giggled. "I love it," she signed.

A dim yellow light on the overhang illuminated the walkway in front of Room 7. There was a straw mat in front of the door and a sturdy-looking wooden chair under the window next to it. They were unable to look through the window because the drapes were closed. Rudy put the key in the lock, opened the door, and went inside.

"A bit musty," he said as he flipped on the light switch. Sandra came in behind him and looked around. There was a slight smoky smell, but the place was clean. The focal point clearly was the double-sized bed, its simple wooden headboard abutting the wall. The mattress was covered with crisp white sheets, two pillows, and a worn brown comforter. Rust-colored rugs lay on the floor on both sides of the bed.

On the other side of the door was a chipped valise stand. Two worn easy chairs with brown cushions, a floor lamp between them, and a bedside table with a lamp on it constituted the other furniture. In the back, a door led to a tiny bathroom that looked to be as plain and clean as the room.

They looked at each other. Both tried to act nonchalant.

"You won't find this place in your mother's magazines," Sandra said.

Rudy laughed, a nervous laugh.

"How did you know about this place? You been here before?"

Rudy nodded. "But not to rent a room. I've never done that. The summer after my junior year of high school, a friend of mine had a part-time job here as a handyman. I picked him up after work a couple of times."

She headed toward the bathroom. "I'll only be a minute."

Rudy turned on the bedside lamp, switched off the overhead light, and fluffed up the pillows. The window shades were already drawn. Soft lamplight made the room more inviting. With nothing else he could think of to do, he sat on the edge of the bed.

Sandra emerged from the bathroom and stopped a second to study Rudy's features. Clearly masculine, yet distinctive, his skin color much lighter than hers. She noticed the slight stubble of his beard, the wavy black hair slicked straight back, and dark brown eyes. Especially those eyes. Warm and deep, full of anticipation and emotion. He sat so stiffly on the bed.

For a second, guilt flashed through her mind. What would her parents think if they knew where she was now? Then the warm glow from their togetherness the previous evening took over as she looked at him. *Dear Rudy. Dear, dear Rudy. My awkward congressman-to-be.* This was his last night, the last chance she'd have to be with him for who knew how long. Perhaps forever, God forbid, if he got killed. And in spite of her nervousness, she was sure now that she was in love. There was no doubt about that. Rudy was the man she wanted to spend the rest of her life with, the one she wanted to be the father of her children.

Sandra went over to the bed, repositioned a pillow against the bed frame, then lay back next to Rudy. She looked at his face just in time to see his lips move. Those lips she knew so intimately, expressing his thoughts and exploring her with kisses.

"I wish there was a way I could get more time off before our outfit goes to Europe. So I could come back to Michigan, to see you again. But I'm sure there's no way that'll happen."

"I'll come visit you." She watched the lamp shadows on his face.

"Maybe you could. But I wouldn't be able to get time off to see you. Besides, there'd be a lot of resistance from both our families if you did that, wouldn't there?"

"That wouldn't stop me."

"I know, I know." Rudy lay down next to her and was silent. A car moved around the motel parking lot, which only he heard. He put his right hand on Sandra's arm. "Yes, I know it won't stop you. Still, that doesn't change the fact that all hell would break loose when they found out you came."

He sighed, a young man contending with the world and its problems. Sandra would remember that look always, his profile outlined in the lamplight.

His voice waxed philosophical. "People are people. They just don't tolerate those who are different. Never have and probably never will. At least not in our time on this earth. It isn't fair, but it's life."

Sandra slid down so their heads were at the same level. "Rudy, let's not worry about that right now. That's for the future. Tonight, let's enjoy what we have. We've got the whole night ahead of us together, just you and me. And no one is going to disturb us here."

Rudy let his eyes take in her body, lying so trusting next to him. He felt an overwhelming desire for her, despite all the turmoil their relationship generated.

"So what do you think?" Sandra wondered, her eyes watching him.

"You're beautiful."

He leaned over to brush aside a few strands of her hair. Then he kissed her gently.

"You know I love you, Rudy."

He responded by kissing her again, this time harder. A hunger consumed both of them. No words, no signing. Just touching and exploring. They clutched each other, enjoying the closeness of their bodies. Slowly they found themselves drifting deliciously into the realm of oneness, where it was only he and she. The two of them entered that special state of mind where nothing else matters but the person one is with. Togetherness. Then slowly and lovingly, touch by touch, they found each other.

It was the first time for each of them. But their love for each other, especially in the shadow of his going to the European front, overcame any uncertainty. A fiery passion arose, from a depth neither one of them had any idea existed. They explored each other's bodies tenderly with their mouths and hands and skin, investigating every crevice they could find, wondering what would happen next.

Sandra lay half-dressed next to Rudy, reveling in his smell and touch. She examined his body, tracing with her fingertips, marveling at how pale his skin was compared to hers. She explored the soft hair on his chest.

"Sandra?" he asked.

"Yes?"

"What's going to happen to us?"

"I don't know. I look at the stars hanging in people's windows and—"

His fingers touched her mouth, quieting her. "We have tonight."

"Yes, we do. And who today can plan for more?"

The rest of their clothes slowly came off, and the wondrous feelings that emanated from the movement of their hands and mouths spread into every corner of their bodies, creating sensations they'd never imagined possible. Though Sandra couldn't hear him, she sensed Rudy's pleasure from the way his body responded.

Together, they caressed each other more and more, their desire rising ever higher until they couldn't hold back anymore. Then, in the glow of the moonlight filtering in through the semi-opaque curtains, they came together in a perfect fit as if they had been made specifically for each other. They made love with a passion neither thought possible. Their bodies were filled with the oneness that they had become, souls and hearts blended together. Swells of emotion swept over their bodies, growing with each wave, heightening the sense of their mutual destiny. Finally, when it seemed they would drown under the starlit sky, their oneness exploded in ecstasy, followed by an utter sense of peace and bliss.

Afterward, they lay quietly, their bodies snuggled together, reveling in the feeling of utter contentment. Life was so peaceful like this, Sandra thought, just the two of them alone, him and her. Why couldn't it also be this way when they were with their families and friends? She wished the world wasn't so regimented, so opinionated, throwing up so many barriers in the way of their being together.

"Sandra?" He got her attention, and she looked at him. "Did the earth move for you too?"

"It sure did. And so did the stars."

After another period of quiet, she asked, "Rudy, tell me more about your dream of going to Washington."

"Aw, c'mon. First you love me as a big war hero, and now it's as a congressman."

"It's going to happen, Rudy."

"How do you know?"

"I just know."

He looked at the ceiling, his arms behind his head, a faraway, dreamy look coming on his face. "To me, no job could be more exciting than that. If I were a senator, I'd be one of only two from my state. I'd meet all kinds of interesting people from around the whole country, the movers, decision-makers. Indeed, from the entire world. I'd have my own desk in the Capitol building with the other ninety-five senators. We'd work with the President to make this country a better place." He looked back at her. "Does that sound corny?"

"You know it doesn't."

He sat up a little. "Sandra, just imagine what being a U.S. senator would allow me to do. I could help the little guy, the average American who's been hurt by the Great Depression we've had the past twelve years. What we need to do is to provide more jobs for them. Roosevelt has the right idea. If enough people got jobs and could provide for their families again, it would start an era of prosperity. People would have money to buy things again, and this would create more jobs. If enough people were involved, it would become self-propagating. Then, over time, the depression would be just a bad memory. Of course, there'll be some senators who for whatever reason won't support creating more jobs, but I'm convinced I could get a majority of them on my side. I can just see the debates, working with the President, the all-night discussions, before finally coming to a consensus—all about important matters that would improve our country, make it as vibrant as possible."

He turned on his side. "Honey, I just realized I may have been talking too fast. Did you get all that?"

She nodded.

"Good. Have you ever been to Washington, D.C.?"

She shook her head, watching this different kind of passion moving through him, the drive to help, to care.

"Oh, it's the most beautiful place. The Capitol building itself is a huge, dome-shaped, white structure that sits on a hill. All around it are other white buildings, with lots of green grass and trees between them. It's just a short walk from the Capitol to the White House, where I'd sometimes meet the President. Behind the Capitol, there's a huge green mall, and at the other end of it is the Washington Monument."

He leaned back on the bed, lost in thought. "There are cherry trees all around. And in springtime, when they're in bloom, people say it's spectacular. And behind the Monument is a long, narrow lake. It's just beautiful, honey. You have to see it to believe it."

Honey. He had called her "honey" twice. She smiled at him as he talked, fired up in the small room with the old furniture. She would remember this moment always.

"But that's not all. There's so much else to see and do in Washington, too. Like the Lincoln Memorial, the Jefferson Memorial, the Supreme Court, the Smithsonian, and more. Sandra, it's simply magnificent. I'm sure you'd love living there too."

"Wouldn't it be something if you really did become a senator?"

"It's gonna happen, Sandra. It's gonna happen. I'm very serious about becoming part of Congress. Even if it's just in the House of Representatives. In fact, I've already planned how I'll get there." He stared into the future again, his brown eyes intense. "When I finish with the Army, I'm going to go to college, then get a good job and become involved in the local Democratic Party. That way I'll get to know people and make some contacts. Then, to get some experience, I'll run for a seat on the city council, then state representative."

His eyes found hers. "I'm sure I'll make mistakes at the beginning. But you've got to start somewhere. Running a successful campaign requires a lot of skills, including the art of persuading others, as well as making a lot of connections. You need to be quick thinking on your feet, and able to persuade people to vote for you. My wife will also need to be a good speaker..."

His voice trailed off. He looked at Sandra. A small fly buzzed under the lampshade. She knew what he was thinking. The silence stretched as the fly moved about. Rudy stared at the wall. For a second, Sandra worried that he was thinking about Susan Oakley, then decided not. There was no way that could be true. Not after what they'd just experienced. She watched him.

Finally, the prolonged silence, normally a deaf person's comfort, reached the point where she couldn't tolerate it any longer. "Rudy, deafness is part of who I am. I can do something about my speech, though. And after what we've gone through the past couple of days, I've already decided to go back to speech therapy. Work really hard on improving it."

He looked at her warmly, but still didn't say anything.

"I know I can do a better job of speaking." She was begging. That was not part of who she was. She didn't like it, and she stopped. She waited for Rudy to say something, something supportive.

"You know, Sandra, no matter how much you plan for how you interact with the world, it often won't go as you planned."

"I'll learn how to deal with it."

Rudy shooed the fly. It darted away across the room. He didn't say anything.

"And after you get elected to the state house," Sandra wondered, "then what?"

"I figure I'll probably spend two terms there, maybe even run for state senator. Then I'll run for Congress. I estimate it'll probably take me ten, maybe fifteen, years before I become a U.S. senator." He turned to her and ran his fingers through her hair. "But enough about me. Tell me more about your dream of becoming a veterinarian."

A shift in subject. Probably the best thing to do now. "I've always loved animals," she began. "We've had a dog ever since I can remember. They're so trusting, so forgiving, and they'll do anything for you. I love horses too. When I was younger, one of my friends had three of them on her grandparents' farm out in the country. We'd go there a couple weekends every summer and ride them most of the day. It used to fascinate me how each one had its own personality, just like every dog does. I can't think of anything I'd

163

rather do than work with animals. And to help them when they're sick."

"It's a great dream, Sandra."

"Yeah. But I'm realistic. As I've said before, I know I'll never get a chance to be a veterinarian. I'm hoping, though, to maybe be a vet assistant."

"You're not even going to apply again to the university?"

"Why waste the time? Rudy, the education I got at the Deaf School was nothing like the kind you got in the regular public schools. In some ways, it's worse than the schools they have for colored people down south." She bit her lip, remembering. "We had basically no education. Except for a few teachers, no one taught us much because they didn't expect anything from us. So, even though I got all A's, it didn't mean a lot. That's why I did so poorly on the entrance test for the university. I hadn't even heard of half the things they asked about. I was lucky to get into junior college, and only managed to do well there by studying all the time."

"Maybe you're right, Sandra, and they'll never take you. But if you give up, you'll never know for sure. I think you should study for the entrance test and take it again." He found her hand. "Tell you what. When I get back from the war, I'll help you with that. We'll get you in."

She glanced at his face. He was so supportive, but just didn't understand. "Let's say I did get a top score on that test, Rudy. It still wouldn't make a difference. Even if I did well at the university. I could see where a vet school might be willing to take a woman who does well. But a Jewish woman? And even more, a Jewish deaf woman?" Her mouth twisted around her words. "No way. Someone who teaches at the vet school at Michigan State told my father that regardless of how well I did in college, or on the admissions test, they wouldn't take me. And that guy didn't even know I was Jewish! He was just talking about my deafness and being a woman."

"Okay. Let's look at it straight on. Maybe he has a point. I mean, since you can't hear, how will you listen to an animal's heart or lungs?"

"I'd figure out a way. Maybe by feeling the chest I can tell if the animal has a problem. If that doesn't work, there's got to be some other way to figure out what's going on."

"Okay, let's say you figure that out. What about talking with the owners of the animals? Most of them will be hearing persons. How will you do that, especially when some of them will be people who are not easy to lip-read?"

"People have been telling me for years I can't do something. Each time I proved them wrong. Being a vet? It wouldn't be easy, but I'd figure it out." Sandra looked closely at Rudy and tensed. "Why are you saying this now? Before, you told me to not let anything stop me. Are you trying to suggest you really don't think I could be a vet?"

"No, I just said hit it head on. Know what you're up against. That's how you'll beat it. Have you ever thought about first being a vet assistant, and seeing how that works before trying to become a vet?"

"That won't help. I know I want to work with animals, but being a vet assistant won't help me become a vet. That's kind of like telling someone who wants to be a doctor to first be a nurse. Sure, some nurses become doctors, but most doctors don't become nurses first."

"Okay. Good point."

She pulled back a little to better see his face. "I'm thinking that you have doubts whether I could be a vet."

"No, no, no. I know you can do it. What I was thinking was as a vet assistant you could get to know folks, like I'll have to when I run for office. Someone might be in a position to help you. Sandra, if any deaf person can become a vet, you can. It would be a huge battle, but you could do it."

165

"Yes, it would. I just need to have a chance to show them I can do it."

"Now that's the part that's not fair. They should give you a chance. It's just not fair."

"It's not, but that's the kind of thing that happens to every deaf person. All the time. For as long as they live. As you said once, 'It's not fair, but it's life.'"

He pulled her towards him. "Look, Sandra. When I become a senator, I'm going to change that. I'll get Congress to pass a law making it illegal for anyone to discriminate like that. Then people of every religion, or sex, or race, or disability or whatever they are will have a chance to do what they want."

They lay looking at each other. Sandra said, "Rudy, I love you so much."

"I love you too, Sandra."

He gathered her to him, and they let soft touches take the place of words. Sandra pulled her head back to see his face again. "Take me back to North Carolina with you."

He looked at her intently. Unusual for her, she couldn't quite interpret his body language.

"I know it'll be hard for me there," she said, hurrying on while she had the courage, "that I'll be alone most of the time because you'll be busy. And that you'll be going to Europe in a couple of months. But the times we are together, we'll make up for all that."

No answer. And no body clues.

She slumped back onto the bed.

He turned her head gently. "Sandra, I love you more than I thought I could ever love anyone. But I can't do that now. It wouldn't be good for you there since I'll have almost no time for you. And I'm just not ready. I need to think through some things. But please understand. It's not because I'm not interested in you. I've never known a woman I wanted to be with so much before."

"Then I'll just come visit for a few days. Okay?"

He shook his head. "Please, don't come. Give me some time."

166

This time, she could read his body language and didn't like what it said. Before she could respond, he drew her next to him and hugged her tightly a long time. In the silence they gathered remnants of dreams, now bruised by realities. Then they discussed life and the world. About how it was unfair that people had to be so prejudiced. That maybe after the war in Europe, people would be more understanding and accepting. Both knew the odds were great, but they didn't care. It was a time to dream, a time for bruised dreams to heal, a time to share inner thoughts, and a time to learn about and savor each other. It might be their only chance to do so.

They were older now, each facing uncertain futures. Like others in the war-torn world.

After awhile, they made love again, and the earth and sky moved once more.

The Aftermath

Autumn 1942

Twelve

It was after six in the morning. Dawn had begun to color the eastern sky. Sandra walked through the front door of her house to see her parents waiting in the living room.

"Where have you been?" Mr. Horowitz signed angrily.

"Out with Rudy," Sandra replied as she started toward the stairs.

Her mother grabbed her arms. Hands trembling, she spun her daughter around. "Out with Rudy? You've been gone all night! If only we'd been so lucky to drop dead than spend the whole night worrying the worst had happened to you. What's got into you? Two nights ago you came home at three in the morning, and last night you stayed out all night. And both times with a hearing goy you barely know."

Her father waved his hand to get both women's attention. "We had just decided to go to the police when you walked in."

"I'm sorry. I didn't mean to upset you, but there was no way to let you know I'd be late. Everything's all right. It was Rudy's last night of his leave. He goes back to North Carolina this morning at seven. We wanted to be together since it'll be a long time before he comes back home."

Mrs. Horowitz's eyes widened.

"Mom, please don't worry. He treats me with great respect."

"So he won't be back again in Michigan soon?"

Sandra eyes misted. "No. I'm sorry to say it'll be a long time, a real long time, because his unit will be going to Europe soon. How long he'll be there depends on what happens with the war. He's expecting to be there at least a year, probably longer."

Mr. Horowitz moved closer to his daughter, worry lines deepening in his face. "Sandra, I know you're old enough to make your own decisions. But please, please think about what you're doing. Please. I know you've seen me tell you this until you're sick of it, but you and he are very different. It may not seem important now, but down the road those differences will cause major problems. Your mother and I want you to be happy, you know that. In the long run, I don't see how you can be happy with him."

"Oh, come on, Dad. Just because he's not Jewish doesn't mean there's something wrong with him."

"He's not deaf either."

"So what? We communicate fine."

"What about your family or friends? They can't understand him. Even I could only occasionally lip read him."

"He's easier to lip read than most hearing people. I think that after you're around him awhile, you'll find that to be true. Besides, he's planning to learn sign. In fact, he's already started."

"You know that's easier said than done. And tell me, how will you communicate with his family and friends?"

"I'm going to take more speech therapy."

He moved both hands up and down, palms up, the sign for "possibly." "Another if. Maybe you can do what most deaf people can't and learn to talk intelligibly. That doesn't solve the religion problem, though, does it?"

Sandra saw her mother nod in agreement.

"Look, I'm getting tired of being grilled about this. Rudy and I are adults, not children. We respect each other and care for each other very much. We understand how different our backgrounds are. We've talked about that a lot. And we believe we can work through them. This is, after all, 1942, the modern world. Times have changed. It's not like it used to be. One's religion or how much one hears doesn't have to take precedence over one's feelings."

"I'm sure you do respect and care for each other," her father said. "But how are you going to feel when he wants a Christmas tree at—"

"I'm not going to watch this again." Sandra cut off her father with an angry motion and stomped upstairs to her room. She slammed the door shut and flopped on the bed. Then she realized the room was pitch black. She leaned over and turned on the small bedside lamp, which brought back memories of the motel room, before falling back on her mattress. How different this pillow was. And how lonely without Rudy besides her. She felt confused, torn, pulled in multiple directions. Her stomach turned, a physical ache.

Thoughts rushed wildly through her mind. Her father's comments had really hit home this time. Communication and religion, essences of human closeness, would always be major issues if she and Rudy became a couple. But would they be insurmountable? She remembered his reaction when he'd realized she wouldn't be able to help with his political campaigns the way he had dreamed his wife would. Susan Oakley shimmered in her restless thoughts. Was she the reason Rudy had said he had to think through some things?

Tears wet her pillow. She pulled a slip of paper from her purse and read Rudy's address in the Army. Words she already knew by heart. North Carolina. So far away. What was Rudy doing now? Going to the bus? Or already on it? Was he thinking about her, wondering when he'd see her again? Or had Susan shown up at the bus station?

She cried uncontrollably. A year. Perhaps even more before she'd see him again. An eternity. And she had thought two months away from Jacob was a long time. How was she going to get through all the days until Rudy got back? And when they finally did get together again, whenever and wherever it was, what would things be like? Would their minds and emotions connect as they had last night? Would Rudy even love her after spending a year fighting a war? What if he met a girl in Europe? What if? What if?

Anxiety gnawed at her. Sandra turned and twisted, succumbing to the emotional morass. She struggled to reconcile things, find some kind of peace inside. Finally, the overwhelming fatigue took her. She slipped into a troubled sleep.

The following Monday, Sandra began her new job at Huron Kennels. It turned out to be enjoyable and a distraction. She didn't have to interact with hearing people much, so the communication barrier was rarely a problem. She cleaned the runs and fed the animals. Sandra noticed many of the dogs seemed lonely, distressed at being away from their masters. So she went out of her way to play with them when she could, and felt good helping them feel less abandoned.

But at the end of the day, when work was done and she had time to think, her thoughts drifted back to Rudy. She felt alone too, like the dogs, yet at the same time comforted by her memories. Having someone she loved, someone she thought about almost every waking moment, filled her time in surprising and wonderful ways. She daydreamed about what it could be like when they finally got together again. Hopefully, it would be a time in the not-too-distant future, as well as a time when they had the support of their families.

She knew Rudy would survive Europe. She felt it deep inside. This conviction, plus her dreams about how life could be when they were together again, was a mixed blessing. At times, it gave her an inner strength. It enabled her to deal with the emptiness. But at other times, when she recalled how he had discouraged her coming to North Carolina, she knew that there might not be a future with him. He clearly loved her—of that she had no doubt. There was so much good between them, even as they explored and learned about each other's worlds. Still, he also worried about the problems they would face. For her, the thought of not seeing him again was almost unbearable.

It helped that her parents didn't mention Rudy again. They kept that burden to themselves. Besides, they knew he wouldn't be back for a year at least. They obviously hoped that as time passed, their daughter would slowly forget about the young soldier. Or that he would find someone else. And Jacob Winter would return from New York before long. They prayed every day that Jacob's presence would bring Sandra to her senses. He was a good man, financially stable in addition to being deaf and Jewish. Just the kind of husband any parents would wish for their daughter, and that any reasonable woman would want as a husband.

Every day, Sandra wrote Rudy a letter. Most deaf Americans in the 1940s never learned to write English well. To them it was a foreign language with a different syntax and grammar than their native American Sign Language. Sandra was an exception. This was both because of her father's insistence that she learn English, plus her years of studying to become a veterinarian. Her letters were long and eloquent, always several pages, filled with details about her life and work and remembrances of their time together. Sometimes she asked about visiting Rudy at Fort Bragg before his unit went overseas, hoping he would change his mind.

Rudy wrote her as well, but less frequently, perhaps three times a week. His letters were shorter but just as sentimental, which pleased Sandra. However, he remained steadfastly opposed to her visiting the base. Sometimes he gave her a reason, such as Army training had him out on maneuvers or the timing wasn't right. Other times he just discouraged her from coming. Each time this happened, Sandra would again feel overwhelmed with sadness, and her doubts would return. As time went on, his letters became less frequent. Rudy still wrote warmly, but his letters were fewer and shorter. And it took all she had to push away the creeping doubts that their relationship would never work.

Sandra stored every one of his letters in a shoebox. She kept it hidden on the top shelf of her closet. Most days, especially in the evening after dinner when the dishes were done, and it got dark and chilly outside, she would go to her room, shut the door, get out the box, and lovingly re-read all the letters. Then she would stare out her window and wonder what Rudy was doing at that moment. She often imagined him sitting alone like her, perhaps in his barracks, or out somewhere looking at the sky and thinking about her.

Sandra also spent many hours reading the book of poems Rudy had given her. She checked more poetry books out of the library. At first she had a hard time figuring out a cadence to many of the poems. But the more she read, the more naturally they came. She liked the variety, not only of the rhythms, but how some poems told stories while others offered ideas. She read some poems many times, each time getting more out of them. She was moved by Robert Frost in particular, but all the poems opened new worlds that drew her from her loneliness.

At the end of each day, lying in bed before falling asleep, Sandra would put her hands behind her head and recall her times with Rudy. She'd replay them like a movie. The photo taking, the rides in the Studebaker, the time at the lake. With their families. In the motel. Each time she relished any forgotten detail. And no Susan. Then she would once more imagine them together, in the future, and how wonderful that would be. With that image comforting her, she would smile and fall asleep.

And so went her life, at least for the time being.

Thirteen

"Sandra," her mother signed one evening three weeks later, after dinner. "Can you come into the den for a moment? Dad and I want to show you something."

They walked into the small room at the back of the house. Mr. Horowitz was sitting at the far end of the couch, an envelope in his lap.

"Sit here." He pointed at the space next to him. Her mother sat on the other side of her.

"Sandra, Mom and I have noticed how unhappy you seem to be."

"I'm fine, Dad. I'm fine."

He nodded. "Tell me, if that's so, why didn't you eat tonight?"

"My stomach felt sick and I wasn't hungry."

"That's exactly what I'm talking about. And you don't talk to us much anymore. You spend a lot of time in your bedroom instead. It's just not like you."

"I know, but I'm fine. I've just been busy, just doing a lot of reading and writing."

Her father glanced at his wife, then focused back on his daughter. "Your mom and I splurged on something that we hope will make you feel better." He handed her the envelope while signing, "These are round trip train tickets for you to go New York City to visit Jacob this weekend."

"Really?"

He nodded.

Sandra opened the envelope and looked at the tickets, her mind conflicted. It was obvious what her parents were trying to do. Her first reaction was to turn them down, telling them she had no interest in going to see Jacob. And she really didn't, not after those days with Rudy. But then she thought about it a bit more. Perhaps she should go. It was clear she wasn't going to be able to see Rudy for a long time, if ever. He kept refusing to have her visit, and he had been responding to her letters less and less. Doing something else to take her mind off him might actually be a good thing. And it would be fun to see New York after all she'd heard about it. But she was concerned that going there might be interpreted as her still being committed to Jacob.

"You shouldn't have done this. Jacob will be back in a month or so."

"We know, but we thought you'd like to see him."

She turned the tickets over in her hands. "Where did the money come from? I know we've had a hard time paying some of our bills lately."

"Don't worry about that, honey. It's our pleasure."

Sandra paused again, feeling a little guilty that she wanted to go, feeling she was betraying Rudy. And she knew how scarce money was. The fact they'd bought the tickets meant her parents must be really worried about her.

"There are a couple of problems with my going, though." They waited, faces showing their concern. "First, we don't even know if Jacob has time to see me. He may be too busy or have some business to do this weekend."

"He knows you're coming," her mother signed as she smiled, leaning forward to touch Sandra's arm, "and is very excited."

"When did you ask him?"

"Does it matter, Sandra? He's really looking forward to seeing you."

Sandra looked at her mother, reading the warm expectancy there. "Okay. The other problem is a bigger one. I just started at Huron Kennels and don't think I'll be able to get the time off, especially with such short notice."

"We've taken care of that too," Mr. Horowitz signed. "We had someone talk with your boss. He agreed to give you the time."

"You're kidding me."

He shook his head, smiling.

"Wow. You really thought of everything, didn't you? I had no idea you were doing this." She looked at the tickets again. "Is this an overnight train?"

"Yes. It leaves Detroit tomorrow around 5 PM. It gets to New York Friday morning."

"Okay, I'll go."

Mrs. Horowitz stood up. "C'mon. I'll help you pack."

Sandra got on the train feeling fragile and sick to her stomach, feeling unfaithful to Rudy. She kept telling herself it was okay that she was going, especially since Rudy was keeping his distance. For all she knew, he could be seeing Susan Oakley. And she had to admit she was really looking forward to seeing New York. It would be an adventure, away from her room with its private worries. Perhaps her parents were right.

Once the train left the station, Sandra forced all thoughts of Rudy out of her mind and dwelled on Jacob. The telegram he'd sent had been charming. It clearly showed his excitement that she was coming. He'd bought tickets to the last Yankee home game of the year, although the Tigers weren't in town, and had made other plans for their time together.

Sandra looked out the train window at the changing scene of houses and country. Jacob was a good man. Kind and considerate, he had always treated her respectfully, looking out for her welfare. He had a good job that would be able to support a family. He was

Jewish, and deaf. And he could communicate with her family. Yes, she thought, Jacob would make a good husband, and would be a wonderful father.

But... he wasn't Rudy. And deep down inside she knew he wasn't for her. He didn't grab her like Rudy had, not even close. There was no excitement, no talk of changing the world, no striving for bigger things. He was just quiet, with strict boundaries in his life. Not what she wanted.

It was darkening outside. Lights were appearing, a prelude to her first visit to New York. She'd been to Chicago twice and wondered how New York compared. She loved Chicago, with its beautiful lakeside parks, downtown Loop, and fashionable stores. Especially Marshall Fields, with those clocks on the corners of its building. Excitement just seemed to spark in Chicago. It made Detroit seem like a small town. New York, she had read, had its own glamour, excitement. *Life* magazine once had a photo of the Empire State Building on its cover. Spectacular! And things there were supposed to move at a very fast pace, even faster than in Chicago. At any rate, it would be different from home, a nice break from the stress of the last few weeks.

Rudy's presence came to her in the gentle rocking of the carriage. She pushed him away, this time with less guilt, as she focused on Jacob again.

Jacob was waiting for her at the train station. He looked exactly as she remembered: hair unruly, shoulders a little slumped, somewhat overweight. He enveloped her in an affectionate hug, then gave her a surprisingly passionate kiss, which brought a smile to passersby.

"I'm so glad you're here."

"Me too," Sandra signed, catching her breath a little, glancing around, then watching him sign.

"You look much prettier than I remembered."

"I'm glad, because the last couple of weeks I haven't felt that good."

"Why? Something wrong?"

"Nothing much." She made a genuine effort for this good man. "Oh, Jacob, it's so nice to be here in New York with you."

He hailed a cab. "Let's go to my apartment. It's quite spacious for Manhattan, so you should be comfortable there." Sandra held his hand in the back seat, mesmerized by the impacting sights of the city. The buildings dominated, so tall she couldn't see the tops of some of them. Glass and steel and concrete offered themselves against a rising sun. People churned and maneuvered through the streets, heads down, newspapers under arms, briefcases swinging. Steam came from several grates as from some netherland. A man with a pushcart sold coffee and Danish. Another had a cart full of fruit.

At a stoplight, Sandra noticed people hurrying down a stairwell surrounded by a wrought-iron fence on three sides. At the top of the staircase there was a pole with a sign that said BMT. She nudged Jacob. "What's BMT?"

"The subway. It stands for the Bronx-Manhattan Transit and is one of the two major subways here. The other one is the IRT, and you'll see that on other corners. They go to different places."

"What if you accidentally go down the wrong stairs?"

He smiled. "No problem. In some places there's a tunnel that connects them. If there isn't, you can always walk back up. After awhile you learn which stairs to use."

Sure enough, at the next stoplight Sandra saw an IRT entrance. They were heading north on Seventh Avenue, and the blocks seemed so long, the streets so wide. Then they turned onto 47th street. Everything changed. The street was much narrower, the blocks so close together. She watched, amazed at how New Yorkers managed the crowds. Their faces preoccupied, they just weaved past each other in some instinctive mutual consent. Two teenage boys ran across an intersection, beating the unstopping cars. Everywhere she saw a mass of moving humanity and automobiles.

Soon they came to the East River and went onto the Brooklyn Bridge. Sandra craned her neck, looking down first at the water under them, then at the panorama of Manhattan and Brooklyn. A barge loaded with iron passed underneath. Now the buildings changed. There were more single homes, and even an occasional open lot. She saw a line of women at the butcher shop, clearly impatient with the wait. They passed a group of youngsters playing a ball game in the street, and Sandra felt Jacob's touch.

"Remember reading about stickball being played in New York streets?"

She moved her fist up and down.

"That's it."

By the time Sandra looked back out, they had passed the boys and were in a different neighborhood. But there were kids playing stickball there too.

Fleeting thoughts of Rudy came, warm and exciting. *What sound does the ball make in the glove?* With a bit of effort, she focused again on Jacob by smiling at him. She would have to be careful she didn't daydream here. Jacob didn't deserve it.

The next few days were a whirlwind. High sensation, pressure and pulse—the big city's lifeblood. New York was as invigorating as Sandra had hoped, as stimulating as Chicago, but a different world. They took in the game at Yankee Stadium, ate in restaurants that dazzled her with their elegance, window-shopped Fifth Avenue and Times Square, and strolled through Central Park. Jacob showed her Radio City, where a long line was waiting for the afternoon show. They went to the top of the Empire State Building to claim its panoramic view. They lunched at a Horn and Hardart automat, its thousands of choices in dazzling, spotlessly clean array. In the evenings, after dinner, they retreated to the calm seclusion of Jacob's apartment, where they alternated between comfortable conversation and gentle caressing, often into the early morning hours.

Being with Jacob was safe. He was kind and solicitous, but unbidden memories of fire and ice with Rudy would intrude, and those memories owned her. With Jacob there were none of the feelings of being complete, of being swept up into another human being, a lover, a confidant, a friend. She made every effort to be kind to Jacob, who obviously loved her.

When they went to sleep in separate rooms, Sandra would recapture those four days with Rudy... and especially their last night, when she had given herself so willingly. So very willingly. How wonderful life could be with Rudy. She would debate sending him a postcard, and if he would even care. Or if he was thinking about Susan. Always, always the intruding presence of Susan, who was of his religion, and who could hear, who could hear Rudy's voice. She cried quietly, until she finally fell into a troubled sleep.

"It's your last night here," Jacob signed.

"I know. I can't believe how fast time flew by."

"I made reservations at my favorite restaurant here. It's a steak place."

"Oh Jacob, you didn't have to do that. It's been a wonderful three days. I've really enjoyed being here."

He beamed, a loving maestro who had orchestrated the city of New York just for her.

It was chilly in the cab. Sandra snuggled closer to Jacob. He put his arm around her. It was dark, but Sandra could still see the city. Lights all around, at the corners, and in the windows, illuminating storefront signs. She saw a woman wearing an unusual, jaunty hat with raspberry ostrich feathers. It must be that Tilt hat she'd read about. Another wore a black felt hat with a turned-up brim. Several men smoking cigars sat on a bench. There was a gravitas to them, a solemnity, as they watched New Yorkers hurry by.

The curb gutters were littered with cigarette butts and papers, a careless discard of humanity in a hurry.

The Brooklyn Bridge. No boats on the water now. Jacob pointed at the Manhattan skyline, and Sandra caught her breath. It sparkled like a just-cut gem. She felt his nudge.

"Ever think what it would be like to live here?"

She shook her head. "Wouldn't it be expensive?"

"It sure would. But it's a great city, always things to do."

Rudy had talked about another great city, Washington, D.C. She wondered a moment how the cities compared, then again pushed Rudy from her mind. Jacob was taking her somewhere special. She needed to give him all she could, companionship and closeness, temporary but affectionate.

The restaurant was beyond Sandra's expectations. They were seated in a large room with several chandeliers packed with crystals that sparkled in the light. Several waiters, not one, doted on their every need. She looked around the room, savoring the mood: soft, serene, elegant movement around her. No hustle and bustle here. Dinner guests rather than diners. Conversation Sandra sensed as subdued, delicately lifted soup spoons, the dab of napkins. Heavy oil paintings hung from walls.

Sandra turned back to the menu and was immediately at a loss. Jacob waved at her. "What are you going to have?"

"Any suggestions?"

"They are known for their prime rib."

"Then that's what I'll have."

He nodded. "Good choice," he signed for emphasis.

They both noticed the stares. The hidden pointing. Of people watching them, just because they signed. They were used to that, though. That happened in Michigan too, everywhere they went. Odd, Sandra thought. She had considered the people around her as elegant, sophisticated. But here they were, the same old rudeness. If they could only be deaf for a day and live life on the other side. How to lift a soup spoon would come in a distant second.

184

The waiters came, and they placed their orders. After a couple of moments of silence, Sandra signed, "So again, how much longer will you be in New York?"

"Not much longer. Perhaps another month." Jacob carefully dabbed at his mouth, trying to fit in.

"Then what?"

"I'll come home and work for my father. It's a good company he has."

Sandra scanned the room once more, then unobtrusively squared her body to face Jacob's. "What do you think you'll be doing five years from now?"

He didn't hesitate. "I hope by then I'll have a family. Of course, I'll still be working for my dad."

"Do you think you'll be involved in anything else?"

Curiosity creased his brow, his eyes focused around her words, habits from business deals. "What do you mean?"

"Like helping others. Or building something important. Or taking a leadership role in the Deaf Club."

Jacob's brow smoothed out. He shook his head. "No. I'd rather be home with my family."

No grand dreams, Sandra thought. No ambition beyond the traditional. She tried hard to keep Rudy's image at bay. There was nothing wrong with Jacob's plans, Sandra admitted, feeling a little snooty even. They were similar to those of most people she knew. But they just seemed so routine, so boring compared to Rudy's dreams. Rudy had jarred her complacency, made her challenge her self-imposed limits.

The food came in four courses, each exquisitely displayed. First an onion soup. Next a salad spiced and seasoned like she'd never tasted before. The main course was the finely prepared prime rib. One bite and she understood why the restaurant was known for it. She signed with Jacob, ignoring diners around them, until they had worked their way through the final touch, the tiramisu for dessert. And the wine. A lot of it. Before and during the meal, enhancing and preparing their palates. It was an experience to be remembered for a poor girl like Sandra.

"So what did you think?" Jacob signed, leaning back.

Sandra didn't have to respond. Her body language was answer enough. She felt a little giddy from the alcohol.

As Jacob escorted her out, Sandra felt lightheaded. When she steadied herself on the table, she felt Jacob's guiding hand, surprisingly delicate and unobtrusive. She saw him giggle, and realized that he was also taken by the wine.

He offered her his arm and they made their way outside, where he hailed a cab. Sandra rested her head against his shoulder, eyes closed. She felt warm, her head light. And strangely carefree. Then she felt his lips on hers. His breath smelled like alcohol. But she didn't care, and responded quickly.

They were both unsteady when they got to his place. The two flights up took longer than usual. Laughing, stumbling, they finally made it. Neither of them was familiar with this feeling. Jacob led her to the couch, where she lowered herself down carefully. He opened a bottle of Sambucca and poured two shot glasses.

"This stuff is good. I first had it a week ago at someone's house. Have some."

"I think I've had enough alcohol," Sandra managed to sign. "I can barely walk."

"You don't have to walk. We're back at my place." Jacob's logic pleased him. Sandra smiled.

He took a sip, then put his fingers on his lips and quickly brought them forward, making a very satisfied face to go with his sign saying, "This is really good."

"Really?" She watched him sitting on the couch in Manhattan. How very sophisticated New York was, she thought. No cleaning out dog kennels. Just skyscrapers and four-course meals.

"You don't drink this fast, or it will burn your throat," Jacob explained. "Just an occasional sip." He handed her a glass. She took a sip. The liqueur was strong, but the licorice flavor was interesting.

"It's a good year for licorice," she signed.

He laughed at her joke. She smiled back. Their worlds were light and filled with giddy optimism.

She took a few more sips as they signed. But she didn't remember what they signed about. The last thing she remembered was wondering if Rudy had ever tried Sambucca.

It was morning. Sandra woke up, her head throbbing. She opened her eyes, but the light was blinding. She closed them again until she could get used to it. Where was she? What time was it?

She stretched and her leg hit something. Someone. She turned and squinted. Jacob's beefy shoulder. Memories came back to her pounding brain. Sitting on the couch. Drinking Sambucca. Then... nothing. She looked back at him. He was sleeping.

She sat up. Dizziness whirled the room. Her stomach churned. Then she saw her naked breasts. Her hand slid down her trunk. No underwear. She lay down again, suddenly frightened, pulling the sheets up to her neck, looking across at Jacob's shoulder and mussed-up hair. *Oh God...*

None of it came back. Only dinner, alcohol and the couch. She looked at Jacob again. Still asleep. He had to be naked too, but she was too scared to check. Her stomach churned worse. Her face felt sweaty. The room was way too humid.

Sandra looked at the bedside clock. It was noon. Two hours before her train left for Detroit. Her heart started to race as she tried to plan. She needed to get up. Get dressed. Only then would she wake up Jacob so he could get her to the station in time.

She started to get up, nude in the humid room, then stopped. Where were her clothes? He mustn't see her nude. Her deeper thoughts told her it was a little late for that. She found her clothes, piled on a chair by the side of the bed. She never piled clothes like that.

She looked back at Jacob. He was awake, watching her. His eyes were wide.

Sandra checked the sheets. She was covered. "What am I doing here?" she signed.

"I was going to ask you that. What happened last night?"

She looked at him closely. She couldn't see enough to assess his body language. But he did seem sincere. Then she reminded herself, who was she to judge?

"Last thing I remember is taking a sip of Sambucca. We had too much to drink."

"Way too much."

He suddenly realized he was naked. And that she was too. No wonder she seemed so frantic. He wanted to reach out, reassure her. But he was afraid she'd take it wrong. Her body language was clear. She was not happy.

"Sandra."

She looked at him.

"I'm so sorry. I mean, I didn't mean for this to happen. I wanted you to have good memories of your trip here."

His body language was clearer. Contrite. Concerned for her. "Let's just get dressed. There's time for talk later. Right now, there's a train to catch."

There was silence. Then Jacob signed. "Did we... did we do it?"

"I don't remember."

"Well, if we did, I don't regret it. Do you?"

"I like to know what I'm doing. This not remembering bothers me." She pointed at the clock. "My train leaves in less than two hours. Let's get moving." Sandra started to get up, then stopped and turned back to Jacob, who was watching her. "Promise me you won't tell anyone about this."

"Of course not."

"Promise, I said."

"Promise," he signed.

"Good. And look the other way. I don't have anything on."

"But Sandra—"

She cut him off with a wave of her hand. "Since neither of us remembers anything from last night, I want to keep it that way."

Three weeks later. Three long, long weeks. Three weeks of misery, of sleepless nights full of guilt. She had slept with Jacob. The thought of it nauseated her. How had she ever let herself get so drunk that it had happened? Jacob hadn't intentionally seduced her, so she hadn't intentionally betrayed Rudy. But she felt awful. The truth of it taxed her heart and seared her conscience.

It was all she could do to go to work every day. The slights and stares she got in public for being deaf rankled her more than usual. Like the drugstore clerk who waited on people who'd come in after she had. Or the man who'd pointed at her, telling his girlfriend that she was "deaf and dumb." Everyday slights for a deaf person. But they hurt more than ever. Even at work, seeing the happy body language of the dogs at seeing her, Sandra just couldn't stop compulsively going over what she had done.

And it didn't get better with time. She became increasingly nauseated, losing her appetite. She couldn't sleep. She cried all the time. And she wondered what she'd say to Rudy. Or if she'd even say anything when she saw him. Either way, it overwhelmed her.

Her parents, who'd hoped that sending her to New York would cheer their daughter up, were infected by her despondency. It was obvious something had happened there. But Sandra refused to talk about it, and Jacob's parents hadn't heard anything either. Jacob himself wasn't due back for another three weeks. Finally, they decided something had to be done.

"Sandra," her father said one evening as she washed dishes after dinner. "This has gone on long enough. Something's clearly wrong. What is it?"

"Nothing, Dad, nothing. I just don't feel good."

"What's the matter?"

"I feel a little sick. But I'm sure it'll pass."

He held her shoulder with his left hand and looked her in the eyes as he signed with his right. "Does something hurt? Your head? Your stomach? What is it?"

"No, nothing like that." She forced a smile that didn't fool them. "I'm fine."

"If you're fine, then why are you acting so down? You didn't eat dinner. You just sit there and don't even sign to us. Something's not right."

"Dad. I've just got some things I'm thinking about."

"About Jacob, or that soldier?"

"There are a lot of things I'm thinking about."

"Well, why don't you tell your mother and me about them? Maybe we can help."

Sandra shook her head. "No, I'd rather not."

"Did things go okay with Jacob?"

She nodded. "He was a great host. And he seems to be doing well." She started for the stairs. "Thanks for being concerned about me, but I'm fine. Really." She went up to her room, leaving her parents staring at each other.

When her queasiness didn't get any better after a few more days, Sandra decided to visit her family doctor. Maybe he had something that could help her calm down. He ordered a urine test and had her come back for the results. She sat in his waiting room, squirming in discomfort, wishing he'd just give her something. He knew she didn't have the money for tests. Maybe he thought it was a bladder infection. Then another wave of nausea. She closed her eyes and breathed deeply, trying to calm her stomach. It took time for the sick feeling to go away.

The front door opened and a woman entered the office carrying her crying baby. The mother sat on the other side of the room, cooing at her child, trying to console it. Sandra picked up another magazine and skimmed it impatiently, looking at the pictures. She got up and went to the bathroom for the second time since coming back to the office. Maybe it wasn't a urinary tract infection. Maybe it was a gallbladder problem, like her cousin had just had.

There was another possibility too, a possibility she had shoved down into the farthest reaches of her thinking. Her period hadn't come... She prayed silently on the toilet, fear mixing with the nausea. "Not that. Not that."

When she came back into the waiting room, a nurse beckoned her into the back. Sandra followed the woman to the doctor's consultation room. Dr. Stein came in. He'd always been their family doctor, and had in fact delivered her over twenty years ago. She felt very comfortable with him, particularly since he had the kind of face that was easy to speech-read.

He sat down behind his desk, faced her directly, and spoke slowly and distinctly. "Your urine test came out positive."

"What do you mean?"

"It means you're pregnant."

Sandra licked her suddenly dry lips, struggling to remain composed. "How far along am I?"

He told her his estimate, but the response barely registered because she was focusing so much on suppressing the tears. Sandra felt weak and was glad she was sitting down. Suddenly she had to get out, as quickly as possible. She stood up, said, "Thank you, Dr. Stein," and hurried from the office.

It wasn't until she was a block away that she slumped down on the curb, nausea roiling inside her. She tried to think about the life inside her, but couldn't. She saw only a frightening future as cars and buses went past her.

* * *

Two days later, she sat at her bedroom desk. What was she going to do? Pregnant. Dr. Stein's lips still moved in her memory's eyes. "You're pregnant." She, the one who'd always done things right. Who had worked hard to get ahead so she'd have a good job. Now here she was, unable to think. Except for the one word. *Pregnant.* The thought hit her just as hard now as it had every time the past couple of days. Should she tell him immediately or wait awhile? She knew how he'd respond.

She walked over to her bed and slumped down on it. Thank God she had a job. It gave her something else to distract her during the day. Being with the animals helped. Their eyes brightening, bodies shaking, tails wagging. But during the lunch break, and especially when work ended, events closed in again. She would come home for dinner, and every day her parents would ask if she had heard from Jacob. Her mind would rack her with thoughts of being pregnant, its consequences. She would see again Dr. Stein's lips saying, "It means you're pregnant."

There had to be some way out. Sandra went over the possibilities again and again, desperately seeking an answer. As with scores of times before, there was none. Then, she'd obsess about how Jacob and Rudy would each respond when they found out. Or how devastated her parents would be when they learned the real reason for her moodiness. Her despair spiraled down to new lows.

Pregnant. What was she going to do?

Sandra found respite at work or in poetry. The rest of the time she obsessed, still trying to find a solution or a sense of what she was going to do. How would she tell people? And when? Jacob was coming home in two to three weeks. Should she wait until then, or tell him now? And somehow, eventually, she'd have to tell Rudy, one way or the other. He was leaving for Europe soon, if he hadn't already shipped out. Once he did, who knew how long a letter would take to get to him, even a V-Victory air letter.

She had planned to wait until she was further along before telling anyone, just in case she miscarried. If that happened, then all would be solved. Guilt reared up as she thought that. But waiting could cause other problems. She wished there were someone she could talk to. Someone who could help her sort out the options. She couldn't tell her parents. And the only friend she'd have felt comfortable confiding in had moved to California a few months earlier. No. She had to make the decision alone.

She read again the book of poetry Rudy had given her, finding comfort in holding the buckram binding, solace in some of the now-familiar lines that nurtured her torn spirit. She connected closely with the poems. They were a salve for the flood of emotions she now felt. One evening, she came again to "The Highwayman," the love story Rudy had read her. The poem with a sad ending. As soon as she read the first paragraph, she remembered how it had really touched her when she had listened to Rudy's recitation. And now she read the poem again, twice, slowly, recalling Rudy's face. The last two stanzas really struck home this time now as her heart struggled:

> And still of a winter's night, they say, when the wind is in the
>   trees,
> When the moon is a ghostly galleon tossed upon cloudy seas,
> When the road is a ribbon of moonlight over the purple moor,
> A highwayman comes riding-
> Riding-riding-
> A highwayman comes riding, up to the old inn-door.
>
> Over the cobbles he clatters and clangs in the dark inn-yard,
> And he taps with his whip on the shutters, but all is locked
>   and barred;
> He whistles a tune to the window, and who should be waiting
>   there
> But the landlord's black-eyed daughter,

Bess, the landlord's daughter,
Plaiting a dark red love-knot into her long black hair.

She wondered why Rudy had pointed that poem out to her. Had he foreseen the difficulties their relationship would lead to? The problems with communication, religion, prejudice? The poem echoed so much of her present situation. Two people in love but unable to be together—if in fact he still loved her. The underlying mood of unhappiness was so overwhelming she couldn't read any more.

She closed the warm covers of the book and let her mind once more dwell on her time with Rudy, taking temporary solace in the memories of those four wonderful days and final night. They had changed her life forever. And she wouldn't have traded the experience for anything, for wealth, for being a veterinarian— anything. Sandra recalled when he'd shared his life's dream to become a United States senator, his enthusiasm, his face animated with goodness and commitment. She loved him too much to even consider forcing him to choose between her and his dream.

Thoughts of having the baby out of wedlock insinuated themselves. She rejected them, pushing them back for later, always later. She'd known two deaf women who'd taken that route and had seen what happened to them. It wasn't an acceptable life. She could take the ostracism, but she didn't want to subject her child to it. No, having the baby by herself wouldn't be fair to the child, and it could cause life-long emotional scars in him or her. Besides, Sandra knew that if she told Jacob, he'd be excited to marry her and raise the child, and no one would know she had gotten pregnant first. But then she'd lose Rudy forever. Of course, she could tell Rudy the baby was his, but then he'd be forced to choose between her and his dream. There was no way she could do that to him, even though Sandra was confident he'd do the right thing.

What about adoption? She had considered it earlier, but knew she just couldn't do that with her own child. Not after bearing it for nine months. How about an abortion? The forbidden thought reappeared, a swirling discomfort to it. There were doctors who did them. It could be done secretly, too, as she'd suspected had happened with several women in the deaf community. If done early enough, no one would ever know. Then she'd be free to resume her life. Then she could wait for Rudy. And when he came back to her later, if he did, it would be of his own free will. If he didn't? Then whoever she did marry wouldn't be saddled with a child they hadn't planned from the beginning.

Tears welled in Sandra's eyes. She'd never imagined she'd ever consider an abortion. But none of the other options seemed any better.

Fourteen

The Tuesday evening County Deaf Club meeting was under-
way. The club president stood at the front of a group of forty
people under the bright lights, his sweaty face serious as he waited
for a response to his question. Several hands shot up around the
room, each waving to catch his attention. He pointed to a man
near the front and everyone looked at that person.

"We need to put an end to this," the man signed as others
nodded. "What happened to Charlie is outrageous. Just because he
didn't hear the cop call to him is no reason for a gun to be stuck in
his face. It's not like he'd done something wrong."

A woman across the room stood on a chair and signed. "What
can we do? If we complain to the police or try to sue them, they'll
be mad and go out of their way to bother us even more. I think we
should accept their apology and watch and see how things go."

"I agree," a man next to her signed animatedly. "The last thing
we want to do is bring more negative attention to deaf people."

Sandra saw multiple people signing at the same time. While
she was trying to read all of them, the president banged on the table
and everyone stopped, having both seen the motion and felt the
vibrations. "One at a time," he ordered. "Matthew first, then Rose,
then Benjamin, then Stella."

"I have no idea what happened at that house that drew the police there, but my son had nothing to do with it." Matthew walked
up to the front of the room as he signed so all could see his hands

and body. "He was walking on the sidewalk to Sandy's place, when the next thing he knew, one cop grabbed him by the arms and the other stuck a gun in his face. They patted him down before they realized he couldn't talk and that he was deaf. Charlie came home so upset he didn't stop shaking for hours."

It was Rose's turn. "Last month, they pulled me over at night when I was driving because my dome light was on and I was signing to my brother in the passenger seat. They thought I was drunk..."

The discussion continued as different people told their stories about police misunderstandings. Sandra remembered a similar meeting a couple of years earlier when the then Deaf Club president complained to the police, with a hearing member of a deaf family as his interpreter. There had been a temporary respite then, but the problems soon started again.

Sandra had continued attending the weekly Deaf Club meetings since Rudy left because it helped her feel less lonely. She'd known the people who went for most of her life. They were her friends, her community. Now, being with them helped distract her thoughts from the pregnancy; no one knew about that or her time with Rudy, so no one asked about them.

After the club business was finished, people broke into small groups, mostly by age but, to some degree, by gender. The lighting was bright, as would be expected at a deaf gathering, and Sandra found herself with four people in their twenties. One was Ruth, the woman who had recently moved to Springville from Battle Creek.

"What's up?"

"Not much."

"Are you feeling at home here yet?"

"Getting there. Everyone in the deaf community's been so nice to us, having us over for dinner, showing us around, helping fix up our place."

"Good."

"I do miss bowling in Grand Rapids. What night is deaf bowling here?"

"Thursday. It starts in two weeks, and if you're interested, talk to Henry over there. He's the short, bald one in the blue shirt. He'll be happy to sign you up. We go to Gabby's. It's cheaper than the new place in Jefferson. And also, because we've been going there so long, they give us the time and lanes we want."

Matthew, her hearing friend of deaf parents, got their attention, then signed, "Hey, Sandra, when's Jacob gonna be back?"

Sandra felt her stomach give an extra turn. The nausea had decreased lately, but the reminder of Jacob and the life she was carrying brought it back in force. She tried to present a cheery front. "Not sure. Last I heard he's still got another two to three weeks in New York."

"Bet you're looking forward to him coming home."

Sandra nodded, then changed the subject. A few minutes later, still feeling upset, she excused herself, saying she had work to do at home. She left the building, struggling not to cry. She felt so alone. So pregnant. There was no one to help her figure out what to do, or when she should tell people her secret. She took several deep breaths, trying to calm herself as she walked home. Trying to tell herself it was all going to work out in the end. Then the now too-familiar image of Dr. Stein's lips saying, "You're pregnant," moved behind her eyes. Tears rolled down her cheeks, cool in the night.

Throughout that week, Sandra came to the conclusion there really was only one solution that would work. But the thought of doing it was so devastating she held off as long as possible before committing to it. She sifted through the options one last time, trying fervently to come up with a better answer, wishing again there were someone she could confide in. But all of her friends were part of the deaf community. That meant anything she said would never remain a secret. The deaf community was too close-knit. If one person found out about her pregnancy, everyone would know.

She cried a lot, but only when alone. And she wondered why God had chosen her of all people to be faced with such a predicament. Sandra even speculated whether this was his way of punishing her for having premarital sex, then decided against that. New York had been a total accident. She had not planned to get drunk, to be totally oblivious of her actions. Her night with Rudy was another story. Yet there was no way something that wonderful could be wrong. No way. She was sure God understood how much in love they had been, and why they had made love when they had.

One evening, her father entered the den and saw Sandra alone, leaning back on the sofa, head resting against the wall, staring into space. Despite being deafened later in life, he had developed the body-language reading skills that all deaf people have. He read the aura of sadness around his daughter.

He sat down next to her. "What's wrong?"

"Nothing. I'm just thinking."

Mr. Horowitz just looked at her, his eyebrows raised.

"Really, Dad. Nothing's wrong. I'm just trying to sort things out."

"About what?"

"My life, and what I'm going to do."

He nodded and sat quietly, something else deaf people are comfortable with. When Sandra didn't sign any more after a couple of minutes, he asked, "Anything in particular you're thinking about?"

She made the sign for no.

"Is it about Jacob?"

"Not really."

"I see. You said you had a good time in New York with him. Are you looking forward to him coming back?"

She turned her body more towards her father so she could better see him. "You'd like me to marry him, wouldn't you?" She made her signs non-confrontational.

199

"It doesn't matter what I want. You're the one who has to decide."

"I know, but it's pretty clear to me by the things you sign that you and Mom really want me to marry him."

"Well, I will admit that I think he'd be a good catch."

"Why?"

Their comfortable silence returned. "The most important reason is that he's a good man, someone who'd treat you well. And since you're my only daughter, that's real important to me. It doesn't hurt that he makes a decent living, either. You'll be much better off than Mom and I ever were."

She studied her father's face. "Dad, what was it about Mom that made you decide to marry her?"

"Why do you ask?"

"I'm just wondering."

"She was just... I don't know, she just made my heart go flip-flop when I was around her. No one else I met ever did that, before or after I lost my hearing. I just wanted to spend the rest of my life with her."

Sandra nodded, but signed nothing. She struggled against her tears, to keep her composure.

Her father put his arm on her shoulder and squeezed as he leaned toward her a bit. "You okay?"

Sandra nodded. When she looked at her dad again, he signed, "You know, these last couple of weeks Jacob has in New York will be over before you know it. Then when he gets back, you can see how things go with him."

There was no reply. Mr. Horowitz sighed. Sandra couldn't hear it, but saw it. She got up and signed, "I think I'm going to go for some fresh air."

He stood too. "Honey, I'm so sorry the soldier left you and hurt you the way he did. It was bound to happen sooner or later, though. He's hearing. It always seems to happen that way when deaf people date hearing people. I know you feel you'll never get over it, but you will. Give it time. Just try to learn from it so you don't make the same mistakes again."

She signed curtly, her emotions clear from her body language and hand movements. "Dad, that's not what happened. You shouldn't be making assumptions about Rudy that aren't true."

"I apologize if I am wrong. I just thought... what really happened then?"

"I'm—" Sandra caught herself just in time. "I... I need to be by myself for awhile," she motioned as she walked to the front door.

It was not the only time Sandra went for a walk. She did it most evenings, going through the neighborhood after dinner, coming back after dusk had gently embraced her, hoping that being out in the open space alone, away from everyone, would help her see things more clearly and figure out a solution.

She stopped and leaned against a tree, lost in thought. It had become ever more clear. There were indeed only two workable options. Time was running out, and she had to make her decision. Then she needed to tell both men what she had decided. As she fought back the tears, which had been her constant companion in these lonely, aching times, she knew what she had to do. It would be the right thing, and it would be the best thing in the long run. Well, for everyone except her. There was just no way she could have the baby out of wedlock, give it up for adoption, or any of the other options. But the best choice, the one she was going to do, was not what she wanted to do.

The hardest part was deciding how and when to tell Jacob... and Rudy. But especially Rudy. She wanted him to know what had happened, but was also afraid to tell him. Although she had continued to write him daily since returning from New York, she hadn't said anything about the baby. Telling him about her decision, regardless of which option she chose, wouldn't be like any letter she'd ever written.

She procrastinated longer. When she got back home, she sat down to write two letters, one for each scenario. When she read each of them, however, she didn't like the way either sounded. So she wrote them again and again, never being satisfied with what they said.

Three weeks later, after Jacob had come home, Sandra finally told him she was pregnant. Time had run out, and she needed to act. He was shocked yet excited at the same time, as she knew he'd be. And just as Sandra had expected, Jacob did the right thing, so that no one else would know when the baby had been conceived. They got married two days later, eloping, telling their families they'd decided they didn't want to wait any longer.

It was after she told Jacob she was pregnant, but before they got married, that Sandra wrote her letter to Rudy, telling him what she was going to do. Things had gone exactly as planned, though not as she desired. Everyone would think that the baby was conceived after she and Jacob had gotten married. So the child already growing inside her would have a normal life. She did not allow herself to dream one last time about how life might have been had she married Rudy. That was over, and she needed to move forward. She turned her attention again to the two versions for the letter. She'd learned over the past year that dreams don't come true. At least for deaf people. And especially for her. There was no turning back now.

Sandra read both versions, trying to be objective. She finally chose one, and hid the other that she wasn't going to send. She just didn't have the heart to throw it away. It was the letter she had really wanted to send, but it wasn't meant to be. She turned her attention to the letter she was going to send. She didn't like the way it sounded. It seemed so trite, and she realized that writing this was going to be even harder than she had ever thought.

She wrote more versions during the two days before marrying Jacob, agonizing over every word of each one, only to tear them up and throw them into a paper sack to discard later, privately, away from discovery in a wastebasket. It wasn't until after she and Jacob had eloped, when it was clear there was no turning back, that Sandra forced herself to finish the letter and drop it into the mailbox. And then she felt an emptiness inside her that made infinity seem small.

Autumn 2008

Fifteen

Somehow, Chuck Winter managed to get his hand up and signal his mother to stop. He sat there, sign-less, staring at her, stunned. It was several moments before he was able to move his hands enough to sign.

"Let me be sure I got this right."

His mother looked at him.

"I don't know why you're telling me all this. Are you trying to tell me that... that Dad wasn't really the real love of your life but... that this... um... this Rudy Townsend was?"

She nodded, watching her son grapple, aching for him.

There was another stretch of inactivity as Chuck struggled with her revelation. "Did Dad... did he ever find out about this Rudy Townsend?"

"No."

"And did you ever... um, love Dad?"

"Yes, I did, Chuck. He was a wonderful husband and father to all three of you. I grew to love him very much."

"But you didn't when you married him."

She didn't respond.

Her son put both hands to his forehead, closed his eyes and leaned forward, trying to come to grips with the sudden upheaval in his well-ordered life. Sandra Winter leaned forward with much effort. She put her hand on his cheek. When he opened his eyes, she signed, "I just wanted you to know about my relationship with Rudy before I died. It was an important part of my life."

"So you say. But I can't believe you're telling me this now. Why tell me now about your real feelings for Dad?" He pushed her hand away more roughly than he realized, stood up and took a couple of steps away. "He was my father. Why are you putting him down like this?"

"Chuck, it wasn't an easy decision back then. I thought it was best for everyone that way. Times were different then, not like now when it's common for women to have babies without being married."

Her son's hands shook a bit as he signed from his newly broken world. Yet Sandra understood him clearly. "I can't believe you never told me before." He started to walk to the door, then turned around to face her. "This man, this Rudy Townsend... is he still alive?"

His mother shook her fist up and down vigorously, triumphing over her waning strength.

"Does he know what happened to you?"

"I sent him birth announcements for each of you."

"Where is he now?"

"In Washington, D.C." She paused a moment, permitting herself a moment of selfishness and celebration, because she had earned it. "He's now a senator."

Chuck stared. "You mean... he's that senator from New Jersey you've always been so interested in?"

She moved her fist up and down more slowly this time. Her secret was out.

No wonder his mother had always been crazy about that man, even now, on her deathbed. And it explained the senator's persistent advocacy for the rights of people with disabilities and minorities. But when he saw her slow smile, he interpreted it the wrong way. "Do you really expect me to have any interest in him? No way.

Dad will always come first. Always. He's my father. And I just can't believe you had to tell me that you loved someone else more."

Sandra leaned over slowly and picked up the picture she had been looking at when her son had first come into the room. She handed it to him. "Remember when I told you about the carnival? Where Rudy and I had our picture taken? This is the one that I kept."

Chuck came back to the bedside and studied the black and white photograph closely. It was of a young woman and man seated next to each other, the man's right hand around the woman's shoulders; both faces had big smiles and both looked happy. His mother looked beautiful and so young, her dark hair long, longer than he'd ever remembered it in other pictures. The simple necklace she wore was a perfect complement to her dress. He had to admit Rudy looked handsome too, hair slicked back, GI posture, straight and proud. But his anger welled up again. He thrust the picture back to his mother. He walked over to the window, struggling to keep his composure.

His mother watched him. When he finally looked at her, she signed, "Chuck, I'm so sorry. I really thought it was best for everyone to keep it quiet until now. But I wanted you to know the truth from me before I died."

Sandra watched the air leave him, his chest collapsing. "I want to know one more thing. After you married Dad, did you ever spend any more time with this Senator Townsend?"

"No, son, I didn't. After I sent that letter, telling him I had married Jacob Winter, he never contacted me again. I wrote him a couple of times before you were born because I wanted to keep in touch, but he didn't respond. I don't know if that was because he was in Europe and never got the letter, or he just didn't want to respond. I suspect it was the latter. I don't blame him. It's what I would have done, I think."

She watched for a response, but he gave none. "Since then, the only time I communicated with him was to send birth announcements when you and your sisters were born." Her filmed eyes captured a wistful look. "You know, I'm pretty sure he was devastated when he got my letter. Think about it. A letter, out of the blue. Telling him I had married someone else. But there was nothing I could say that would make him fully understand, to know why I was doing that, without telling him I was pregnant. And by then I had made my decision to commit my life to Jacob Winter. Besides, I figured he still had Susan Oakley. Turns out, he did end up marrying her."

Chuck paced around the bedroom, trying to calm himself. His life, his whole life, had been knocked out from under him. He had been a boy, growing to manhood, standing firm on a flawed foundation.

"There've been so many times over the years that I wanted to tell you, Chuck. But each time I just couldn't. So many times I wanted to go see Rudy and tell him what really happened. But I couldn't, though I did come close once. Remember when you were in high school and we took a family vacation to Washington? During your spring vacation? And how much you really enjoyed it?"

Chuck stopped pacing. "So that's why you were so excited about going. I thought it was because you were looking forward to seeing all those stupid cherry trees. It was really because you hoped to see the senator. You lied to me."

"I wanted to see the cherry trees too, Chuck. Because I remembered Rudy telling me how pretty they were. He'd already been elected senator, and it would have been easy to find him. But I got cold feet. I was afraid he'd have wanted to meet the family. Then all of you, including Jacob, would've found out about Rudy, and that might have ended up destroying all of us. I decided our family was more important, so I didn't visit him."

A delicate blue-veined hand smoothed her bed covering.

"After your father died, I debated with myself many times whether to call Rudy. I'm not sure why, but I never could bring myself to contact him. I just couldn't face the possibility that he'd long since forgotten about me. Or worse, wanted nothing to do with me. I knew he'd gotten a divorce from Susan Oakley and hadn't remarried." Her smile was tired. "Still, I decided it was better to cherish my good memories than chance finding out he no longer cared for me."

Chuck sat down on her bed. "Mom, it's been sixty years since you last talked to him. You must realize he's a totally different person now. He's a senator. How do you know you still love him? You don't even know him anymore. Maybe you're just loving a memory, frozen in time."

Sandra grabbed his hand, large in hers, and squeezed it a long second before letting go. "Chuck," she signed. "I know my telling you all this is a shock, but I hope you can understand why I did it. I love you. Since I'm not going to be here much longer, I wanted you to know the truth. Whether you tell your sisters about this is up to you."

Before he could respond, Judy barged in the room, signing animatedly. "You two have been alone in this room over four hours! I don't know what it's all about, but that's long enough. Mom, you always told us there weren't any secrets in this family."

"You're right." Fatigue took Sandra as her other daughter Lisa came into the doorway.

"Well, then tell us what you've been talking about."

"Mom was telling me about old times."

"For four hours? Don't lie to me, Chuck!"

Their mother adjusted her pillow and leaned back, her burden finally lifted. Sixty years, Chuck had said. Sixty years.

Chuck turned to his sisters. He nodded towards the door and signed, "Let's go out and give Mom a rest. I'll tell you all about it."

An hour later, Chuck's two sisters and their husbands sat stunned. "I can't believe Mom never told us before," Lisa signed. "She never even gave us a hint."

211

"It's so hard to believe Mom had a lover," Judy added, "much less a hearing person who is one of the leaders of the country."

"I'm glad Dad never found out about this before he died," Lisa noted. "It would've hurt him so much."

Everyone nodded. "Your mom did the right thing by keeping it a secret until now," her husband said.

"I wonder why she told us this now?" Lisa continued, her face still cast in shock. "I mean, if she hadn't, we would've been fine. I just don't see what difference it makes, why she thought she needed to tell us before she died."

Judy stood up. "And why did she only want to tell Chuck and not the rest of us? I mean, I know he was always her favorite, but a secret like this? She should've told us all."

"I'm not her favorite."

"Yes you are, and you know it." Judy's signs were angry. "I always thought it was because you're so different than the rest of us. You're tall, have blonde instead of dark hair, got acne as a teenager, and most of all, you hear. You know, I used to feel so sorry for you because you had all those things."

Lisa got their attention and signed, "Now I understand why Mom always read us poetry when we were younger, no matter how much we complained about it. Remember how she would drill us on the cadence by moving her head to emphasize the rhythm? Like with 'The Raven'?"

Judy nodded, then the two spontaneously started to sign and mouth the words of the first stanza of that poem, moving their heads every other syllable as their mother had taught them. Chuck joined in at the second line. His sisters' husbands just watched, having no appreciation of the poem's cadence.

"Hard to believe we learned how to do that because of this man we never knew," Lisa noted when they finished.

"A man Mother loved. We have to face that," her brother added.

They sat around the well-lit living room, lost in thought, facing each other so they could see when someone signed. Judy signed first. "Mom really looked worn out when we were in there, didn't she?"

"Are you surprised?" Lisa asked. "She'd just told Chuck her innermost secret, one she'd held inside for, what, sixty years? And that even Dad had no inkling about. And remember, it was just a couple days ago that Dr. Benson told us she didn't have long to live. She's obviously been debating with herself for quite some time whether and how to tell us."

"She's getting close to the end now," Lisa's husband signed.

Judy wouldn't stop. "I still want to know why she told Chuck that she loved someone before Dad. I mean, what's the purpose of getting everyone so upset? The doctor said she's going to die any day."

They all shrugged.

"None of us have any idea, Judy," Chuck signed. "Mom knows she's dying and, although I would've had all of us there, I'm sure she had a good reason for wanting to tell only me."

"Oh, my God." Lisa motioned to her watch as she got up. "It's almost nine. Didn't realize it was so far past dinner time. No wonder I'm starving. I'll go make a quick supper for everyone."

Her sister got up. "I'll check on Mom."

"Judy, now's not the time to say anything to Mom about why she told Chuck what she did," Lisa signed.

As Judy nodded, Chuck got everyone's attention with a wave of his arm. "I think I know why Mom may have told me this now. And I have an idea of one last thing we can do for her."

The four lifted their eyebrows at him, the deaf way of silently asking a question.

"I think it'll work," they saw his hands murmur.

"What?"

"I'm going to Washington, D.C., tomorrow on the first plane I can get. I'll see if I can't bring this Senator Townsend back to see Mom before she dies."

"What?" Judy's eyes widened. "What makes you think he'll even want to come? I mean, he's a United States senator, a big shot, one of the most important men in the whole country, maybe the world. Even if he still remembers Mom and wants to see her after what she did to him, he's a politician. The last thing he'll want is for something like this to become public."

"The way Mom described their relationship, Judy, the feelings they had for each other, and from what she said at the end, I'm pretty sure he'll be interested."

"Well, I don't think so. He's hearing and a big shot. He's not going to want to come see some deaf person who's dying, someone he hasn't talked to for all these years."

"That's brutal, Judy."

"It's true!"

"I'm confused, Chuck," Lisa signed. "A little while ago you were upset with her for telling you about this. Now you want to go bring this stranger here for her? Help me to understand why you want to do this."

Chuck nodded. "I guess I've had some time to let it sink in. And I think I know why Mom told me her secret now. She wants to see this senator before she dies. And she knows I can go talk with him better than any of you. Look—I want to try to do this for her."

"Okay, okay. Let's say this senator is willing to come—and you already know my doubts about that. Do you really think you can get him here in time?"

"I don't know, Judy. I'm going to do my best. Just don't tell Mom where I went."

"You say that like you want it to be a surprise," Judy signed. "I must say I've had my share of surprises for the next month. Frankly, I'm not sure I want to meet this senator."

"Fair enough. Let's see what happens when I meet him."

The DC-11 touched down at National Airport with a soft screech of tires and taxied to the terminal. Chuck Winter glanced at his watch: 8:30 a.m. Even though the first flight of the morning had been fully booked, he'd been fortunate to get a standby seat. Now he had the entire day to find and persuade this Rudy Townsend to come back to Michigan with him.

Chuck found a taxi quickly and within thirty minutes was on Capitol Hill. He walked up the steps into the Senate office building and spent more time than he wanted going through security. Then he located the New Jersey senator's suite. Upon entering it, he found himself in a sizeable room with a large, traditional mahogany desk in the middle. A young woman and older man were standing next to it.

"Hello. May I help you?" the woman asked, judging Chuck to be fifty, even though he was over sixty.

"Yes. My name's Chuck Winter. I'd like to talk with Senator Townsend about something urgent."

"I'm sorry. The senator is busy all day today with meetings. He's the majority leader, so when Congress is in session he's there all the time."

"When will he be back here?"

"I'm not sure. It can get quite hectic up there. He rarely sees drop-in visitors. What organization do you represent?"

"None. I need to talk to him about a personal matter."

"If you wish, I'll be glad to send a message to the senator."

"Good. Tell him I'm Sandra Horowitz's son—that's spelled H-O-R-O-W-I-T-Z—and it's very, very important I talk to him as soon as possible."

"Got it." She nodded, her body language officious, dismissive, especially to Chuck, who'd developed some body language reading ability from living with a deaf family. "Does he know you?"

"No. But he knows Sandra Horowitz very well."

"And your name again?"

"Chuck Winter."

"Give me your address, phone number and e-mail so the senator can get ahold of you if he needs to."

"That's okay. I'll wait here for him."

He watched the frown, guarding her powerful employer's time. "I wouldn't do that, sir. I doubt very much he'll be able to see you today. He really is quite busy."

"This is actually a matter of life and death. I'm confident he will, once he gets that message. I'll wait here." Chuck sat down in a chair.

"What do you mean, a matter of life and death?"

"Sandra Horowitz is my mom. She's on her deathbed. She's a good friend of the senator, and I need to give him a message from her, in person." Chuck watched her face, its thoughts reading like a storybook. *I must be careful here. This one is different.*

"Okay, I'll tell him you're here. But you may find yourself sitting there a long time." She emphasized long.

"I'll wait all day if that's what it takes. Like I said, time is running out. Tomorrow could be too late."

"Very well. Your choice. I don't want to seem harsh and uncaring, but you must understand I deal with many types of people insisting on seeing Senator Townsend."

"I understand your position." Chuck managed a smile.

"Would you like some coffee?"

"No thank you." Chuck settled in, glanced through the magazines on the table, then stared unseeing at the wall.

He had been, what, seven years old when he had first been asked to interpret for his parents? Maybe only six. Chuck remembered that day very well, particularly how agitated his parents had been. They'd been at the doctor's office, and he didn't understand most of what they were talking about. All he knew was that the doctor was using these complicated words he'd never heard before, and he was expected to translate those into sign language for his parents. He shook a little even now, just recalling how scared he'd been. His parents had been upset because they didn't understand what he had translated, and the doctor was upset because his parents kept asking the same questions. And Chuck had been caught in the middle. Afterwards, his parents had peppered him with questions about what the doctor had said, most of which he couldn't answer. He remembered how bad he had felt back then. Like he was a failure.

Chuck look around the senator's reception area. The receptionist was working on a computer, angled away from him. He drifted back into his reverie. In a way, things had only gotten worse from there. As the only hearing person in the family, he was increasingly used to interpret for his family's interactions with society. With the doctor or dentist. At the store. The train station. Schools. Gas station. Anywhere. For his sisters. Parents. Even his mother's parents. There were almost no professional sign language interpreters available in those days, so he'd had to do it. Many times his parents had pulled him out of class to interpret for them. Chuck remembered well how he'd hated that. Leaving class in front of everyone. Being taken out of baseball games when they needed him to interpret. He'd hated the fact he had Deaf parents when all his school friends had parents who could hear. None of them ever had to interpret. It hadn't been fair, and he'd thought about running away.

Things got easier as he became older because he understood better what was happening. But requests for interpreting also increased. Others in the Deaf community began to ask him to help, often to make telephone calls for them. Since there was no phone in the house, he'd had to go outside, rain or shine, night or day, homework or not. It had taken away time from friends too. He'd always been expected to help Deaf people interact with hearing persons. Much as he hated this demand on his time, he'd also developed a sense of responsibility to help, especially for his family. It was a fact of life. He was hearing. They were Deaf. He knew his parents couldn't do without him.

What really bothered him as a teenager was what hearing people said about his family. The ridicule. The derogatory comments about his Deaf parents and sisters, which only he heard. Every snide remark hurt, each a little more, building inside him a defensiveness and walled-off privacy. After awhile he just couldn't let it go unanswered. So he began to retaliate, first vocally and then physically, his roiling feelings increasingly obvious for all to experience. That didn't stop the barbs, but at least he felt better inside. Several times he came home with a black eye, worrying his parents. They implored him to ignore the ridicule, but he couldn't do that. He could hear. He knew the depth and breadth of the ugliness.

No, it hadn't been easy growing up a hearing child of Deaf adults, called a CODA by the Deaf community, and he was glad to be his own person now. He still helped out when needed. But with professional interpreters now available, there were fewer demands. Most CODAs he knew had helped as they grew up, but not all. A few had spurned the Deaf culture. And he knew of one who had even refused to talk with his parents.

He was startled out of his reverie when someone walked by. He looked at the clock. Noon. He picked up a magazine again.

Sandra Winter woke up in pain. With much effort, she pushed the bedside button that flashed a strobe light in the house.

Lisa came in. "You called, Mom?"

The older woman nodded, masking her pain.

"How are you feeling?"

"Not good. I'm close now, Lisa."

"Mom! You're giving up. Don't do that. I'll go get you something to eat."

"Honey, I'm tired. I'm old, nauseated, and I hurt all over. I don't want to fight it anymore."

"On second thought, I'll go get Dr.—"

She cut off her daughter with a wave of her hand. "Please, Lisa, don't waste his time. Let it be. I'm ready to go. What I would like is to be together with the family for awhile before I die. Go get everybody."

"Mom." Lisa hesitated, then plunged ahead. "Something important came up for Chuck. He had to leave this morning, but said he'll be back as soon as he can, probably later today."

A little burst of energy ran through her. Sandra tried to sit up. "Oh? What's it about?"

"He didn't say. I think an emergency with his business. You know Chuck. He does this kind of thing all the time." Lisa put on her best annoyed face.

"Where did he go?"

"Um, someplace east, but... um... I'm sorry, Mom, I don't remember exactly where."

Sandra noticed the slight but distinctive change in body demeanor. Signs that Lisa had always displayed since childhood when she was lying. Sandra smiled inside. It didn't matter. She was pretty sure she knew where Chuck had gone. How long had she talked to him yesterday? Four hours?

"Okay, then," she signed with renewed strength. "I'll try to hold out until he gets back."

"Good. I'll go get you something to eat."

The older woman shook her head and touched her thumb and forefinger together, the sign for no, then closed her eyes as she signed, "I'm not hungry. Just tired. I think I'll take another nap. But wake me up as soon as Chuck comes home, so I can have the family around me."

* * *

Chuck got a Coke and sandwich from the vending machine and returned to the reception room. He checked in with the receptionist in what had become an insistent, unpleasant routine, then sat down again.

He'd been waiting over five hours. He thought about his father, Jacob Winter. Tears welled. Good old Dad. He unwrapped his sandwich. Chuck had only a vague recollection of his father running alongside as he rode his first two-wheel bike without training wheels. Later memories were much clearer. Having a catch in the yard, playing baseball at the park with other Deaf people, and going to the Tigers games.

He remembered his father coming home from work every day and asking how his children's days had been. Jacob Winter was a man who took his Jewish heritage solemnly, and Chuck remembered his dad stressing honesty. Many evenings, before Chuck went to bed, he'd sit with his father and they'd talk about life, about the news, and about people. Jacob was not university educated, but he was a well-read man. Chuck learned a lot from those conversations. His father had taught him many things. Perhaps most important, he was always there for Chuck when he needed a strong father, a good and wise father. Despite all his childhood anguish about being a CODA, Chuck loved his parents.

It hurt him to think that his mother had loved another man. Loved him even more than Jacob Winter. He felt a knot in his gut.

When he popped open the soda can, the receptionist looked at him. "Still no word from the senator."

He nodded, lost in thought, not tasting the dried-out sandwich, sipping the soda. He loved his mother, and this was the last thing he could do for her. He didn't want to meet this Rudy Townsend. Or even know that there had been someone else in her life. But the sixty-year-old secret was out. Too late to change that.

The soda can gave under his grip. Why had Mother waited so long to tell him? Why hadn't she just contacted the senator directly, not involving him? Why did she have to throw his world into such turmoil? He'd probably never know the answer. Perhaps in a couple of years, when he found peace with her revelation, when things healed, he might understand it better. But not now. His family history, so loving and caring, had been torn open by the release of the secret. He took a few deep breaths and made himself calm down.

Almost two p.m. He'd been in the senator's reception area over six hours. "Does it usually take this long for Senator Townsend to respond to his messages?"

The receptionist placed some papers in her out tray. "Depends on what he's doing and what the message is. When Congress is in session, especially now with the debate on the tax bill, it's not unusual for him to wait until the end of the day to get back to us—unless it's a Senate emergency." She looked at Chuck with growing concern. "Maybe you should just leave a message. I promise you I'll personally make sure he gets it."

"No. Listen, miss. My mom is going to die soon from her cancer. I've lost six hours during which I could have been with her —that's how important my meeting with the senator is. Are you sure he got your note? I am positive he'll call as soon as he reads it."

Chuck watched her face. Not as expressive as a Deaf person's, but he could still read it. This was not something to be placed in her "Out" tray.

"So it really is about your mother?" she asked.

"Yes. And she will be important to the senator too."

"May I ask—"

Chuck interrupted her, tension surfacing with the strain. "My mother was one of his best friends from many years ago, and he will want to hear what I have to say."

The woman hesitated, a little frightened. People frequently gave dramatic reasons for having to talk to the Senator. Most were blatant lies, attempts to finagle a face-to-face meeting. Over time,

221

she'd gotten good at winnowing these people out and keeping them at bay. She could handle most of them easily. But this man, who sat staring at the wall for hours—he was something different, talking of his mother's imminent death and the senator's place in her life. Even though she'd never heard of Sandra Horowitz in her ten years with the senator, she sensed this man was telling the truth.

"Okay, I'll beep his staff. I'll ask them to personally give him the message now. Now what was your mother's name again?"

"Sandra Horowitz. H-O-R . . ."

Sixteen

It was another thirty minutes before the white-haired senator was handed a copy of the message left on his desk in the Senate chamber. Fortunately no one was watching when he read it because his face became pale. He staggered slightly, the message crumpling in his hand, then he sat down to read the words again, this time more slowly. Sandra Horowitz. Just seeing the name released another round of the intense sorrow he still felt every time he thought of her. Especially when he thought of the letter she'd sent announcing her marriage to another man. A sharp mental picture of a vivacious twenty-two-year-old woman summoned itself as he stood under the Senate Chamber's vaulted ceiling. An image that had haunted him over the past sixty years, since he was a young solider shipped off to European battlegrounds.

He recalled the pictures they'd had taken at the carnival their last day together. He'd kept his on his dresser—since divorcing Susan Oakley. What, he wondered, did she look like now? Their short but intense romance played across his memory. It had been the most wonderful time of his life. Every word she had uttered during those few days was ingrained in his mind and heart, staying with him in battle, in college, and here, in the Senate Chambers. He'd never found another woman like her. That had become clear after he'd married Susan Oakley within a month of coming back from Europe. It hadn't been a good marriage. They had divorced amicably three years later. The women he had dated throughout his professional life had also fallen short. He eventually lost interest in trying to find someone, losing himself in his other passion, helping people. And he had, thank God, known some success.

If only he had grabbed her when he could have! The senator remembered Sandra's plea to bring her back to Fort Bragg with him. It had been a choice between her and his career, and to a much lesser degree, between her and Susan Oakley. He'd made the wrong decision in both cases, not a good record, he noted as he started the walk across the Senate floor. Why did wisdom come so late in life? Tears welled. Soon after, Rudy Townsend got up and left the Senate Chamber before anyone could see his emotions surfacing.

So Sandra Horowitz's son was waiting for him in his office, the senator thought, focusing his politically trained mind to handle any contingency as he walked through the Capitol rotunda. Did his mother send him with a message? Maybe she wanted to see him again. Or, dear God, could it be that Sandra had died…

From the Capitol, Rudy walked to the Senate office building. He then took the stairs to his office, as had been his habit for years, a small investment in cardiac health as he worked his long hours. He paused a moment at his door to put in place the politician's veneer. It was something he had learned early in his career, realizing it was not two-faced. It was a way to hold people at bay until the political considerations were confirmed.

"Senator?" Chuck Winter asked, studying the tall white-haired man.

Townsend weighed up the man before him. Sandra's son was handsome. He had his mother's graceful bearing and was tall, even taller than the senator. He had to be at least sixty, but he looked younger.

"Come into my private office." Townsend beckoned toward his chambers. "We can talk alone there." His eyes found his secretary's worried ones. "No calls."

"Yes, sir."

Once inside, the senator shut the door and gestured to a chair on the other side of his desk. The two sat quietly, facing each other, sizing each other up. Each carried a different burden, but both were weighed down with emotions, making it difficult to think clearly.

It was Rudy who broke the silence. A bland offering, deferential, a little flattering, easing the tension so they could move forward. Rather like his Senate sub-committees. "This is certainly a momentous day. I never thought I'd have the pleasure of meeting one of Sandra Horowitz's children."

"And I never thought I'd be having a private conversation with the Senate Majority Leader in his office."

"Tell me, how's your mother doing these days?"

Winter heard the anxiety echo in the older man's voice and felt an inner sense of joy. The senator still cared deeply for his mother. "I'm afraid she's not doing well, Senator. She's dying of cancer and is very close to the end."

Rudy closed his eyes against the pain. When he looked back at Chuck, he asked, "How much longer does she have?"

"Very little. The doctor says she could die any day." Chuck struggled with how to make his request, then decided to be forthright. "That's why I'm here. I think she'd like to see you before she dies."

Majority Leader Rudy Townsend withdrew into himself, where it was safe and he could think. Something he had learned first on Omaha Beach and later applied in Congress.

"She would? You really think so?"

"I know so."

Rudy measured his words. "I'd love to see her myself. I've always wondered what happened to her over the years and wished we'd kept in touch."

"She feels the same way." Chuck paused a second, then forced himself to say words he didn't want to say. "She told me yesterday she's always loved you. That you were the real love of her life."

Silence grew in the room as the senator gripped his desk. "I don't understand. What about her husband, your father?"

"With respect, Senator, I think you do understand. As for my father, he died two years ago. She loved him, she was a good wife and mother, but you were the true love of her life." Chuck leaned forward. "She told me you were the true love of her life," he repeated, his words echoing their truth from the oil portraits of Washington and Jefferson on the walls.

Rudy remembered the memories. All his life, the memories. The politician's façade reappeared, distancing as he grappled with deep emotions. "How long have you known this?"

"As I said, Mom told me yesterday."

Rudy's eyes watched Chuck. "That must've been a shock for you. Hard for you to hear."

Chuck said nothing, returning the senator's gaze.

"I've yearned for Sandra Horowitz all these years and never knew she still loved me. Not after she sent me that letter."

A flood of emotions flew through his mind. First he was ecstatic. His dreams had come true. Sandra still loved him. Then he felt the stirrings of anger towards Sandra for sending him that letter, for not telling him all these years of her love for him. But he realized she must have had a good reason. She always had a good reason for everything.

He forced himself back to the present and sat straight up, a senator's posture, though he steadied himself with a hand on his desk. "I wish I had known earlier," Rudy murmured, using a letter opener to scratch at some paper on his ornamental blotter. "Why didn't your mother tell me?"

"Because she didn't want to ruin your dream of becoming a senator. She knew if the two of you had gotten married, that would keep you from being elected. So she decided to marry someone else. She told me making that decision and writing you the letter about her marriage were the hardest things she ever did."

"That's your mother," Rudy said. "Acting in my best interest rather than her own."

He knew it was his fault that they hadn't seen each other for sixty years because of how he'd responded to her pleas to get together at Fort Bragg. The silent wish, prayer really, returned now as it had many times over the years. Who knew what might have happened if he'd done that, rather than contacted Susan Oakley? He'd always thought that, between the lines of that last letter, Sandra had been trying to tell him something her words weren't saying. But he'd been too vain. He'd never followed up with her.

The senator unlocked a desk drawer using a key on his watch chain and took out his copy of Sandra's last letter. His hand shook slightly.

"Mom really doesn't have much longer, Senator," Chuck said. "If you want to see her, we should go to Michigan as soon as possible."

Rudy stood up, tucking the letter in his pocket. "What time's your flight?"

"I don't have one. I didn't know how long it would take to reach you." He pulled out a Delta Airlines flight schedule he'd brought with him. "The next one scheduled leaves at five fifty-eight."

"From Reagan?"

Chuck nodded

Rudy looked at the clock: 4:46. He was standing, lost in thought, when his pager went off. He looked at the message, his public face showing. "I would really, really like to see her, but I just don't see how I can come on such short notice." He pointed at the pager. "They're waiting for me to come discuss how we're going to get the votes we need to get for this bill. I just can't take off now. There's a major vote coming up tonight, or more likely tomorrow, which I can't miss. Besides, I haven't seen your mother for decades. I mean, I'm sure we've both changed a lot, and who knows what it'll be like when I come there?" Chuck saw the anguish behind the senator's words. "I'll try to come after the vote, but I have to see how that goes."

Chuck stiffened. "Listen, Senator. The doctor said Mom's going to die very soon. Not in a few days, but very soon. I'm not a doctor, but based on how she looked last night, I don't think she'll make it many more hours. If you want to see her, you must come now."

Senator Townsend shook his head. "I'm so sorry. I wish I'd known about this earlier. It's just too hard in my position for me to drop everything and come rushing there right now, with everything that's going on." He pulled out a slip of paper. "Here. Give me your phone number and I'll call you tomorrow when I have a better idea of when I can come."

"I just want to be real clear here," Chuck said, ignoring the proffered paper. "Mom's about to die. If you want to see her, you will need to come now. And, in case you're wondering, I'm positive she'd love to see you. Call it a dying wish, Senator. How can you put a price on that? If you were hit by a car, Congress would carry on, wouldn't it?"

The majority leader looked right back at him. "I'll see what I can do about getting there tomorrow."

Chuck wordlessly took the paper, wrote his mother's address and his cell number down, and handed it to the senator.

"Thanks. I'll have my people make sure you get expedited security clearance and a seat on the 5:58."

"Senator?"

"Yes?"

"Go fuck yourself."

Chuck reached the airport and got to the gate in time. He used his Blackberry to e-mail his sisters on their Wyndtell pagers that he was coming home and to tell them what had happened. They, like many deaf people, communicated with each other via

IM on their t-mail. Before the days of wireless e-mail, his sisters sometimes would search the entire airport for the TTY phone to call someone on, often to find it broken. Then they'd ask him to make the call on a regular phone.

After Chuck boarded the plane, the captain announced a delay due to mechanical difficulties. The takeoff was postponed two hours. It was almost ten before he arrived at Detroit Metro. Chuck still faced a forty-minute drive from the airport to the Winter home in Springville. When he arrived, the sun had long since set. A streetlamp lit up the area by his mother's home. Chuck parked on the street, sitting in the hot car, his heart still heavy. He had failed. His mother had finally told her secret about the true love of her life, and he had failed. Even if the senator did call in a day or two, he'd never get there in time.

Chuck stepped out into the cool night air and inhaled deeply. Nothing he could do about the senator now. Hopefully, his mother didn't know where he had gone.

He entered the house. Lisa saw him first, reading his weariness and dejection. "Come in, Chuck. I'm so sorry."

Judy walked in. "So, the senator wouldn't come?"

He shook his head. "At first I thought he would, since he seemed so genuinely interested in Mom. But when it came time to leave, he said it had been too long since he'd heard from Mom. And that there was too much going on in Congress. He said he'd call me tomorrow about possibly coming, but I wouldn't bet on it. You were right. Forget him. And don't tell Mom. Better she never know what happened."

Judy signed, "I told you he wouldn't come, but you wouldn't listen to me. Anyway, Mom's worse."

"I'd better go see her now." Chuck rubbed at the fatigue in his eyes.

"Mom wants all of us to go be with her now," Lisa signed, touching her brother's shoulder. "I'm so glad you're here."

They went to their mother's room. Sandra was propped up on a pillow, eyes closed. Everyone stood by. Her children, sons-in-laws. Even the dog lay in the room, head on paws, eyes watching.

Chuck touched his mother's shoulder. She opened her eyes, saw who it was, and smiled. "Thank heavens," she said. "I'm so glad you made it back today." She looked frailer. Chuck thought he could detect a slight glance from her, behind him, followed by a sense of disappointment that he'd come back alone. But he wasn't sure..

The family signed for an hour. Stilted conversation, awkward but well-meaning. Sandra made a point of signing to each one. It was his mother's generosity, Chuck thought, but it was more. A last sharing of her diminishing energy, a reaching out of her spirit.

Senator Townsend sat in the limousine and stared at the scenery going by. He replayed again the day he'd gotten that fateful letter from Sandra. How he'd immediately gone into his survivor mode. That was something he had always been good at—acting like he was in control, projecting an image of calm, even if he wasn't. He had convinced himself he hadn't been that interested in Sandra anyway, and by the end of that day, had written Susan Oakley a letter encouraging her interest in him. And then he had gone off to war.

The images of death and destruction in Europe would never leave him. Even now, sixty plus years later, those images were fresh in their ugliness, their foulness. Blood. Men crying in pain. The controlled chaos of an attack. Noise. Pounding eardrums. Guns, bombs, tanks. Men yelling. The grenade that went off thirty feet from him, killing his platoon leader and taking off legs and arms of others. And when no one took over, how something had clicked in him. He had lost his fear. Why, he did not know. He had gone into harm's way to rescue the wounded...

As he watched through the limousine's glass, he wondered why he was thinking of the war. Then Sandra's words came to him. "You'll be a big hero, and come back and be a senator..." The words hung in the limousine's interior, her voice young, that nasal tone.

The rest of the war also seemed like a dream. During down times, he often thought about Susan Oakley, especially since she had written him. His parents wrote V-mails weekly, too. Mostly, he had dwelled on his political aspirations. How he would get started, and what he would accomplish.

It was just before falling asleep, when his guard was down, that Sandra Horowitz would come to him. And he would feel his emotions gyrate, missing her terribly yet upset by her letter, that damned letter. After brutal days of fighting, perhaps to soothe shattered nerves, he would sometimes allow memories of those four wonderful days to return, their four days in Michigan. Then he could sleep, rifle by his side. Sometimes she spoke to him in that frightened twilight. *"Can you hear the ball hit the bat, Rudy?"*

The limousine accelerated, taking advantage of a lull in the traffic. The scenery was changing. Fields. Farmhouses. Small towns.

Rudy had married Susan Oakley three months after the war. They moved to New Jersey. Things didn't go well from the beginning. Life with her was dull, uninteresting, no challenge of ideas. What colors for the kitchen? Movie stars. Fashion. Her words eventually drilled into him. By the time Susan began to complain about the amount of time he spent campaigning for his first office, he knew it wasn't going to work. But he never contacted Sandra. She was married. Instead, he stayed focused on his political career. It was safer that way, and less painful.

The senator stared out the window as the limousine maneuvered around a truck, pondering the passage of time and the vividness of his memories. Now he was a powerful Washington insider. Majority Leader. One of the most influential men in the country. And suddenly Sandra Horowitz had come back into his life.

The car pulled up to the curb, and the driver stopped the limo's meter. Townsend paid him the fare plus a generous tip, then paused, his heart beating harder and faster. Like the war. Just like the war...

He got out, his knees weak.

Sandra Winter finished talking with Lisa's husband. Smiling, she leaned back on the crisp white sheets and closed her eyes. For a moment, she seemed to stop breathing. When Lisa gasped and reached for her mother, Sandra opened her eyes, her gaze calm. "Are you okay, Lisa?"

"Mom, I love you so much."

"I love you too, Lisa, with all my heart."

The lights flickered on and off. Everyone ignored it, but the flickering persisted. On and off, on and off. Judy finally signed, "Let me go get rid of whoever it is. I'll be right back."

Lisa pulled up a chair next to her mother. Chuck sat at the foot of the bed.

An impish sparkle touched Sandra's eyes. "Let's not rush me." She found her daughter's hand and squeezed it.

Lisa started to sign when her sister came back into the room. They looked at her as she signed to Chuck. "There's a man on the front porch. He insists on talking to you now."

"Who is it?"

"He's hearing. He knows sign, but is not a native. He wouldn't give me his name. Said he'd only tell you." Judy got agitated. "I told him now wasn't a good time, but he refused to leave."

Anger clouded Chuck's face. "Man, some people just don't get it. I'll be back in a minute after I get rid of him."

Judy pulled up another chair. Husbands stood by their wives. People signed in a subdued manner.

When Chuck came back, even a hearing person would've noticed the lightening of his body language. He waved to get everyone's attention. Then looking at his mother, he gestured to his right as he signed, "Mom. Someone's here to see you."

His sisters gave him a surprised look as he stepped aside. An older, elegant man appeared in the doorway. Sandra looked at him, her eyes alive, searching with reborn vigor.

"Rudy." She spoke at the same time as she signed. Her voice had timbre; it carried across the room, its emotion as clear as that in her signing.

Rudy walked forward as the family stepped back. He took one of her hands in both of his, brought it up to his lips and kissed it. "It's so nice to see you again, Sandra," he signed. "It's been too long."

"I see you still remember my sign name."

"How could I forget it?" He leaned over and embraced her gently.

Chuck got the attention of the others and motioned that they should all leave their mother alone with the senator.

"What's going on?" Judy signed. "I thought you said he couldn't come?"

He raised his eyebrows in surprise. "That's what he told me. I guess after I left, he changed his mind. Just now, he apologized. He didn't want to miss the chance to talk with Mom again, and took the next flight out."

"Mom looked bad in there," his sister signed determinedly. "I'm going to go back in. I want to be there if she's going to die."

"Judy." Lisa got between them. "You saw the change in Mom when she saw who it was."

Judy nodded.

"I think she'll be okay for awhile. She'll let us know when to come back in. Let's give them some time alone."

"I still don't get it," Lisa signed.

* * *

It was an hour before Rudy Townsend came out of Sandra Winter's bedroom. "Your mother wants to see you again," he spoke and signed simultaneously to the family.

They entered the room. Something about their mother was different. It was more spiritual than physical, touching all immediately. She looked rested, more at peace. In her lap lay pages of a letter, obviously old. Rudy's photo of the two of them at the fair lay against the sheets.

Sandra motioned everyone over. One by one, she hugged each of her kids before signing with much effort. "I want to tell you how much I love each one of you. I've been the luckiest woman in the world to have had you as my children." She looked at Rudy a moment before picking up the mementos on her lap. "You must take these, Rudy. And thank you so much for coming." She hesitated, then signed, "I'm complete now."

She turned back to her children. "Remember, you're all family. My last request is that you never forget that. Promise me you'll always take care of each other so I won't have to worry about that."

Mrs. Winter's gaze moved among the people in the room, communicating with each person using body language and facial expressions, her deepest feelings. Then she closed her eyes, her breathing light.

Everyone was quite still. A few moments passed. It was Judy who detected her mother's unusual calm.

"Mother's left us," she signed.

The senator's face turned white, drained of all its strength. He trembled, unsteady on his feet for the second time that day. But when Chuck came over, he fell into the younger man's arms.

"She said, 'I'm complete now.' "

Seventeen

News reporters and TV cameras turned the street into a media fair. They had stood vigil in front of the Winter house for two days now, taking pictures and attempting to interview everyone who went in or out of the building. At first the family had been taken aback when the reporters appeared. They quickly realized it was because of Senator Rudy Townsend. And it made sense. People would wonder why he had left Congress so urgently, in the middle of a crucial budget debate, to spend time with a family of no known relationship to him—and a Deaf one at that.

Rudy refused to talk with them. He remained secluded in the house. He had his office issue a brief statement that a close friend of his had died, and that he planned to spend the next few days with the family of the deceased. The constant stream of people coming to sit shiva, the never-ending supply of food, and the ongoing conversations were welcome diversions for him. Because he was comfortable with sign, he could communicate.

Still, he found himself dwelling on Sandra, now gone, and what could have been. His thoughts were vignettes of his time from when they were young and things were simpler. No, he thought, Sandra's deafness and Jewish faith had never made things simple. Fresh, precious thoughts. Replays of their last conversation together. And now new memories, formed in a quiet bedroom. What they had said after her children had left the room.

Rudy had sat on the bed next to Sandra and held her a long time before giving her a gentle kiss. She had spoken first, signing simultaneously. As always, she was easy to understand.

"I can't believe you're actually here, Rudy," were her first words. She used the sign name she'd given him by the side of the lake that long-ago starlit night. "This was my most fervent wish, to see you again."

Rudy leaned forward. "I've dreamed about this so many times too, but never thought it would happen. And not like this."

"You're signing well!" she had replied, changing the subject. There was too much to talk about and so little time. No use dwelling on things that couldn't be changed.

"I try, but I'm not that good. I have taken some ASL courses since you taught me my first signs, and I use it with Deaf people all over."

"You sign very well, honey. You don't even have much of a hearing accent."

"C'mon now. I'm not that good. Now, if I had been smart enough to stay with you, then I might be."

They'd studied each other's faces, noticing how life's trials had left their mark over the years. Rudy had been the one to break this silence.

"I'm upset with myself, Sandra," he signed. "If only I'd been more receptive when you wanted to come visit me in North Carolina, or if I'd had enough nerve to call you before now. At least maybe we could've gotten together when we had more time to talk. Several times over the years I came so close to calling. But, after that letter telling me you were getting married, I thought..." His eyes became moist.

"Oh Rudy, I'm so sorry I hurt you. I am so sorry. It was the last thing I wanted to do. But at the time I didn't know what to do, knowing you were concerned my deafness would keep you from your dream of becoming a senator. I didn't want to destroy your dream. So I did what I thought was the lesser of two evils. I hope you can forgive me."

"It was as much my fault, Sandra. The way I treated you."

She smoothed the wrinkles in his shirt, her hand moving slowly with fatigue. "Sending you that letter was the lowest point of my life, the hardest thing I ever had to do. I must've thrown away a score of drafts. I only got around to mailing the one I did because time had run out. I also wrote another letter, in case things changed and I was able to be with you. But I never sent it." Her hands, despite their weakness, moved with a poetic touch. "Tell me, Rudy. What did you do when you got my letter?"

"I just remember the shock. My life knocked out from under me." He smiled wanly as he adjusted the sheet, tucking her in a bit, a small loving touch. "I tried to pretend I didn't care. But it took all I had to carry out the daily training at camp. It wasn't until we got to Europe that I got a focus on in life. I convinced myself then that Susan Oakley was who I wanted. We got married after the war. Big mistake."

Sandra's eyes were kind. He found he could go on.

"You know, Sandra, much as it hurt me to get that letter, I kept it. I had this feeling deep inside that you were trying to tell me something between the lines. Many times over the years, when I wondered about what might have been had I been smart enough to have you come to me in North Carolina, I'd pull the letter out and re-read it. Each time I got the same sense that something else was going on. But I could never figure it out." He pulled out the letter from his pocket then. "I brought it with me in case you wanted to see it."

"My letter."

He nodded. She held the two yellowed sheets carefully, survivors of many foldings and unfoldings. They read the sentences together.

My dearest Rudy,

It's hard for me to think straight right now, let alone write this letter to you. I've been sitting in my room for the past few days, reliving our time together, and crying so much that I've had to restart this page three times just because my tears had ruined the paper. Every single moment of those wonderful four days I spent with you are ingrained in my memory, so deeply imprinted that nothing will ever erase even a single detail. It was a time like I never thought possible. I now know that two people can truly draw together as one.

The sun is shining brightly outside and the weather is close to 70, an Indian summer day here in Michigan, possibly the last before winter sets in. But this gorgeous day doesn't even begin to soothe the ache inside me, a hole so deep that it seems bottomless, one I'm sure will never heal. For I love you, Rudy, more than you will ever realize. And yet, because of circumstances beyond our control, what I wanted more than anything in the world will never come to pass. Instead, I have gotten married this past weekend to Jacob Winter.

Rudy, I know this comes as a shock to you, and hope with all my being that you'll understand that it's something I have to do. Certain events have occurred recently that left me no other option. You are, and always will be, the true love of my life. I want more than anything to be getting married to you instead. But it just isn't destined to be. Perhaps sometime in the future, when you come back from Europe and we've both gotten on with life, we'll chance to meet again. If so, maybe I'll be able to tell you what happened and why I married Jacob Winter. But for now, we'll need to be content with cherishing the memories of the time we had together, and to imagine what might have been.

Rudy, I have no doubt that you will succeed in realizing your dreams. I will be watching the newspapers closely so that I can follow your progress toward reaching your goal, and look forward to reading about the great things you will most definitely do as a famous senator in the United States Congress. You can be certain that I am now, and will be then too, so proud of you and everything you stand for and will do. And I will always, always, regret that life is so unfair, and that it kept me from standing at your side as your partner in this world.

With all my love, forever and ever,
Sandra

The letter hung loosely in Sandra's hands. She looked at Rudy. "I remember the day I finally mailed it, and how devastated I was. I wanted so much to be with you. I wanted to have your children. And yet I was determined not to interfere with your desire to go to Washington. But back then, life was different. My being both Deaf and Jewish would've kept you from being elected. Still, it was so hard to pledge my life with Jacob. Until I realized that truly loving you meant putting your interests ahead of mine. But I never stopped loving you. Never."

Rudy found her hand, warm against the cool sheets.

He leaned back so she could see his face and hands. "Sandra, only once in my life have I been as overwhelmed as during the past few hours. That was our night together in the motel. Even when I was elected senator for the first time, or when my colleagues elected me majority leader, I wasn't affected as much. And now, just seeing you again is... is so incredible. And then to discover you still love me..." His hands quieted, unable to capture the inexpressible.

The senator felt someone shaking his shoulder, snapping him out of his reverie.

"You hungry?" Chuck asked. "You haven't eaten much for two days."

The senator shook his head.

In the evenings, Rudy Townsend found some time alone with Chuck. They grew closer across a common, searing loss. Chuck asked about life in Washington, as well as about the senator's past. And the senator probed Chuck, this man who had stood up to him, senator's trappings be damned. His answers about his life growing up gave Rudy a sense of the life the Winters had led. A modest home filled with love and warmth. It had also become clear how Sandra had been the linchpin of that family as a dedicated mother and wife. Chuck's stories about the difficulties his family—and especially Jacob and his sisters—had interacting with the hearing

world, and how Chuck had often had to act both as an interme-
diary and interpreter, hit home with Rudy. The senator wondered
how much different things might have been had he been there.

It was time to leave for the funeral. Ignoring the reporters'
shouts, Senator Townsend entered the front passenger seat of
Chuck's car. Chuck backed out of the driveway and followed his
sisters' cars toward the synagogue. Rudy noticed how the area had
changed since he had last been there decades ago. He didn't recognize many of the buildings. They passed a *USA Today* news-
stand by the road and Rudy saw the headlines:

SENATE MAJORITY LEADER HAD DEAF LOVER

So the word was out. There would be hell to pay from the
Republicans when he got back to Washington. He didn't look
forward to it. Not because he was embarrassed about Sandra, but
because he was tired of the sordid quest on Capitol Hill to find dirt
in the personal lives of its legislators. It had gotten worse over the
years since he'd first been elected. He had no desire to deal with
that kind of trash anymore.

Then he noticed the street they had turned onto—the one
Gabby's had been on. He looked up eagerly and saw the building.
When they passed it, he noticed the bowling alley was gone; the
structure had been remodeled and converted to a restaurant with
some shops on the side. The entire area had become more upscale.
A new world, far removed from the Springville of his memories.

Gabby's… His mind drifted back to Sandra and their time
together the night she had died…

"Has Chuck ever been married?"

Sandra shook her head. "He's had a lot of girlfriends, and
there was one he'd dated for ten years, but then he broke up with
her. Decided she wasn't the right one. To be honest with you, I'm

glad. I didn't like that woman at all. I guess maybe he's just not destined to get married. He's sixty, after all."

"Our parents weren't enthralled with whom we had chosen either."

Sandra nodded, smiling. "I learned from our experience. Even though you weren't there to remind me of our pact, I remembered it. So, I never told Chuck what to do. In fact, I always told the kids that if they really wanted to do something, and it was the right thing for them, they should go ahead and do it, regardless of what people thought. They heard me say many times, if they did things only to make other people happy, they'd end up being sorry."

"Like us."

She looked at him. "At least like me. You did go to Washington like you always dreamed of doing."

"True. But I'm a wiser man now too. If I were given the opportunity to do my life over and choose between that and you, there wouldn't even be a choice."

Sandra's eyes misted. "It's not your fault, Rudy. As they say, hindsight is 20/20. Besides, if you had married me but hadn't been elected senator, you very well might not feel this way. You may have felt you made the wrong choice then too."

And she had been right. Ambition and regrets might have blinded him to what was really important in life. Either way, he might have been destined to regret his decision.

"Another thing I've learned, Rudy, is that deaf people really can do anything they want. I could have been a veterinarian. Did you know there are deaf vets now? There are even deaf doctors. Deaf people everywhere appreciate the laws you've gotten passed. Laws that gave us a chance. That was all we needed. A chance."

"Don't sell yourself short, Sandra. You were the one who made me understand how unfair society was to deaf people. You also taught me anything is possible."

"You know, it's amazing how certain things can change the rest of your life in totally unexpected ways. If either of us hadn't gone to the bowling alley that day, we'd never have met. Then I would have never learned to love poetry. And my life would have been so different." She looked him in the eyes. "Do you know what my favorite poem is?"

He made the sign for no.

She reached behind her, pulled down a book of poetry and opened it to a well-worn page. Rudy looked at the title: "The Road Not Taken."

He knew the poem well as it was also one of his favorites.

Two roads diverged in a yellow wood . . .

"We choose our roads, Rudy," she had signed when he finished. "And I'm so glad I agreed to go on that first date with you."

"Remember having cherry Cokes at Gabby's, when you asked me if I was afraid of dying if I went to war in Europe?"

She bent her fist up and down.

"I said no back then. But I have to confess when I got over there, I was terrified of dying. Especially when so many of my buddies were killed, and many more were maimed. Now it's my turn to ask you that question. Are you afraid of dying?"

She shook her head. "I'm ready. But it's a very different situation for me than it was for you back then."

"True, true. I must admit, I don't know what the Jewish religion believes about life after death. Do you believe in a heaven?"

Sandra signed no by bringing her first two fingers down to her thumb. "Jews don't believe in a specific place in the afterlife like that."

"What do they believe in then?"

"That no one knows what happens when we die. I guess I'll find out soon enough, eh?"

Chuck's voice drew Rudy back into the warm car interior. "We're here."

Townsend looked up. They were just turning into the parking lot of Temple Beth Shalom.

Eighteen

The family sat in the front row of the right side of the sanctuary, waiting for services to start. Chuck looked around. A large crowd, much bigger than he had expected, of friends, family, and well-wishers of Sandra Horowitz Winter had gathered to pay their last respects. The room was quiet, as most were signing. He didn't know most of the people. But quite a few of them had come up and told various family members how his mother had helped them in their lives. Many mentioned how she had encouraged them to pursue their dreams, overcoming their misgivings. The size of the throng was a testimonial to the influence his mother had had on the lives of others.

Senator Rudy Townsend also watched the gathering. He sat quietly in the front row between Chuck and the rest of the Winter family to his right, and Sandra's brother David's family on his left. The senator knew almost no one. He kept an eye on a few people in the back who had the universal posture of reporters. He sensed many in the crowd knew who he was, and he ignored their stares. He wondered how much of it was due to the *USA Today* headline. As he waited for the service, Rudy's thoughts found comfort in his memories of Sandra.

He remembered that when he'd first met her, back in the 1940s, she'd been frightened of communicating with hearing people. And he had taken her to a party. He smiled, saddened at his ignorance of what he had put her through and at the behavior of his "friends." How ignorant he had been, safe in his hearing world.

Her fear of being with hearing people had changed over the years. She had told him that near the end of their last conversation, in her bedroom.

"I remember when Chuck was eight months old and we found out for sure he was hearing. Everyone in the family was upset because he would be different from the rest of us. And we'd be forced to deal with hearing people. But because of my time with you, I was the exception. I decided I could learn to do that and vowed to become comfortable being with hearing people.

"It was also the first time I really understood something else you had taught me. Something no one else in the family seemed to appreciate."

"What?"

"That whatever religion or physical attributes we have, we all have the same needs."

"And that will never change, Sandra, unlike some other things. Such as the telephone. Remember when I asked to use the telephone at your house?"

She smiled.

"I was pretty stupid! But now that's available to all deaf people via the relay system. And with that, plus wireless e-mail and online chats, deaf people can get the same information as hearing people do."

"The playing field is more level now, Rudy," she signed carefully, "but the telephone is still an issue for many deaf people. Being able to talk on the phone is something some of us wish we could do. And there are many other areas in which we still don't have equal access."

"I understand, Sandra. I'll tell you something else that has changed. Baseball."

She laughed. "I guess I was wrong on that. It sure did. Who would've guessed sixty years ago that we'd have a designated hitter who didn't play in the field?"

"You still like the Tigers?"

"Do you still like hot dogs?" She smiled at him. "I just wish they'd won a few more pennants and World Series in my lifetime."

"Don't we all. We've had some exciting times, though. Remember Mickey Lolich leading us to victory in the Series? And who could forget Kirk Gibson's home run?"

"Now that was exciting!"

"Who's your favorite Tiger of all time?"

"It's still Hank Greenberg. And yours?"

"Al Kaline."

There was a pause, then Rudy signed, "Sandra, what kind of work did you end up doing over the years? Did you ever go to Gallaudet?"

"I worked at the kennels for nine months, until I had Chuck. Then I stayed at home to raise the children. Jacob had a good job and made enough money to pay for everything. So no, I never ended up going to Gallaudet." Her eyes took on a sparkle. "But you know what I did finally end up doing? I got my driver's license. And I have never had an accident. Remember we talked about whether deaf people were more likely to have accidents or not? When we were going out to the lake?"

"Of course I remember." He hesitated. "We had the top down on the Studebaker."

"Studebakers. Another thing that has changed."

He nodded. "Your hair twisted in the wind. You'd smooth it back, like this." His hand brushed at his shock of white hair.

"You do remember."

"Yes, Sandra, I remember. I remember so much about you."

"I saw an article a few years ago," she signed slowly, gently changing the subject, "that showed that deaf people are actually less likely to have car accidents than hearing people, whether they are deaf or Deaf."

"Just like you guessed."

"I was sure of it. Anyway, after my three kids had all grown up, I volunteered at the local Humane Society and worked there for almost twenty years."

"Sandra, that's wonderful. They were lucky to have you. I remember how much you wanted to help animals."

"I felt like I really made a difference, Rudy. Especially looking back on it now. You wouldn't believe what some people had done to animals."

"Just like people do to other people."

They looked at each other for a few moments. She kissed him gently on the lips, a comforting sense of peace inside her. "Rudy. Can you ask the kids to come back in? I need to see them."

"Sandra, not yet. Please. Now that I'm finally with you again, I need more time with you. There are so many things I want to talk to you about, tell you about."

She grasped both his hands and for the first time began talking without signing. She said slowly, "Rudy, believe me. I've been dreaming about doing this all those years too. And I also have a ton of things I'd love to talk about. I really, really wish I could give us more time." Her smile brightened. "I'm just so thankful that I got to see and talk to you as much as I did tonight." She pressed his arm. "Just one more thing."

He remembered the look on her face when she had told him her last secret. It was if she was glad to be finally telling someone about it, giving it release, like flight to a dove. "Now, honey, please call my children. I must see them."

Rudy felt an arm go around his shoulders. He looked up to see Chuck. "You okay?" the younger man asked.

The senator pressed back the welling tears. "Yes, Chuck. Thank you."

"Reporters bugging you?"

"Not with you around."

The rabbi stood up and raised his hand. Gradually everyone stopped signing or talking and focused on him. He conducted a short, traditional Jewish service, accompanied by a sign language interpreter. Before reciting the Kaddish, he asked if anyone wanted to come up and say a few words. Chuck gave the first eulogy, talking about his mother and how she had been such a nurturing presence for everyone. He was followed by several family members and friends.

Then a silence fell. The rabbi waited. Rudy sat there, surrounded by Sandra's loved ones, thinking about the love of his life, about how even at the end of her life she had been full of wisdom and insight. What could he say that hadn't been said?

Just as the rabbi started to rise, the answer swept through the senator's mind. Rudy got up and walked slowly up the steps onto the bima. He turned and stood straight, instinctively, his years of experience speaking to large groups assisting him through the constraint of emotions. He looked at Chuck, then Sandra's brother and daughters. His quiet nod acknowledged them. A moment of anger as reporters pulled out cassettes and notebooks. He scanned the audience. Then he began to speak, signing as he did so.

"I met Sandra Horowitz Winter sixty years ago, when I was a young man on leave from the Army and she had just graduated from junior college. I remember, clear as can be, the first time I saw her. We met by chance, at a bowling alley called Gabby's. It was in a building just a few blocks west of here. Some of you may remember. There were many differences between us that could have kept us apart. She was Deaf and communicated in American Sign Language. I was hearing and spoke English. She was raised Jewish. I was born Catholic. She was poor. I was upper middle-class. Her deafness, her religion, and even her gender prevented her from attaining her dream of becoming a veterinarian. Even today, I have never faced discrimination of any kind during my life."

Every face in the room watched the senator intently. Two reporters whispered to each other. "There were other difficulties too.

247

Our parents and friends strongly discouraged us from being to-gether. I was naive in those days, and might have given up trying to fight these obstacles. But Sandra was wise beyond her years. Indeed, wise beyond most people in those days. She taught me a better way. And so the barriers people put up didn't stop us. She knew that despite all our differences, every one of us is unique, a creature of God. She knew that the so-called differences between us were not those that should come between people. So she en-gaged me in conversation, and over the course of my remaining four days in Michigan, we became friends."

The cold headlines of the newspaper offered one gift: he could speak honestly. "Indeed, we became best friends." He paused, a pause of political caution, during which his survival instincts told him that this was not the time to acknowledge publicly that he had been her lover. His voice became stronger. "And in the process of knowing her, I learned things I never would have otherwise. I learned from the ways other people treated her how cruel and in-sensitive prejudice can be. And I learned from the way in which she acted toward others how supportive and caring people can be, and how love is the strongest and most meaningful force in the world."

Rudy looked around the assembly. When he felt in control again, he continued. "Unfortunately, and to my everlasting melan-choly, after I went back to Fort Bragg I didn't see Sandra again for sixty years. Sixty long years. That was my fault. I had been blinded with ambition. I had put that ahead of my friendship with her."

His eyes welled up, but he didn't care anymore. He'd reached the point in his career where he was ready to go with his con-science, not voting blocs.

"One of the last things Sandra did before she left us was to tell her son that she wanted to see me one more time. So, he... came to Washington to find me. And..."

The senator looked at Chuck. The younger man nodded. When Rudy spoke again, his voice was quieter and his signs less dramatic, but understandable. "I came back to Michigan and was

248

lucky enough to spend some time with Sandra before she died. I apologized for not keeping in touch with her. And like the understanding person she's always been with each one of us, she forgave me."

He compelled himself to look at each row, including the far back with the huddled reporters. His voice gathered its strength. "I will miss Sandra Horowitz more than I ever thought was possible. I suspect most people here will. But her passing need not be in vain. We can all adopt the principles she lived by. I know I'm going to. We can strive to eliminate prejudice, to provide every person on this earth with an equal opportunity to seek their dreams." His signs took on a grace, and his voice resonated across the gathering. "If Sandra were here, she would say it much more eloquently than I."

He scanned the audience again, his tears held back, the way Sandra would have wanted.

"Please, come join me in this vision where everyone has an equal chance. Together, working hand in hand, we can make things better in this world. I can't think of a better remembrance we could give than that... Yes, that would be a fitting—and everlasting—memorial to Sandra Horowitz Winter."

Chuck sat quietly. A grievous ache took him, and he felt like he was falling, with nothing to hold him. It was how his mother must have felt in her dream. That day she had shared her dream, the overexerted horse, the earth giving way... a goal unreached.

The rabbi chanted the Kaddish. Solemn, reverent tones. Ancient truths carried from one generation to the next, and now here today. Then it was finished. There was a sense of movement, scraping and murmuring, as people got up and prepared to leave. Chuck looked around, feeling suddenly cold. It was all he could do to nod his thanks to those who stopped to offer their condolences. He looked around. His sisters were quiet, subdued.

When the rabbi stopped by to say farewell, Chuck stayed seated. Melancholy wracked his soul, leaving him feeling alone, fragile and vulnerable. In the span of two years, he'd lost both his parents. First, his father, Jacob. Now, his mother, Sandra. Those pillars on which he had built his life. He closed his eyes and wondered why life had to be this way, why people had to grow old and die.

He felt a hand on his shoulder. It was Senator Townsend, sitting down next to him. Although Chuck could hear normally, growing up in a Deaf family speaking sign language had made him adept at reading body language. He could sense the anguish in the senator. And he could read it in his face and eyes all too well.

"A bad day, Senator."

Rudy nodded. "A very bad day."

"There is one thing I can salvage from it."

"Yes?"

"Mom saw that I connected with you. Someone who was part of her life."

"That she did, Chuck. That she did."

Chuck looked up and smiled ever so faintly in the direction of the heavens to let his mother know he now understood, just in case she was indeed looking.

Nineteen

The two men left the synagogue after everyone else had gone. The family had agreed to meet back at Sandra's house. Chuck pulled out of the parking lot while Rudy sat in the passenger seat, staring out the window.

It was at the second stoplight, waiting for a red light, that the senator saw they were at the old Gabby's. Just as he had been compelled to speak at Sandra's service, so now he had to follow up on Sandra's last secret. He opened the door and got out.

"I just need to be alone for awhile."

Chuck nodded. "I can come back and pick you up. How much time do you want?"

"An hour will be enough."

"I'll pick you up at this corner."

Townsend watched the younger man drive off, then turned and looked back at what once, when he and Sandra were young, had been a bowling alley. Memories rushed in: a bowling alley on a hot summer day, droning ceiling fans, sweaty clothes, a musty smell. The big band music overhead he had tapped to. A darkened interior and worn benches. Two lanes being used, the rest empty. Three pool tables, one newer and fancier. A young soldier on leave from the Army, playing the newer table, unaware of that quiet young woman in the light blue cotton dress, watching him. And that the next four days would change his life forever.

A wafting breeze made the air seem cooler. Rudy looked up again at the sign above the main door, the same door he'd entered many years ago to play pool. THE WHITE FROG BREWING COMPANY. It was exactly as Sandra had said. He remembered her words, when she had told him her remaining carefully guarded secret. Then asked him to bring her children back into the room...

"Rudy. Remember the building where Gabby's used to be?"

"Of course I do. How could I forget?"

"Well, it's not Gabby's anymore. When they closed a few years ago, it was converted to a restaurant and some shops. The restaurant changed everything about the place. It's called the White Frog Brewing Company. You wouldn't recognize anything about it if you went in. Except for one thing. They kept our pool table."

"They did? That fancy Brunswick table?"

She nodded, then signed, "But it's not in the same place you remember. Now it's in the far right corner. No one uses it anymore. It's mainly there for decoration. Which is good."

"Good? Why is that good?"

"Because that's where I put it."

"Put what?"

"You know, Rudy, I went to Gabby's quite a few times after I found out I was pregnant. I was trying to decide what to do. I liked going there because that's where we met. Usually there was no one playing pool, so I'd go to our table and just walk around it, remembering our time together. Something about being there felt comfortable. I could sense your presence and was able to think more clearly."

She paused. He waited.

"The day I mailed that letter to you," she nodded at the papers in his hands, "I went there for the last time. And while going around the table, I noticed this drawer at the bottom. I opened it, and in it found a horsehide brush for the felt, some extra chalk for the cue stick, and in the back, a thin paperback book of rules for playing pool."

"Drawer? That's kind of unusual in a pool table."

"Whatever, it was there. The book was like new. I don't think anyone had ever opened it before I did. So I stuck it in the middle of the book."

"Put what in there?"

Sandra kept talking, releasing herself from this long-held secret. "I don't know if it's still there after all these years. You might want to go take a look."

"Sandra, what are you talking about?" His voice carried a hint of impatience.

She smiled. "It won't be the same if I tell you, Rudy. You need to see it for yourself. Besides, there's not enough time left now to talk about it, and deal with all the implications. Just remember, I love you. Now go call the kids in."

A car horn blared at the intersection, pulling Rudy back. He walked through the front door of the restaurant and looked around. Sandra was right. He didn't recognize anything in the large room, with its many tables and dividers. But in the back he saw their pool table.

"Can I help you?" The hostess smiled tentatively.

"I'm just looking around to see how much it's changed since I was here sixty years ago," the senator said, then pointed. "Would it be okay if I look at that pool table? I remember playing on it back then. I've a lot of fond memories with it."

The place was not busy, so the hostess agreed. He walked to the table. It looked as grand as ever, though it was at least seventy years old. Two cue sticks lay on the table, slightly crossed, with the balls nestled in the triangle between them. Rudy ran his hand slowly along the smooth wood, relishing the feeling of craftsmanship that had become increasingly rare in the modern world. He walked around the table until he found the drawer. He looked up to check on the hostess, who was organizing menus. He opened it. The brush and chalk were there. And so was the book.

Rudy held the leather-bound book a moment, gathering his courage. Then he opened it. It contained a sealed envelope. On it was written, in Sandra's handwriting, "If this envelope is found, please return it to Sandra Horowitz." It bore the address she had lived at when Rudy first met her. He glanced around the restaurant again. No one was watching him. He put the envelope in his inside pocket, then replaced the book and closed the drawer.

"Thanks," he said as he left. Rudy made his way to a small park a half-block away and found a quiet bench. He was alone. Perhaps the relatively cool autumn weather was keeping others away. He pulled out the envelope and fingered it gingerly, his heart suddenly thumping. It had aged, despite being in the drawer all these years. He held the envelope between his two hands and closed his eyes. *Sandra...*

He remembered her request. Quickly, Rudy slid his finger under the flap and opened the envelope. It was a single sheet of paper, writing on both sides, the handwriting familiar from the letter he'd kept all these years.

My dearest Rudy,

If you are not sitting down now, please do so before you read any further. I have big news for you, and I want you to know that I've been thinking for days about how to tell you about it. You know, of course, that I will support whatever you decide to do when you hear this. For I love you, Rudy, and I miss you with every iota of my being. Every waking hour I think about those wonderful days we spent together, days which showed me how wonderful love can be. And now, I'm excited to tell you that that was only the beginning.

Rudy, I'm pregnant! Yes, I'm pregnant, and you're the father. I'm pregnant with our very own child! I'm so excited to think that I will have your child.

I know this will be a shock to you. I didn't expect it either. But I missed my period that was due two weeks after our night at the Lake Hotel. I saw the doctor and he confirmed that I am pregnant. It was clearly meant to be, Rudy, and I hope that once you get over the shock, you will be as excited as I am. Any child born of the love we have will be a special child, especially since it will have a father like you.

Rudy, I know you are worried about my being deaf, and how it will impact your dreams for a political career. I have no doubt that you will succeed— even if you agree to have me as your wife. I will do everything in my power to help you succeed, and look forward to the great things you will most definitely do as a famous senator in the United States Congress! You once said that "If one thinks one can, one can. And if one thinks one can't, one can't." You can do it, and I am so looking forward to the chance to be alongside you as your partner in life. We will show the world that anything is possible. That a deaf person and a hearing person, a Jew and a Catholic, can indeed be happy together and raise a family.

Rudy, you will be going to Europe soon. I will leave it up to you how you want to do things now. If you want me to, I'll come down to North Carolina immediately and we can get married. That way, no one will know when the baby was conceived. If you want me to wait until you get back from the war, I'm willing to do that too. I know war is dangerous, but I also know, deep in my heart, that you will be coming back. You are, and always will be, the true love of my life, and I'm willing to wait as long as is necessary for you.

With all my love, forever and ever,
Sandra

Rudy looked up from the letter, hot tears welling up, then falling free from his new profound knowledge. He had a son. The child he'd always wanted. And it was by Sandra, the love of his life. The next question came to him—Did Chuck know? Then the senator decided he didn't. Rudy had been there several days now and Chuck hadn't said anything. There's no way he would've kept quiet about it all that time.

He read the letter again, clinging to each word. The memories flooded in again. He closed his eyes to watch the remembrances. Then he read the letter one more time. So this must be the other letter she'd written, the one she never sent. He smiled. It was so incredible to think that all these years, he'd had a son. He wished he had known, so he could've been there as Chuck grew up. He thought about Chuck's sisters, and realized how different Chuck was from them. Sandra had had to live with that. Alone.

The senator checked his watch. Chuck—his son—would be coming to pick him up. He folded the letter and carefully put it in the envelope, then stuck it back in his inside pocket. He got up and walked slowly back to the corner, wondering when he should tell his son what he had learned. How would Chuck respond? Rudy now understood why Sandra felt there wasn't time to talk about it at the end of her life. She was right; there were a lot of implications.

Up ahead, he saw Chuck waiting at the corner. Chuck, his son. The senator walked up to the car and stopped beside it. He took a deep breath and knew then exactly what he was going to do. Life was short, and there was a lot of catching up to do. He opened the door and got into the passenger seat. Then he faced his son, smiling.